Lori

P9-CSV-881

HUNGRY
LIKE THE WOLF

PAIGE TYLER

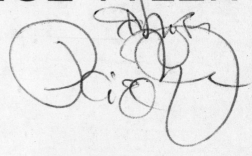

sourcebooks
casablanca

Copyright © 2015 by Paige Tyler
Cover and internal design © 2015 by Sourcebooks, Inc.
Cover art by Kris Keller

Sourcebooks and the colophon are registered trademarks of Sourcebooks, Inc.

All rights reserved. No part of this book may be reproduced in any form or by any electronic or mechanical means including information storage and retrieval systems—except in the case of brief quotations embodied in critical articles or reviews—without permission in writing from its publisher, Sourcebooks, Inc.

The characters and events portrayed in this book are fictitious or are used fictitiously. Any similarity to real persons, living or dead, is purely coincidental and not intended by the author.

Published by Sourcebooks Casablanca, an imprint of Sourcebooks, Inc.
P.O. Box 4410, Naperville, Illinois 60567-4410
(630) 961-3900
Fax: (630) 961-2168
www.sourcebooks.com

Printed and bound in the United States of America.
RRD 10 9 8

With special thanks to my extremely patient and understanding husband. Without your help and support, I couldn't have pursued my dream job of becoming a writer. You're my sounding board, my idea man, my critique partner, and the absolute best research assistant any girl could ask for.

Love you!

Prologue

GAGE DIXON STRAINED AGAINST THE HEAVY BARBELL, relishing the resistance as the stacked metal plates on either end of the solid steel bar made the whole thing flex. The bar quivered slightly as it reached that sweet spot of the lift where his pecs stopped doing all the work and his triceps and shoulders kicked in. But he'd already been punishing his body for over an hour, and this time the bar momentarily stopped moving upward, gravity insisting that down would be a much better—and easier—direction to go.

He grit his teeth, let out a growl, and forced his muscles to keep pushing until his arms locked out straight. He racked the load with a clatter of metal on metal. Even then, the bar still bowed and flexed—loading 525 pounds on a barbell would do that.

Gage sat up and looked around the small weight room he and the other members of the Dallas Police SWAT Team had set up. It wouldn't measure up to any of the fancy gyms in the area, but considering they'd paid out of their own pockets for the mirrors, heavy-duty lifting equipment, and free weights, it wasn't too shabby. It would have been nice if it were bigger, though. The presence of the four other men reminded him just how small the room was.

Then again, his men made most rooms seem small—special weapons and tactics teams tended to attract big, muscular men, and his particular team happened to be bigger than most. No surprise there either—alpha were-wolves were always big as hell.

Gage wiped the sweat off his face with the back of his arm and took a moment to appreciate the relative peace and quiet. Regardless of the room's size, it was rare for there to be only a handful of men in it. But with half the team out helping run weapon qualifications at the police academy and most of the others out conducting joint training with the ATF, the compound was practically empty.

Across the room, Diego Martinez spotted for his best friend and teammate, Hale Delaney, as the man tried to go for a personal record on the other bench press. At the same time, Gage's two assistant squad leaders, Mike Taylor and Xander Riggs, were hanging upside down from the ceiling-mounted chin-up bars, seeing who could do the most crunches. Alphas didn't need much of an excuse to turn everything they did into a competition.

They hadn't gotten around to cutting an opening for the air-conditioning units they'd bought for the room yet, so it was pretty warm. Which meant that all of them were sweating like crazy even though they weren't wearing shirts.

Gage was wondering if he should spring for some gym towels when he heard the sound of fast-moving boots coming down the hallway.

The other werewolves' keen hearing had also picked up the sound, and everyone was looking toward the doorway expectantly by the time McCall poked his head around the corner.

"Got a bad one, Sergeant," he said to Gage. "Hostage situation over on Belmont. Multiple injuries, at least two dozen hostages. Five shooters being reported."

"Well, there goes the workout," Delaney muttered, getting up from the bench.

Gage stood. "Five shooters, huh?"

At McCall's nod, Gage glanced at his two assistant squad leaders. "You two mind doing some entry work for a change while I run the show?"

"Hell, no," they said in unison, excitement clear on their faces, even though they were still hanging upside down. *Kids—they're so easily excitable.* Mike and Xander jumped down, joining Martinez and Delaney. Sweat was still running down their bodies, but they were eagerly awaiting his next order.

"Then gear up," Gage ordered. "I want us out of here in less than five minutes."

The four men cleared the room in seconds, leaving Gage with his weapon's expert. "Sorry," he told McCall, "but you're stuck here on the phones until we get some people back."

McCall grumbled—none of them liked to pull desk duty when there was a mission to do instead. But McCall knew it had to be done. "I'll get Martinez's and Delaney's assault weapons out for them" was all he said as he left.

Gage was only thirty seconds behind the rest of the team, but by the time he got to the second floor of the admin building, the other four men were already gearing up. He joined them as they yanked on navy blue T-shirts, matching military-style uniforms, and black boots. Then came the heavy black Kevlar vests, with tactical web pouches attached. The sounds of Velcro being yanked open filled the room as they adjusted their vests, ammo pouches, and holsters to a snug fit. The gear wasn't the most comfortable stuff to wear,

especially during the hot Texas summers, but it came
with being in SWAT.

McCall met them heading down the stairs, tossing
Martinez and Delaney their military grade M4 carbines,
while giving Gage more details on the situation. The
kidnappers were serious—there were cops and civilians
already on the way to the hospital in serious condition.

As they moved outside, Gage's men carefully checked
their weapons, yanking slides and bolts back to inspect
chambers, then dropping magazines and clips to check
their loads before slamming them in with a firm click.

While they'd been working out in the weight room, there
had been a lighthearted sense of competition about them.
They'd even joked and laughed while they'd gotten dressed.
But as they moved toward the operations vehicle and the
white SUV that McCall had ready and running for them, the
tone had changed. A charged intensity filled the air, the kind
you sometimes feel right before lightning strikes.

They were heading out to face a group of men who'd
already shown a willingness to shoot cops and innocents.
They likely wouldn't hesitate to shoot a SWAT officer,
given the chance.

Everyone turned to look at Gage just before climbing
into the vehicles. He glanced at his watch—barely over
three minutes since the call had come in. Good.

"We're going in a little undermanned on this one," he
announced, though it wasn't something that needed to be
said. "There's a department negotiator heading for the
scene, and we'll give him every chance to get control of
this situation. You heard what McCall said, so you know
as well as I do how this one is likely going to turn out.
These men are killers, so if we have to go in, don't take

any chances. Hit them hard and fast, and let's get everyone out of there alive and in one piece—us included."

With that, Gage climbed into the passenger seat of the white SUV, and Martinez had it moving for the gates before he even got his seat belt on.

Chapter 1

"HEY, MAC. WE GOT SOMETHING."

Mackenzie Stone jerked her gaze away from the fenced-in compound and its collection of mismatched concrete buildings. In the driver's seat of the *Dallas Daily Star* undercover van, her photographer, tech guy, assistant, and all-around best friend Zak Gibson yanked the buds from his ears and switched the police scanner on the dash to the external speakers. The blare of a fast-talking dispatcher spouting code numbers and addresses filled the van.

He glanced over his shoulder at her. "There's a hostage situation over on Belmont Street and the on-scene commander has requested SWAT to respond."

About damn time. "Excellent. Let's go." She climbed around the console and into the passenger seat as he cranked the engine. "It'll take a while for them to gear up. If we hurry, we can get there before they do."

She and Zak had been slowly roasting in this dang surveillance van for two days in a row, trying to figure out how to get inside the SWAT team's inner sanctum. She'd been so close to walking up to the gate and ringing the freaking bell. It probably wouldn't have gotten her anywhere, but right about now she was willing to try anything.

Mac clicked her seat belt into place just as Zak slammed on the brakes. She was thrown against the restraint, then flung back. "What the hell?"

Zak pointed at the monstrous vehicle barreling through the gate, cutting them off. A white SUV bearing a matching SWAT insignia followed, lights flashing as it raced down the road.

"How is that even possible? They just got the call," she said to Zak.

"Fast response time?"

She snorted. Just one more thing that didn't add up about the Dallas Police Department's SWAT team. She considered scrapping the idea of following them in favor of sneaking into the compound and snooping around, but the gate had already closed. Inside, a cop the size of a linebacker scanned the fence line, then headed back into the building. Just her luck, one of them had stayed behind.

Damn.

She tucked her long, dark hair behind her ear and sank back in the seat. She wouldn't have to be so underhanded about this whole thing if the police department had agreed to a ride-along with SWAT. Or at the very least, an interview with their commander. Why wouldn't they want her to do a story about the team unless they were hiding something?

Investigating cops who might be corrupt was never a good idea. But she'd earned her reputation by sticking her nose in places other investigative journalists were too afraid to go. She'd covered everything from gangs killing each other over territory and coyotes who robbed illegals blind to the murderous Mexican drug cartels and dirty politicians. She went wherever the story took her and never flinched when things got rough. She'd helped to make the *Dallas Daily Star* synonymous with fearless, Pulitzer-worthy journalism. So when she'd told her editor she wanted to go after SWAT, he gave the okay. Even if he did think she was wasting her time. There wasn't a division in the Dallas Police Department that had a better—or cleaner—reputation than SWAT.

It didn't help her cause any that everyone except the criminals SWAT put in prison thought the tactical team was damn near perfect. They'd taken on some of the toughest and most ruthless crooks, gangbangers, and cartel goons in the city. You name the bad guys, Dallas SWAT had taken them on and taken them down. Considering the load of major shit storms the group had been involved in, they had a ridiculously low number of complaints filed against them. There'd been allegations, but nothing had ever come of them—not since the new team leader, Sergeant Gage Dixon, had taken over eight years ago. Since then, the SWAT team had been beyond perfect.

By itself, that was enough to make her suspicious. All organizations tended to screw up occasionally, no matter how dedicated and capable they were. But that rule didn't seem to apply to the Dallas PD SWAT.

The police chief held them up as an example for the rest of the department to emulate, and for reasons she couldn't figure out, the other divisions seemed eager to try. The mayor even used their exploits to roast other civic leaders across Texas and the southwest. Hell, even the Girl Scouts wanted to be associated with them, and SWAT was happy to oblige by lending their muscle-bound presence to the annual cookie sale kickoff every winter. As far as everyone in Dallas was concerned, the SWAT team was better than sliced bread, PB&J with the crusts cut off, and sex in an air-conditioned room—combined.

"Just what do you expect to find, Mac? That they don't floss after eating popcorn?" her editor had asked in his deep Texas drawl. "Maybe the Dallas PD finally got something right for once. Maybe this city just has the best damn SWAT team in the country."

Mac had good reason to believe the SWAT team was crooked and a danger to everyone around them. But she had to be damn careful how she sold it to her editor. She had a hard time believing the story, and she'd heard it firsthand from an eyewitness named Marvin Cole.

Marvin was a two-time loser currently out on bail awaiting trial, this time for kidnapping, assault, and resisting arrest. Normally, Mac wouldn't have given the guy the time it took to call security to escort him out of the building. But then he had something on the one group of people in Dallas who were damn near untouchable—SWAT.

She was intrigued, so she'd bought him a cup of coffee in the newspaper's break room and listened to his story. She figured it was sour grapes—they had busted his ass, after all—but she pretended to pay attention as Marvin described how two big SWAT guys had smashed in the reinforced door of his secret hideout, tossed him around like a rag doll, and took the kid he'd been holding for ransom.

She didn't exactly swoon from excitement, but then Marvin described how one of the SWAT officers had growled like an animal, then grabbed him and shoved him up against the wall, holding him there with one hand as his feet dangled above the floor. The only reason that got her attention was because Marvin weighed about 350 pounds—and most of it was muscle. Still, SWAT guys were big and tough—everyone knew that. Marvin must have seen how skeptical she was because he opened his shirt and showed her the two sets of four parallel scratches gouged in the muscles of his enormous chest. He looked as if he'd been clawed by a big animal.

"Son of a bitch did that with his bare hands. I lived on the streets my whole life, so I know when someone's messed up," he said as he slowly buttoned his shirt and sat down. "Those SWAT dudes that everyone's so freaking impressed with? They're on something."

She lifted a brow. "You mean like steroids?"

Marvin shook his head. "Hell no, lady. Shit, I take steroids and I ain't never acted like that. No, those cats are on something really serious. Something that makes them crazy strong."

The idea that SWAT members were on some kind of designer drug was insane, but Marvin wasn't making up the ragged marks on his chest.

"What do you hope to gain from telling me this?" she asked him. "Even if this is a case of police brutality, I don't think it's going to keep you out of jail."

Marvin shrugged. "Probably not. But maybe it might land one of them in there with me."

She'd sat in the conference room for a long time figuring out what to do. The possibility that Marvin was right had buried itself in her soul too deep to let go. But while convincing her boss to let her run with the story had been easy, getting close enough to any of the guys on the SWAT team to find out what they were hiding, if anything, was damn near impossible. As far as she could tell, they only hung out with each other, and it wasn't at any bar or club she could find. They only worked out at their own facility, so she couldn't bump into them at the gym or along a running path somewhere. And if they bought their groceries from a store anywhere in the Dallas area, she couldn't figure out where.

Well, today she was going to talk to the elusive SWAT commander even if she had to take the man hostage.

Okay, maybe not. But she *was* going to talk to him, damn it.

Even though Zak drove like a madman, they couldn't keep up with the SWAT vehicles, so the scene was already well established by the time they pulled up to the industrial district on Belmont. There was crime tape going up everywhere, but fortunately Zak found a space near the curb only two blocks down the street from the SWAT tactical operations vehicle. It was usually impossible to get this close to an active shooter situation. That probably meant there weren't enough uniformed officers available to both set the perimeter and evacuate the surrounding buildings. No doubt the cops would remedy that soon. Until then, she might be lucky enough to get a few action shots and gain a bit of insight into how the mysterious SWAT team worked.

Zak leaned forward to get a better look, making a face when a pair of EMTs ran across the street half carrying, half dragging a man covered in blood.

"You think maybe we should move a little farther back?" he asked as the EMTs put the man in the ambulance and jumped in after him. The ambulance peeled away from the curb.

"I don't think so. It looks like all the action out here is over with. We'll be fine." Mac held a pair of binoculars to her eyes and scanned the area in front of the building. "So, what's our situation?"

Zak pulled out the buds he'd stuck back in his ears so he could listen to the scanner on the drive over. Thank God he was good at figuring out all those silly-ass codes and cop acronyms because it was like a foreign language to her even after ten years as a journalist.

"Sun Community Bank over on First and Devon got hit by a crew about an hour ago." He fished his camera out of the back and swapped out his normal lens for something bigger. "Someone got to the silent alarm and the cops were waiting for the bank robbers the second they walked out. That's when all hell broke loose." Zak stopped as he fiddled with one of the option settings on the top of the camera. "The cops ID'd at least seven bad guys armed with automatic weapons, some of whom were set up outside the bank while the rest went inside."

Mac set down the binoculars and climbed in the back to grab her own gear. "That doesn't sound like your ordinary bank robbers to me." She took a binder out of her bag and started flipping pages. "More like a gang with military training."

She'd spent enough time investigating gangs on both sides of the border to recognize their handiwork. Some of them could rival the U.S. military when it came to weapons and tactics.

"You could be right," Zak agreed. "Regardless, the responding officers got hit hard. There were multiple injuries, including some innocent bystanders. Cops took down at least two of the robbers, but the rest got to their vehicles and turned it into a car chase." He pointed at the industrial building in front of them. "They're holed up in there."

Mac didn't recognize the name of the place, and sure didn't know what kind of product E-Brand produced, but the bad guys had decided the three-floor brick building made a good defensive position. Probably because it didn't have any windows.

"They already shot four people and are currently holding thirty employees hostage," Zak continued.

"What do they want?" she asked as she scanned the pages of the SWAT personnel folder she'd put together. It wasn't much more than fluffy Dallas PD public affairs crap at this point, but it was a start.

"That's anyone's guess," Zak told her as he started snapping pictures of the scene. "But I think we can assume it's not world peace since SWAT was called in."

As if hearing the introduction, the door of the tactical operations vehicle opened and three big men stepped out. Dressed head to foot in black with heavy tactical vests, helmets, and automatic weapons, Mac would have known they were SWAT even if she didn't have their pictures. She had to admit their public affairs headshots didn't do them justice.

Maybe it was just that a simple two-by-three-inch photo couldn't capture how big the three men were—at least six-three or six-four with broad shoulders and biceps she wouldn't be able to get her hands around. Or maybe it was that all guys simply looked hotter dressed up in tight-fitting tactical gear.

She dragged her gaze away—a little reluctantly—to scan each cop's bio.

Officer Diego Miguel Martinez, ten years on the force, the last four with SWAT. More commendations than fingers.

Officer Hale Delaney, eight years on the force, the last three with SWAT. Taught martial arts to underprivileged children in his free time.

Senior Corporal Michael Lavare Taylor, eleven years on the force, the last five with SWAT. His records had a big gap missing, indicating he'd probably been an undercover officer before he joined SWAT.

Mac studied the three men as they stood talking. No doubt going over last-minute details before entering the building. They didn't look like they were on drugs. They were too relaxed and sure of themselves. If they were juicing, their hands would be shaking or something, wouldn't they? For the first time since talking to Marvin, she began to think he'd been full of crap.

"If these guys are up to no good, they're the hunkiest dirty cops I've ever seen," she said.

Zak shrugged. "I guess some women might consider them attractive."

She raised a brow. "Some?"

He went back to snapping pictures, this time getting close-ups of each SWAT member. "The ones who're only interested in muscular men who kick in doors and shoot things."

Her lips twitched. "Versus men who do what? Take pictures and eavesdrop on police scanners?"

"And program their own phone apps," he told her. "Trust me. That skill is in high demand these days."

Mac shook her head. Zak had nothing to feel inferior about, but they'd been ragging on each other since college, so she couldn't resist teasing him.

She was about to remind him he'd been talking about hitting the gym more often when the door on the operations vehicle opened again and an even bigger man stepped out. She pointed at him. "I want pictures of him. Lots of pictures."

"Yeah, yeah," Zak groused, thumbing a button on his camera and taking rapid-fire shots of the primary focus of her investigation.

It was possible the SWAT commander wasn't even

aware someone on the team was using drugs to improve his performance, but instinct told her if there was something going on, Sergeant Gage Dixon knew about it. Which was why Mac had put his name at the top of her list.

Three other men followed the SWAT commander out of the vehicle, but it was almost impossible to do anything but ignore them—Dixon was that mesmerizing.

Dixon was the type of man who made it hard to notice anyone around him, even the other members of the SWAT team, who looked as if they should each have their own month in the Hot Cops of the Dallas Police Department calendar right along with him. It wasn't simply that Dixon was tall, muscular, and sinfully gorgeous. It wasn't even that he was a charismatic leader. It was that he had a presence, which made every head turn his way—male and female.

Sergeant Gage Dixon, fifteen years on the force, the last ten with SWAT. Previous military experience as a U.S. Army Ranger, two years in the narcotics division, and commendations out the wazoo. She didn't have to refer to her personnel record to remember those facts. She'd learned everything about him she could, including the fact that he'd replaced every single member on the tactical team with his own handpicked people after taking charge when he was promoted to sergeant eight years ago.

That by itself gave her reason to think something was fishy. Organizational trends being what they were, it was highly unusual there'd be a one-hundred-percent turnover in such a peach assignment in such a short period of time—unless someone pushed to make that happen. And that someone was Gage Dixon.

She finally forced her attention to the other men

who'd come out of the operations vehicle behind Dixon, trying to figure out who they were. The one wearing a uniform was obviously a cop—a lieutenant she guessed— probably the on-scene commander who'd called in the SWAT team. The shorter guy next to him was also easy to ID. The white shirt, hard hat, big radio on his belt, and a familiar logo above the pocket on his shirt indicated he worked for the local power company. The last guy had her stumped, though. He had unkempt hair and wore a cheap herringbone sports coat, but he didn't have a side-arm or radio that she could see. Whoever he was, he got along well with Dixon. They shook hands, then did one of those weird shoulder-squeeze things men did when they were giving an enthusiastic hug.

Zak was snapping photos of the man-fest, so Mac asked him, "Any idea who that man is in the sports coat? I don't recognize him."

"Not surprising. He doesn't get a lot of press. He's one of the department's new civilian crisis negotiators."

"But SWAT has its own negotiators."

Three of them, to be precise—Diego Martinez, Trevor McCall, and Zane Kendrick.

Zak shrugged. "Maybe the department brought him in to soften up SWAT's image."

And he was on good terms with the commander of the unit? What was next—dogs and cats sleeping together?

Dixon finished up his conversation with the lieutenant and two civilians, who disappeared back into the oper-ations vehicle. The SWAT commander then turned and said something to Taylor, who nodded. Damn, she wished she could hear what they were saying. A few moments later, Taylor and the other two SWAT officers headed for the brick building, reaching under their helmets to pull knit caps down to cover their faces as they went. Before they got there, the three men split up, each disappearing around a different part of the building.

"You'd think they would go in with more people than that," she said.

"Maybe some of them entered the building before we got here," Zak suggested. "You know, like an advance recon team."

Mac blinked. Where the hell had that come from? "An advance recon team?"

He stopped taking pictures to give her a superior look. "Hey, I play video games. I know the lingo."

She shook her head. Men.

Mac turned back to see what Dixon was up to and saw him looking over at their undercover van. Crap. She started to duck down in the seat but caught herself. What the heck was she worrying about? The windows were too tinted for him to see anything at this distance.

His gaze lingered on them for a moment longer before he said something to the two patrol officers nearby, then climbed into the operations vehicle.

Mac grabbed the door handle.

"Where are you going?" Zak asked in a voice that said he knew exactly where she was going, and that he also knew he couldn't stop her. He'd given up trying a long time ago.

"I'm going to look around, see if there's anything interesting happening. Maybe get a few pictures."

Zak frowned but held his tongue. Another thing he'd learned over time. "I'll go with you."

She reached into her bag for the digital camera she

carried on little sneak-and-peek missions like this. It was small, simple to operate, and took higher-quality pictures than her cell phone. She tucked it in her back pocket.

"Nah, I'm good. I'll be back in a few minutes."

She slipped out the door and closed it before Zak could insist. And he would, on principle. But she didn't like him getting involved in this kind of stuff. She was willing to be stupid with her own neck, but she sure wasn't going to let him risk his. Zak was good at a lot of things, but he sucked at the sneaky, Danger Mouse stuff. Fortunately, he knew it and never tried to force her to take him along.

"Be careful," he called out.

She nodded and hurried down the block, away from the scene. As soon as she reached the end of the block, she started jogging. Cop cars zipped past her, lights flashing and sirens wailing, but nobody paid attention to a woman who seemed to be doing the sane thing—running in the opposite direction of trouble.

The moment she was out of sight, she turned down an alley and worked her way back toward the rear of the building where all the crap was going down. If she could sneak inside and find a place to hide, she'd be able to observe the SWAT team in action and see how messy things really got.

And she had no doubt things were going to get messy. Why? Because she was here now, and things always seemed to get messy when she showed up. Zak said it was because she had a nose for finding trouble. Maybe he was right. That used to scare her parents to death when she was a kid—it probably still did—but it proved to be an invaluable talent for a journalist.

She looked left, then right, then darted across the

street. She couldn't believe the SWAT team didn't have anyone covering the back door of the building, but there wasn't a cop in sight. Maybe they weren't the hotshots everyone made them out to be.

She was just about to grab the handle when the door burst open.

Mac barely had time to gasp before a man with a baseball cap on backward and a chest full of tattoos lifted a big rifle and aimed it at her. Her heart stopped. Instinct told her to run—or at least scream for help—but before she could do either, a SWAT officer in tactical gear dropped from above and knocked the thug to the ground with some kind of martial arts chop to the back of his tattooed neck.

She stared at the man lying unconscious on the ground, then at the cop before looking up to see a rappelling rope swaying back and forth against the side of the three-story building. How the heck had he dropped down fast enough to do that?

Mac opened her mouth to identify herself, but the SWAT officer closed the space between them in the blink of an eye and slapped a gloved hand over her mouth. She automatically reached up to grab his hand, but then froze as she locked eyes with his. He was wearing his ski mask, so all she could see were those eyes and a small amount of smooth brown skin around them. It had to be Mike Taylor or Jayden Brooks, the only two African American members of the team. Since she hadn't seen Brooks go in, it had to be Taylor. But for the life of her, she didn't remember his eyes being a shocking shade of gold in his personnel file photo.

Movement caught her attention and Mac darted a quick look to her right to see two uniformed officers appear out of nowhere. When had her SWAT savior called them?

"Get them out of here," the golden-eyed man said softly. "And keep her quiet."

And just like that, one of the uniformed cops wrapped his arm around her waist from behind and picked her up, putting his hand over her mouth when Taylor pulled his away. She watched helplessly as the other cop grabbed the unconscious gunman and heaved him over his shoulder in a fireman's carry, then ran toward the front of the building. When she looked back, the SWAT officer was nowhere to be seen. Where the heck had he gone? If all the guys in the tactical unit were this fast and powerful, she could imagine why Marvin thought they were on something. Nobody should be able to move that fast.

Her captor followed his partner, running down the alley with her like she was an unruly kid in a movie theater. She was so shocked she didn't even struggle, and by the time she thought about it, they were at the SWAT operations vehicle. The minute he planted her firmly on her feet and took his hand away from her mouth, she whirled around to chew him out for manhandling her and was amazed to discover he was the same uniformed cop Dixon had spoken to earlier. Had the SWAT commander seen the news van and told the cop to keep an eye on her? But that was impossible. No one had eyesight that good.

The officer reached around her and opened the door of the operations vehicle, then motioned her in.

She'd about had enough with the caveman crap for today. "I'm not going in there."

"In here, or in the backseat of a cruiser until this is done," a deep voice said from inside. "Your call, Ms. Stone, but make it quickly."

The cop raised an eyebrow, gesturing with one hand toward the open door and the other across the street where his cruiser was parked. Well, she'd wanted to get an inside look at how the SWAT team operated.

Mac ignored the hand the cop put out to help her and tried not to stamp her foot as she stepped into the vehicle.

"Please close the door, Officer Danner," said that same deep voice.

The door slammed shut, making her jump.

Mac pushed her sunglasses up on her head and surveyed the inside of the huge vehicle. The three men she'd seen earlier were eyeing her curiously. Gage Dixon, on the other hand, wasn't paying attention to her at all. He stood with his back to her, his focus locked on the computer monitors attached to the far wall of the vehicle. All six screens were on, but the images on four of them were moving and changing so fast it made her dizzy to look at them. It took her a moment to realize she was seeing live feeds from cameras mounted on his men's helmets. Funny, she hadn't seen one mounted on Taylor's.

Who the hell was she kidding? She hadn't noticed much of anything besides his big muscles and seriously mesmerizing eyes. He might have been naked for all she knew. Nah, she would have noticed that. She never missed a naked man.

But the four moving cameras meant Zak had been right—there were more than three SWAT officers in there. There were four. Not that four seemed like enough to her, either. She'd want like fifty or so to do the job.

The other two screens were stable, showing the inside of the building from two different angles. Mac took a step closer to get a better look and saw people lying facedown on the floor. At first she thought they were dead, but then she picked up movement.

She surveyed the inside of the operations vehicle and was disappointed to see it was nothing more than an RV without all the good stuff that came with it. That wasn't to say it was empty. There were racks for equipment, racks for weapons, and racks for radios, computers, and cameras. There were even two whiteboards and a corkboard. A rather detailed drawing of the exterior of the building had been drawn on the whiteboard. Double red lines marked what looked like entry points.

Mac glanced at Dixon and the other men. They were all staring at the monitors. Figuring this was her chance to pick up some intel, she slid her hand into her back pocket for her camera.

"Please put your camera away, Ms. Stone," Dixon said.

Mac froze. Damn. Everyone turned to look at her—well, everyone except Dixon. He was still glued to the monitors.

She pushed the camera back into her pocket. How the hell had he known what she was doing?

Dixon reached out and thumbed a switch on a box near the monitors. "We just got audio from the room where they're holding the hostages."

The sound of quiet sobs and pitiful moans—punctuated with a whole lot of shouting for the hostages to "Shut the eff up!"—filled the operations vehicle.

When the hostages were only silent, black-and-white video images, it had been possible for Mac to distance herself from the fact that the people lying on the floor—most of whom were women—were real, live human beings with mothers and fathers, sisters and brothers, boyfriends and husbands, maybe even kids. And that they were scared to death. But now it was impossible to remain detached.

Mac edged closer, holding her breath without even meaning to. One of the gunmen weaved in and out of the hostages, kicking them in an attempt to get them to move…somewhere. Most of the women just curled up in the fetal position and cried harder, which only seemed to infuriate the guy kicking them even more.

Cursing, he grabbed one of the women by the hair and dragged her out of the camera's view. The woman's terrified screams echoed through the speakers, chilling Mac to the core. She'd seen a lot of violence in her line of work, but that didn't mean she was used to it.

She covered her mouth with her hands to keep from shouting at Dixon to tell his damn SWAT team to do something to help. She was a journalist. She was supposed to stay neutral in every situation and just observe. But it was damn hard when she knew that thug in there was moments away from killing that poor woman—or worse.

"Shit, this is bad," the hostage negotiator said. "Those animals are on the edge and ready to go over. If your team is going in there, they'd better be quick."

Dixon didn't answer but just spoke softly into the mic he was wearing. A moment later, he turned to the man from the power company. "Are your people ready?"

Hard Hat looked nervous, but he nodded. "When you say the word."

Dixon turned his attention to the uniformed officer. "I know you were hoping we wouldn't have to do this, but I need to get my people in there."

The man didn't look happy about it, but he nodded.

"Do whatever you have to do. Just be careful. There're a lot of hostages in there."

Mac wasn't sure in a case like this who got to make the call as to when SWAT went in. But regardless, Dixon had smoothly put the lieutenant in the decision loop, making sure he didn't step on any toes he didn't have to. She'd used that trick herself a few times in the past to keep herself on people's good side, even when she could have trampled all over them. He was pretty smart for a big, muscle-bound trigger puller.

Dixon threw a glance at Hard Hat. "On my mark. In three...two...one. Now."

At the SWAT commander's signal, Hard Hat said a single word into his radio. All at once, every screen on the wall went black. For a moment, Mac thought the SWAT vehicle had lost power. Then she heard screaming over the speakers and realized they'd cut the power to the building.

Half a second later, gunfire erupted.

Mac couldn't see a damn thing on the monitors except the occasional bright orange flashes that reflected off the walls.

But while she couldn't see much, she could hear plenty. Women screaming, men cussing, the thud of heavy stuff hitting the floor. And interspersed between all of it, the growls of what sounded like a pissed-off SWAT team. Man, these guys really got fired up when they went in. It sounded as if they were ready to tear the place apart. Maybe that was what Marvin had meant when he said they were on something.

Right now, she couldn't care less about her story. She only prayed the hostages made it out of this in one piece, although she couldn't imagine how that would be possible. Not with all that gunfire.

But as fast as the shooting had started, it stopped.

Mac stared at the pitch-black screen, straining her eyes for something—*anything*—that would tell her if the hostages were still alive.

Gage pressed his index finger to the small bud in his right ear as if listening, then he turned to Hard Hat. "Flip on the power."

The monitors trained on the interior of the building lit up, but not the ones connected to the SWAT officers' helmet cams.

Mac sagged with relief. The women were huddled together in the center of the room, clearly traumatized but alive. Three men were on the floor nearby. They were still moving, but it didn't look like they'd be going anywhere. One member of the SWAT team was covering the downed bank robbers, while two others moved among the women checking for injuries. Mac didn't see the fourth member of the SWAT team. He must be dealing with the other thugs out of the camera's view.

"Copy that," Gage said into his mic, then glanced at the lieutenant. "Scene secure. Five suspects down, four WIA, one KIA. No hostages seriously wounded, but a few got trampled in the panic."

Four bad guys wounded, one dead.

The lieutenant looked as relieved as Mac felt. "I'll get in there with some uniforms and EMTs, start getting everyone out."

He brushed past her at a run, slamming the door of the operations vehicle behind him. A few moments later, Hard Hat and the hostage negotiator left as well, leaving her alone with the SWAT team leader.

Curious despite herself, Mac moved closer to the man

so she could see the monitors better—or at least that was the excuse she was going with.

She watched in silence as police officers and EMTs rushed into the room to take custody of the bank robbers and give first aid to the hostages. Dixon's team fell back, disappearing out of the camera's view.

Only then did Dixon take off his headset and turn to face her. "So, Ms. Stone. Did you get what you were looking for?"

This was the first time Mac had seen Gage Dixon this close up. Saying he was gorgeous didn't even begin to cover it. With his dark hair, chiseled jaw, and sensuous mouth, he was downright devastating. She was especially captivated by his eyes. They were the color of dark honey. Or maybe fine whiskey. Either way, it was too easy to get lost in their depths.

She gave herself a mental shake and forced herself to look away, if just to catch her breath. "What are you talking about?"

He smiled at her in a way that made her wonder if he knew how off balance he had her. That bothered her—she was used to being the one who put other people off balance.

"It's obvious you've been snooping around for a story," he said.

"When your man grabbed me, you mean?" She shrugged. "That was a complete accident. I got turned around and ended up back there."

He chuckled. "Right. Just like it's a complete accident that your unmarked news van has been parked outside my SWAT compound for the last two days?"

She tried not to let her surprise show, but failed

miserably. Mouth twitching, he turned and switched off the monitors.

How the hell had Dixon made her so easily? She and Zak weren't that sloppy, were they? Dixon turned off the monitors, then picked up a cloth and wiped down the whiteboard.

"Okay, you caught me," she said. "But I only resorted to that because the department turned down my request for an interview and a ride-along."

He stopped wiping and turned to her, his brow raised in a way that did interesting things to her tummy. Damn, the man had quite the smolder. "Most reporters would be able to infer from that answer that they should go after a different story."

Mac knew it was crazy, but if she didn't know better, she'd think Dixon was teasing her—if not outright flirting. Well, she could play that game, too. But while she wasn't above using her feminine wiles to get a story, she needed to make sure she was right about him first.

She moved a little closer. If he backed up, she'd assume she read him wrong and would retreat accordingly. If he didn't, she might be able to work him a little bit.

Dixon did neither. Instead, he took a step toward her so that they were standing even closer together. She hadn't realized how big the SWAT officer was until that moment. He towered over her by almost a foot, and his shoulders were nearly twice as wide as she was. She decided she suddenly liked really big men.

Damn, it was going to be hard remembering this guy was the target of her next in-depth investigative article.

"I've never been very good at picking up subtle hints." She gave him her best award-winning smile—the one she used on her editor when she wanted a really juicy story—and moved a fraction of an inch closer. He smelled nice. "I was simply waiting outside the compound so I could talk to you and straighten out the obvious misunderstanding the department had."

"Of course." He returned her smile with one of the sexiest grins she'd ever seen. "Because it must have been a mistake. After all, what cop wouldn't want to talk to the ever-insightful Ms. Mackenzie Stone, right?"

"Exactly."

Mac gave him a real smile this time. It was hard not to. He was one of those rare men who could be charming with a few carefully chosen words. And he seemed attracted to her—at least she was pretty sure he was.

She was just trying to figure out how to use that attraction to weasel an invite for an in-depth interview with the hunky SWAT commander when the door to the operations vehicle opened and two of his men climbed in. They hesitated for a moment when they saw her, as if surprised to find their superior alone with a woman in the back of the operations vehicle. She wasn't sure why. It wasn't as if they could know she was a journalist looking for a story.

One of the men was Senior Corporal Michael Taylor—the man who'd saved her life before. The other wasn't one of the three she'd ID'd earlier, but she recognized him from the files anyway—Senior Corporal Xander Riggs. He must have been the one who'd slipped into the building before she and Zak got there.

Dixon took a step back, putting some space between them as Taylor closed the door behind him and Riggs.

"This is Mackenzie Stone from the *Dallas Daily Star*. Ms. Stone, meet Mike Taylor and Xander Riggs, two of my senior team members."

Being surrounded by three guys so big and muscular in a confined space like the operations vehicle should have made her feel claustrophobic, but that definitely wasn't how Mac felt right then. She had to make a serious effort to keep her mind in gear as she shook their hands.

She had a hundred questions about the operation she'd just witnessed, but there was one thing she needed to get straight first. "Sergeant Dixon said that one of the bank robbers was KIA. That means he was killed in action, right?"

Riggs glanced at his boss, his dark eyes questioning. Dixon nodded, signaling it was okay to talk to her. "Yes, one of the suspects was shot and killed by a member of the team. He left us no choice. When the power went out, he grabbed a hostage. We ordered him to drop his weapon, but he pointed it at the woman's head and was about to pull the trigger. A disabling shot wasn't an option because he was behind the woman."

Mac noticed Riggs didn't say which member of the team had shot the suspect, but based on the level of detail he provided and the way the muscle in his jaw flexed, she guessed it was him.

"That must have been a pretty tough shot, considering how crazy it was in there," she said. "And in the pitch black, too."

Xander's eyes narrowed, but he didn't say anything. She thought he would have taken it as a compliment, but instead he looked uncomfortable. Why did men find it necessary to downplay every heroic thing they did?

"We have excellent night vision goggles," Taylor said. "They help."

"Of course." She smiled at him. "By the way, thanks

for helping me out back in that alley. It's possible I might have been in a bit of trouble."

Taylor's mouth curved. When he smiled, he seemed a lot less intimidating. "Something tells me you find yourself in trouble like that frequently."

Mac shrugged. "Every now and then," she said before turning back to Riggs. "I didn't see you enter the building with the rest of the team. Did you go in before I got here?"

Riggs threw Dixon a sharp look. Instead of giving the corporal the okay, he answered her question this time.

"We dropped Corporal Riggs off a few blocks out from the scene. He hoofed it in over the rooftops while we were getting into position outside. He went in and set up the remote cameras and microphones while everyone inside was focused on us and the other police officers."

Riggs and Taylor stared at their commander, clearly shocked by how open he'd been about their tactics to a member of the media. Mac was stunned, too. She'd been fishing when she'd asked the question. She hadn't expected them to actually answer her.

Dixon chuckled. "You don't have to look so alarmed. It's not like I shared state secrets. Besides, Ms. Stone will be coming by the compound later today to take a look around and see how we operate."

Mac did a double take. "Seriously?"

His amber eyes met hers. "That's what you wanted, isn't it? An in-depth look at a day in the life of a SWAT officer?"

She was more interested in finding out if they were hiding something, but she didn't tell him that.

"I figured if I didn't make the offer, you'd only hang around outside the compound for months until I agreed to let you in. Or until you tried to sneak into the middle of the next hostage situation," he said. "This way we can do our job without worrying about you popping up out of nowhere, and you get to do yours without risking your life." She opened her mouth to thank him, but he held up a finger. "There's one condition, though."

"Name it."

"You agree not to detail any of our tactical procedures or techniques like the one I just told you about. You print those and you'll get my team killed." He lifted a brow. "Do we have an agreement?"

Mac nodded eagerly. "Yes."

She'd agree to whatever he wanted if it got her in the compound—even if it meant going back on her word later. Although, after today, she wasn't sure there was a story. She seriously doubted these guys were doing drugs, regardless of what Marvin said. But that didn't matter. No way was she passing up an opportunity like this.

"I'll see you at the compound this afternoon then," Dixon said as he opened the door for her. "Say three o'clock?"

She smiled up at him. "I'll be there."

Mac had to resist the urge to do a little happy dance as she hurried back to the news van. She wasn't sure how it had happened, but somehow she'd gotten herself an engraved invitation to get up close and personal with the country's most elite tactical unit—the Dallas PD SWAT.

Chapter 2

ZAK WAS FLIPPING THROUGH DIGITAL PICTURES ON HIS laptop when she climbed in the news van. He took a lot of shots of the on-scene lieutenant and the uniformed cops running into the building, then coming out with the hostages and the handcuffed bank robbers. He even had some pictures of the SWAT team coming out. But he wouldn't send those in. Her boss considered it bad policy to print pictures of cops if it tied them to specific crime scenes. He thought it might lead to retribution against them. Mac wasn't sure if she always agreed with that, but she abided by it.

He glanced at her, his eyes full of amusement behind his wire-rimmed glasses. "I thought I was going to have to bail you out of jail."

She made a face at him. "Very funny. I'll have you know I got an invitation to visit the SWAT compound this afternoon."

His eyes went wide. "Seriously? You think that invite includes me?"

She considered that. Dixon hadn't specifically said to come alone, but she didn't want to press her luck by bringing her photographer. Especially since the SWAT commander wasn't crazy about cameras. "Probably not right away. Let me work my magic on Dixon first."

Zak looked bummed at that, but nodded as he went back to surfing through his photos. "So, did you enjoy being carried to the operations vehicle like a sack of potatoes?"

Mac's face heated at the memory. Damn, she should have known Zak wouldn't have missed that. She gave him her best I'm-offended-by-that-comment look. "I was not carried like a sack of potatoes. Officer Danner simply escorted me to the operations vehicle to meet with the commander of the SWAT team."

Zak snorted and spun his laptop around so she could see the screen. There was a picture of Officer Danner running across the street with her in his arms, his hand over her mouth. Her color deepened. He kind of was carrying her like a sack of potatoes. God, that looked bad.

"Maybe you could keep that one off the shared drive?" she asked Zak.

He laughed. "Sure thing. But it's definitely going on the *Best of Mac Stone* disk."

Mac stuck her tongue out at him. Zak loved reminding her he had visual evidence of all of her most embarrassing moments—and that she shouldn't forget it.

He was still flipping through photos when something caught her attention. "Stop. Go back a couple pics."

Zak didn't ask why, but just scrolled back a half dozen pictures.

"Stop," she said. "Go slow from there."

He clicked one picture at a time, giving her a chance to look at each of them before moving to the next. She studied each SWAT officer's photo as it filled the screen. Zak had captured them coming out of the brick building. They had their ski masks pulled up, and under their helmets, each man's handsome face was covered with a light sheen of glistening sweat.

Zak moved from the SWAT guys to random pictures of hostages, EMTs, and bank robbers. When he got to the end, she had him back up and scroll through the same pictures again.

Mac leaned closer, focusing on the photos of Martinez, Delaney, Taylor, and Riggs. She didn't know what it was, but something was gnawing at her.

Then she had it.

"These were taken the moment the SWAT team first came out of the building, right?"

"Yeah. I was focused on those doors from the moment the cops and EMTs ran in until you came out of the truck. That's where all the action was." He frowned at her. "What's up?"

Mac studied the pictures one more time, just to be sure she hadn't missed anything. But she hadn't. None of the men were holding anything other than their weapons. And none of their tactical vests had pouches that could hold what she was looking for.

Zak looked from her to the photo of the four highly trained officers coming out of the warehouse, then back to her. "What is it?"

"They shut down the power to the building before they went in. It was pitch-black in there. I saw it on the monitors in the truck. But the SWAT guys aren't carrying any night vision goggles."

Zak glanced at the picture again. "Maybe they left them in the warehouse?"

She shook her head. "No way. Those things cost a fortune."

"So, what are you saying? That these guys can see in the dark?"

Mac didn't answer. Thinking the SWAT officers could see in the dark without the aid of night vision goggles would make her sound crazy, especially since she hadn't told Zak about the drug angle yet. But what if Marvin was right and the SWAT guys were using a performance-enhancing drug that let them see better in the dark? Crap, that was even more outlandish than a drug that made them crazy strong.

She was busy examining the photos for the missing night vision goggles when something else caught her attention.

She pointed at Diego Martinez's right hand. "What does that look like to you?"

Zak leaned close to the computer screen. "What the hell?" He fiddled with the keyboard, zooming in on Martinez's hand. "It looks like blood."

"That's what I thought." She turned to look out the window at the big operations vehicle just in time to see Martinez and Delaney climbing into the cab. Was Martinez holding his arm a little funny?

"Did we just see an injured police officer drive off when there are half a dozen EMTs who could have looked at him?" Zak asked.

"I think we did."

"Why the hell would they do that?"

"I don't know...yet."

But she was damn sure going to find out. She had a sneaking suspicion it was because Martinez was worried about whatever drug he was on showing up in his blood. If she was right, then there really was a story here.

‹‹‹‹‹‹‹‹‹‹‹‹‹

"Are you sure this is a good idea?"

"I'm sure," Gage said. "Martinez was barely scratched by that bullet. He can get patched up at the compound."

Xander swore. "That's not what I'm talking about and you know it."

Gage waited until the news van drove away before he turned to his senior squad leader. He knew Xander wasn't worried about the minor graze wound Martinez had sustained during the entry. It was almost closed up already and would barely leave a scar if they took care of it right. But Xander definitely wasn't too thrilled at the idea of having a reporter—a woman reporter at that—sticking her nose in their business. Gage hadn't expected him to be. Xander didn't like outsiders in general, and female outsiders in particular. In his opinion, both were bad for the Pack. And if something was bad for the Pack, Xander was never shy about letting him know it.

Gage glanced at his other squad leader. "What do you think, Mike?"

The big man shrugged. "I gotta agree with Xander on this one, Gage. You know Mackenzie Stone has a reputation for digging pretty hard to get the story she's after, right?"

Gage went out of his way to let his two assistant squad leaders have a say in how the team did things. But when you lead a group of alphas the way he did, it wasn't possible for everyone to agree on everything all the time. And that's when he had to pull rank.

"I know all about her reputation," he said. "She isn't looking to write a fluff piece on how we do our job. If she's sniffing, it's because she thinks there's a story here. And if she thinks that, she isn't going to stop looking just because we make it hard on her. If anything, that will only make her dig deeper."

"So what, we just make it easy for her?" Xander demanded.

"No, we don't make it easy," Gage said. "We bring her in and control the flow of information she receives. We show her what we want her to see, when we want her to see it. We make sure she gets the message—and only the message—we want her to get."

Mike raised his brows. "You honestly think that'll work? She doesn't come across as the kind of person you can mislead easily."

"I'd rather have her where I can keep an eye on her instead of constantly worrying about where she's going to show up and what she'll find on her own."

Mike regarded him thoughtfully. "You sure this is just about keeping an eye on a possible threat?"

Gage pinned him with a hard look. "Meaning?"

Mike didn't back down. "Meaning, I couldn't help but notice how nice the inside of the operations truck smelled when we walked in. In fact, it wouldn't be a stretch to say Ms. Stone has a scent our kind might find irresistible. Sure that doesn't have something to do with your sudden interest in her?"

Gage did his best to keep his face unreadable and his heartbeat steady, but it was damn tough. Mostly because Mike was right. Gage *had* noticed how good Mackenzie Stone smelled. Her scent was so intoxicating, he'd almost groaned out loud when she stepped into the operations vehicle. It wasn't some expensive perfume she'd been wearing, either. Just good old-fashioned, feminine pheromones. Luckily, he wasn't ruled by his nose—or other parts of his anatomy—when it came to making decisions. Especially decisions about the Pack.

He knew the threat Mackenzie Stone presented. He'd been on guard from the moment he'd spotted her at the compound in her undercover news van two days ago. Hell, he'd been on alert ever since the public relations department told him she wanted to do a story on SWAT. He'd turned down her request for an in-depth interview and ride-along, hoping she'd take the hint. He should have known better. After the stunt she pulled today, he figured the only way to get rid of her was to give her the interview she wanted.

"I make decisions about pack affairs with the head above my shoulders, not the one below my belt," he said to Mike. "If I think it's a good idea we keep Ms. Stone close, it's because it's best for the Pack, not because she smells good."

Mike shrugged. "Just checking. If you're not interested in her that way, maybe I'll look at her Facebook page— see if she's available."

Mike might have sounded casual, but he was still testing him. He wanted to know if Mackenzie's pheromones were making Gage think with his dick instead of his head.

"You could do that," Gage said. "But I wouldn't if I were you."

Mike tensed, as if bracing for a fight. Beside him, Xander did the same.

"Why's that?" Mike asked.

"Because I don't think she's that into you," Gage told him. "I mean, you're not very attractive and you sweat…a lot. Women find that gross."

Mike stared at him, speechless for once.

HUNGRY LIKE THE WOLF   39

Xander laughed and slapped Mike on the shoulder. "Dude, I've told you that sweating thing was going to ruin your love life. Now even the boss man has noticed. You need to get that looked at."

Mike scowled at him, his brows drawing together to make his already chiseled features look extra fierce. "I don't have a sweating problem, you jackass. I'm wearing thirty-five pounds of Kevlar on a hot Texas day. Of course I'm going to sweat."

"I'm not sweating," Xander pointed out.

"That's because you haven't hit puberty yet," Mike retorted. "But just wait, in another year or two, it will happen—I promise."

Gage chuckled as his squad leaders unloaded their weapons and put away their gear. Another tense situation defused—and he didn't mean the one with the hostages. Keeping his pack of alpha werewolves under control was just as much a part of his job as figuring out when to greenlight an operation or determining the best way to enter a building full of armed thugs. In some ways it was the toughest part of the job. Because nobody wanted to have a bunch of out-of-control SWAT types running around town, especially when they also happened to be werewolves.

Yeah, they were a pain in the ass sometimes. But at the end of the day, they were his pack and he wouldn't want it any other way.

———

"What the hell's going on, Vince?" Gage asked as the Internal Affairs officer ran down the same list of questions for the third time.

After dropping Mike off at the compound, he and

Xander had come to police headquarters for what was supposed to be a quick debriefing on what had obviously been a clean shooting. But they had already been here for almost two hours.

The gray-haired man looked at him over the top of his glasses. "Just being thorough, Gage."

That was a crock of shit. It was standard procedure in an officer-involved shooting to talk to both the cop who'd done the shooting and his supervisor on the scene, but if this was just about being thorough, Internal Affairs wouldn't have put him and Xander in separate rooms for questioning.

"You already have a statement from the woman Xander saved," Gage pointed out. "She corroborated what he said—that the gunman was in the process of pulling the trigger on her. According to the other hostages in the E-Brand building and the employees at the bank they robbed, the guy had been coked up to all hell. Even his own crew admitted he hadn't been in control. How much more thorough do you need to be?"

"Just work with me on this, okay?" Vince sighed. "Trust me. We have our reasons."

Trust and *Internal Affairs* normally didn't go together, but it wasn't as if Gage had much of a choice. Unless he wanted to call in a union rep and really make a mess of this situation. Which he didn't.

So, Gage leaned back in his chair and answered Vince Coletti's questions again. God, he hoped Xander was keeping his cool in the other room. His senior squad leader was smart and had been in these shooting reviews before, so he knew what to say—and more importantly, what not to say. If the questioning seemed like it was heading in a bad direction, he was savvy enough to ask for his union rep. But Xander also had a short fuse sometimes. If IA got in his face, he might tell them to pound sand.

"Okay, I think we're good," Vince said after the fourth rehash of his story. "We're going to need to talk to Corporal Riggs for a little while longer, though."

Gage stared at the man. "Seriously?"

Vince gave him what was probably supposed to be a placating smile. "Don't worry. I'll have patrol give him a ride out to the compound."

Which was IA's way of saying he didn't want Gage hanging around because it was going to take a hell of a lot longer than a little while. But getting into it with Coletti wasn't going to help. While he might be more than ready to rip someone in half right now, Gage reined in his inner wolf. He jerked open the door and stormed out of the interrogation room, almost running over his boss, Deputy Chief Hal Mason. If he didn't know better, he'd think Hal had been waiting for him.

"Why the hell is IA grilling my senior corporal?" Gage demanded.

Hal waited until Vince had gone into the room where they were questioning Xander before answering. "IA is just doing their due diligence on this shooting, that's all. They aren't trying to screw Corporal Riggs, you have my word on that."

Gage snorted. "You could have fooled me."

The way his boss was looking at him made Gage think Hal wasn't telling him everything, but the deputy chief only sighed. "Go back to work. I'll make sure Riggs gets a ride out to the compound when IA's done with him."

Gage hated the idea of leaving Xander with IA, but Coletti could have him in interrogation the rest of the day,

and he still had to tell the Pack about Mackenzie Stone—
who'd be at the compound in a little over an hour.

Shit.

"Tell Xander I'll see him back at the compound."

Hal nodded. "I will. And Gage? Good job out there today."

Gage grunted.

Luckily, there was no sign of Mackenzie Stone's news
van in the lot when Gage arrived at the compound. He
parked the SUV, then went around to the training building, figuring that's where everyone would probably be.

He heard the sounds of growling before he even
opened the door. Officers Landry Cooper and Eric Becker
were sprawled on the couch in the dayroom watching TV
and eating popcorn.

"What the hell's going on back there?" Gage demanded, jerking his head toward the rear of the building.

Cooper, the team's explosives expert and coincidentally—or maybe not so coincidentally—the most
laid-back, in-control member of the Pack, shrugged.
"Martinez and Delaney came back a little fired up from
today's action," he said in his southern drawl. "They got
into an argument with some of the other guys and now
they're just working it out."

Which was code for going at each other like a couple
of MMA fighters.

Gage swore. Sometimes he felt more like a damn school
teacher than the commander of a team of highly trained
police officers. "And Mike didn't think it was necessary to
break it up before they destroyed something expensive?"

Cooper grabbed a handful of popcorn from the big bowl
Becker was holding. "Domestic abuse call came in about
an hour ago. Mike took Duncan and Boudreaux with him."

"Didn't you consider that maybe you should step in and do something?" Gage all but snarled.

Cooper didn't take his eyes off the TV show he was watching—a damn G.I. Joe cartoon, for crying out loud. "Not my argument."

And sometimes it felt like he was in charge of a day care center—for out of control werewolves.

Gage didn't waste his breath asking Becker why he didn't do anything. The surveillance expert was one of the newest members of the team. He might be as big and tough as anyone in the unit, but they weren't going to pay attention to anything he said. Besides, Gage didn't think he could pry the tech and electronics experts away from their tub of popcorn.

He headed toward the back of the building, wincing at a particularly loud thud. There was always a little rough-housing after a mission. It was how werewolves dealt with stress. But usually he, Xander, or Mike were around to keep things from getting out of hand. And when you had sixteen oversized alpha wolves in one pack, things could get out of hand pretty damn quick.

He noticed a couple broken chairs and a crushed desk as he passed the classroom. The disagreement must have started there, then moved to the back of the building where the weight room and gym were. He hoped they were in the gym instead of the weight room—not only was there less stuff they could break, but there were also fewer things they could use as weapons.

But while three members of the team—Senior Corporal Zane Kendrick, Senior Corporal Trevor McCall, and Officer Alex Trevino—were in the gym tossing around a basketball, they weren't the source of the racket he'd heard.

His nose confirmed the identity of the men in the weight room before he got there. All six remaining members of the team were in the weight room. Damn it.

On the bright side, only four of the men were fighting. Two of them—Senior Corporals Jayden Brooks and Carter Nelson—were doing their best to keep the other cops from grabbing anything they could use as weapons while at the same time working just as hard to keep them from destroying the workout equipment.

They were only marginally successful at both tasks.

Gage ducked to avoid a forty-five-pound weight someone threw across the room. It smashed against the wall of mirrors on the far side of the room, completely shattering the floor-to-ceiling piece of glass. Shit, he'd paid for those out of his own pocket.

A low rumble erupted from his lips. This was the reason alpha wolves rarely ever got together in a group—it was damn near impossible to keep them from fighting. But when he'd taken over the SWAT unit eight years ago, he'd made the decision to seek out the best cops in the country and get them on his team. If that meant bringing in other werewolves, that was what he did.

But days like today made him wonder if it was worth it.

Martinez and Delaney had squared off against Connor Malone and the newest member of the team, Max Lowry. Their claws were out, their canines were extended, and their eyes gleamed gold. All they'd done so far was slash each other up, but their faces and jaws were changing shape even now, which meant bites would be coming next, and they were much tougher to recover from. Worse, Malone's back was already starting to bunch up in that way it did before a full shift. And if Malone shifted

into his two-hundred-and-forty-pound wolf form, someone was probably going to get killed.

Gage let out a deep growl and waded into the midst
of the brawl, letting his fangs slide out in a partial shift
as he started laying backhanded swings that sent people
flying. The moment he had them separated, he grabbed
Malone by the shoulders and yanked him off his feet, then
slammed him against the remaining mirror hard enough
to shatter it like the others. Then he bared his teeth and
let loose a snarl loud enough to be heard well outside the
compound. He didn't care who heard—he wanted their
full attention and he wanted it now.

Malone immediately relaxed in his grip while
Martinez, Delaney, and Lowry took a few steps back.

Gage held on to his lead sniper until the man had completely shed any vestige of his wolf form. By the time he
turned to look at the other three, they had shifted back,
too. There was no evidence of the werewolves they'd
been—except for the bloody claw marks covering their
bodies and shredding their uniforms. Gage didn't shift
back. He wanted them to get a good look at his yellow-
gold eyes and gleaming fangs.

"What the hell is wrong with the four of you?" he demanded. "I walk in here expecting to find a team of profes-
sional cops, and instead I find you acting like a bunch of
freaking out-of-control Chihuahuas." He pointedly looked
around the room at the broken mirrors, crushed weight
benches, and torn mats. "We paid to renovate this weight
room out of our own pockets and you've wrecked it with your
bullshit. Somebody here better start talking fast or I'm going
to give in to my first instinct and have you all transferred to
bicycle patrol handing out parking tickets downtown."

"They started it, Sarg." To his credit, Delaney actually looked a little chagrinned at all the damage they'd done. "Martinez and I were talking about him getting shot in the arm, and Lowry said it happened because we didn't know what the hell we were doing."

Gage stared menacingly at Delaney. "The four of you tore up pack property because the new guy was trying to get under your skin?"

"That's not the way it went down, Sarg," Lowry protested.

"No?" Gage hoped like hell this new pup wasn't about to say something that was going to get him buried. "So, how did it go down? Please tell me."

Out of the corner of his eye, Gage saw Brooks and Nelson exchange a worried look. Like they thought he might snap someone's neck. He'd be lying if he said the thought hadn't crossed his mind. He'd never do it, of course.

Unfortunately, these kinds of brawls happened a lot. Regardless of the formal rank structure placed on them by the Dallas PD, his wolves were constantly challenging the pecking order within the Pack as each cop tried to outperform the other and each squad tried to make its group look better. With all the new guys he'd brought in over the years, he shouldn't be surprised the issue had come to a head again. Well, he was going to nip this competition shit in the bud right now. His team would be one, well-oiled unit, or he'd tear it down and start over.

"So?" he prompted Lowry again.

Lowry swallowed hard. Gage knew the man wasn't actually afraid of him, but he was the unchallenged alpha of the Pack, and whether the younger guys knew it or not, that position came with a certain amount of inherent control over the other pack members. Standing this close to his pissed-off lead alpha, Lowry probably felt seriously uneasy for the first time in his life. Gage hated making any of his men feel that way, but he'd learned he had to either lead them by force of will or learn to live with chaos.

Gage didn't like chaos.

"It's was nothing, Sarg," Lowry finally conceded. "We were just messing around and things got out of hand. It won't happen again."

Gage held him there until he was sure all four of them had firmly received the message. Then he lowered Delaney to the floor.

"No, it won't happen again," he agreed. "Because I'm breaking up your teams. Lowry, when Mike gets back, let him know you've been reassigned to Xander's team, and that Delaney's going to be your entry buddy. I want him to put you two shoulder-to-shoulder on every mission from this day forward."

Gage ignored the look of shock on Lowry's face and turned to look at Martinez. "I assume you got that arm looked at before you decided to get in a fight?"

The stocky man flexed his injured arm. "Yeah. Trevino fixed me up the moment we got back. It's fine."

"Good," Gage said. "Because you'll be taking Lowry's spot on Mike's team. Same thing applies—you'll be tied to Malone every time the two of you walk through a hostile doorway."

Martinez opened his mouth to argue, but Gage silenced him with a glare. Malone, on the other hand, was too fuzzy from his recent near-shift to keep his trap shut.

"But, Sarg, I'm your best sniper. I don't usually go through doors."

"You do now," Gage told him. "So, I suggest you

spend a lot of time with your new entry buddy and learn real fast."

"Sarg, you can't do this," Delaney said. "We know we screwed up and we'll fix everything, I swear. But you can't break up Martinez and me—we've been on the same team for more than three years."

"Then you'll be able to bring Lowry up to speed on Xander's tactics."

"But Sarg—"

"Have you ever seen how tight the shorts are on those bike cops?" Gage asked.

Delaney snapped his mouth shut.

Gage looked at Brooks and Nelson. "Next time I expect you two to get in the middle of a fight and break it up—or you'll be wearing the bike shorts. And I'm not sure they make any in your size, Brooks."

The big African American shifted from one foot to the other. The ex–college fullback was probably envisioning himself in tight blue shorts and perched on a bicycle. Apparently, it wasn't a very pretty image.

"Sure thing, Sergeant."

"Good." Gage jerked his head at the four junior officers. "Make sure they get those wounds cleaned up right before they start to heal. And make sure Martinez didn't rip his open again."

All he needed was for Martinez to be the first werewolf who got an infection. Going to the hospital really wasn't something werewolves preferred to do.

Gage started for the door, then stopped and turned back to them. "And get this mess cleaned up. I want everyone in the classroom in fifteen minutes."

He didn't need to see his men's scowls to know he

wasn't their favorite person right now. It made him wonder what they were going to think of him when he told them about Mackenzie Stone.

"Xander isn't getting jacked up," Gage said for the third time.

He'd started their all-call meeting with a quick briefing of the hostage situation earlier, then touched on the detailed level of questioning he and Xander had gone through downtown. At least he'd planned on it being brief. He wanted to get to the real reason he'd called everyone together—Mackenzie Stone—but he couldn't get the team to focus on anything other than Internal Affairs grilling one of their own.

"Then why is IA still questioning him?" Remy Boudreaux asked, a trace of his Louisiana accent coming through.

Gage suppressed a growl. Sometimes his guys were bigger conspiracy nuts than Mulder and Scully. "They're just going over his statement to make sure there aren't any inconsistencies that could end up in a lawsuit. They're trying to help him, not screw him. Besides, he's probably already on his way back."

"Then if you didn't call us here to talk about Xander, what's this about?" Martinez asked.

Gage was pleased to see the cop sitting beside his new best buddy, Malone. On the other side of the room, Delaney and Lowry were doing the same. Maybe they had the ability to overcome their petty squabbles faster than he'd given them credit for.

"Yeah, Sarg." Mike was lounging back in his chair,

a knowing smile on his face. "What are we here to talk about?"

Gage scowled at his squad leader. Mike wasn't going to cut him a break, damn him. And while the rest of the guys might not know what was going on, they'd definitely picked up on the strange vibe. Well, everyone except for Cooper. He was reading a damn comic book.

"I wanted to tell you that we'll be having a visitor hanging around the compound for the next few days," Gage said.

"What kind of visitor?" Cooper asked, raising his gaze from his comic book long enough to show he was capable of multitasking.

Oh hell, no way to avoid this. Might as well rip off the Band-Aid. "A reporter from the *Dallas Daily Star*—Mackenzie Stone."

Gage waited, expecting an immediate firestorm of negative comments. But his announcement was met with complete silence. Though whether that silence was because they were stunned or just indifferent, he couldn't tell.

"I've seen her picture," Becker said. "She's really hot."

Okay, that wasn't the comment he expected. Then again, this was Becker. The information tech and electronic surveillance expert always said the first thing that came to his mind. As if to prove his point, Becker pulled out his iPhone and quickly found a picture of the journalist to show the other guys. They took one look at her photo and agreed that Ms. Stone was "smokin'." Damn, sometimes they could be so shallow.

Cooper passed the phone back to Becker. "Isn't Mackenzie Stone known for her in-depth investigative stories, ones usually involving corrupt politicians or major crime figures? What does she want with us?"

The rest of the unit stopped debating about whether Mackenzie Stone had a boyfriend or not to give Gage a worried look. For all the trouble they caused him with the bickering, the fighting, and the constant effort to move up the Pack's command structure, they trusted him to protect and keep hidden the one thing they cared about—their identity as werewolves. Because if they were scared of anything, it was being exposed for what they really were.

Gage sat on the edge of the desk at the front of the room. "Ms. Stone said she wants to see how we operate so she can write a story on how we work together as a team."

"Do you believe her?" asked Trey Duncan, the unit's other resident medic and entry man.

"Honestly? I think it's a load of crap." At their surprised looks, he continued. "As Cooper said, Ms. Stone specializes in digging into serious stories that grab national headlines. I doubt she's interested in writing a fluff piece about the city's SWAT team. I'm guessing she's seen all our accolades and figures there's something fishy going on. I don't know if she thinks we're crooked or in league with the criminals we take down or what. Ultimately, it doesn't matter what her angle is. I've decided the best way to get her to go away is to bring her in and let her see what we do."

Becker stared at him in disbelief. "You're going to tell her we're werewolves?"

Gage would have laughed if anything about this was funny. "No, I'm not going to tell her the entire SWAT team is made up of werewolves. But I will show her how hard we work and train, how much we care about the people of this city, and what we're willing to risk for them. I'm going to be charming and friendly—we're *all* going to be charming and friendly. By the time she leaves, Mackenzie Stone will realize we're nothing more than hardworking, dedicated cops, not a story for the evening news."

"And what if she doesn't buy that line?" Mike asked from the back of the room. The smile he wore earlier was gone now. "What if she keeps digging?"

Gage met his gaze. "I guess it's on me to make sure that doesn't happen, isn't it?" He scanned the room. "But I need all of your help to do it. As long as Mackenzie Stone is around, you're going to have to stay in complete and total control. No one going half wolf on me, no one jumping a wall they shouldn't be able to jump, no one running faster than they should be able to run. And definitely no fighting. You need to look like the best SWAT team in the country. Got it?"

Slow nods came from around the room, Mike included.

Gage took a deep breath. Until now, he hadn't realized how hard hiding their secret from Mackenzie Stone was going to be. But his pack was depending on him to keep them safe, and that's what he'd do.

As everyone stood up to get back to work, Gage added one more thing. "Ms. Stone will be here in less than an hour. I want that weight room cleaned up before she shows up. Get on it."

That earned him some groans, but not nearly as many as he expected. Maybe this was going to work.

Chapter 3

MAC TOOK HER CAR TO THE SWAT COMPOUND, LEAVING Zak and the news van behind on purpose. She wanted to send a clear signal to Dixon that she was agreeing to his terms—no video cameras, no recording devices, no divulging secret tactical procedures. Of course, she had no interest in secret tactical procedures, and wouldn't have printed them regardless. She was after something else entirely. She rolled to a stop outside the gate and turned off the engine. She didn't know what it was yet, but her instincts told her there was the mother of all stories behind that fence.

She grabbed her purse, but didn't bother with the monster camera Zak had tossed in the backseat. She still had her trusty little camera tucked in her back pocket. And if Dixon wanted to take it from her, she had her iPhone.

She took a deep breath, relaxed her shoulders, and put on her game face. Sergeant Gage Dixon was no idiot. He knew she was snooping for a story. She had to remember not to underestimate the man simply because he was attractive as all get-out.

Mac headed for the gate to ring the bell, only to stop when she realized Dixon was already waiting for her. He was standing there in his navy blue uniform, which consisted of military-style pants bloused above combat boots and a skintight T-shirt that showed off every muscle he had—and there were a lot of them.

She dragged her mind out of the fantasy it was headed for and gave him a smile. "Sergeant Dixon, you didn't have to meet me at the gate. You could have just buzzed me in."

He opened the door, returning her smile with a devastating grin of his own. "What kind of host would I be if I did that? And if we're going to be spending so much time together, maybe you can stop with the formalities and just call me Gage."

Maybe this was going to be easier than she'd thought. "Okay, but only if you call me Mac—it's what all my friends call me."

"I like the idea of being friends, but if it's all the same to you, I think I'll call you Mackenzie." He grimaced. "Mac makes me think of a big, overweight trucker, and you definitely don't fit that image."

Mac couldn't help but laugh. He was the first guy who ever told her he wouldn't call her by her nickname. Most guys would call a woman Hannibal Lecter if they thought it'd get them in her panties. Perhaps it was an indication that working Dixon—Gage—was going to take a different approach. *Not to mention a more subtle touch*, she thought as he led her across the parking lot and into what he called the training-slash-maintenance building. It had a break room, a classroom, a small gym with basketball hoops, and a few rooms for storing tactical gear and other equipment.

"What's in there?" she asked as they walked past a room that had the door closed.

If the door was closed, it was a place she wanted to see. And if he resisted, it meant she *really* wanted to see it.

Gage frowned. "Just another gym." He opened the

door to reveal a weight room. "We had a little accident and some of the mirrors got broken, but we should have it back in shape in a day or so."

So much for a room full of those deep, dark secrets she'd been hoping for. "I guess you guys have to work out a lot, huh? To get all those big muscles, I mean."

She figured a guy his size would appreciate a little love thrown his way when it came to maintaining his physique, but he only chuckled.

"We work out, but not as much as you think. We stay in shape mostly from the training we do. You know—a lot of running, climbing obstacles, carrying heavy gear and each other." When she lifted a brow, he added, "To simulate evacuating a wounded man. The weight room is here more to give the guys something to keep their minds occupied between incidents, as well as help deal with stress afterward."

She wasn't sure how much she bought that. Somebody his size needed to work out—a lot. But she certainly enjoyed the spoils of his efforts. Gage had a nice body. She could only imagine how much better he'd look with his clothes off.

She immediately berated herself for forgetting why she was there. *Focus on the dang story.*

They ran into four members of his team as he took her on a tour of the last storage room in the building. The men were repacking some kind of gear she didn't recognize, but stopped when she and Gage walked in.

"Mackenzie, this is Officer Hale Delaney, one of our specialists in less lethal tactics and martial arts. Officer Eric Becker, computers and surveillance. Officer Landry Cooper, explosives and demolitions expert. And Officer

Remy Boudreaux, shotgun breech specialist and assistant armorer." Gage glanced at her. "Meet Mackenzie Stone from the *Dallas Daily Star*."

Mac already knew their names and their specialties from the personnel file she'd made. She smiled and shook each of their hands. And like the other SWAT cops who'd rescued the hostages that morning, they were all big, tall, and muscular. Not to mention easy on the eyes.

As Gage led her over to the next building, he gave her a tutorial on how the SWAT team was organized.

"We have a lot of flexibility when it comes to how we operate, based on the mission," he said. "We have two separate squads within the unit—Mike runs one and Xander leads the other. They can operate independently or together as part of the full team. If there's more than one incident at a time, or if a particular mission calls for it, we break the team up into thirds, with me leading the third squad."

"Do you always run the operation from the vehicle you were in today?" she asked as they entered the administrative building.

"Normally, no." He gave her a wry smile. "I try to stay as close to the action as I can, but today was a little different because I needed to be there to communicate directly with the on-scene commander and the power company. Plus, we had the department's crisis negotiator there because we were hoping to make a deal with the gunmen and avoid a confrontation, but that didn't work."

When they got to the main office, he introduced her to Officers Alex Trevino and Max Lowry, two of the team's snipers. It seemed odd to see big, strapping men like them sitting at desks filling out forms.

"SWAT officers doing paperwork?" She shook her head. "Tell me it isn't so."

The two men laughed.

"Unfortunately, it's the bane of all police work," Gage said. "The more actual cop work you do, the more reports you have to fill out."

While the admin part of the job might be boring, Mac did see one thing that caught her attention. Next to the office was a room filled with filing cabinets. If there was something interesting to find around here, that'd definitely be the best place to start.

She and Gage were heading out the back door of the building when they passed a set of stairs that led up to the second floor.

"What's up there?" she asked when Gage didn't offer to give her a tour.

Gage paused, his hand on the doorknob. "Some is storage, but most of it is barracks space."

"Barracks space?"

"Yeah. You know—showers, a small kitchen, and a few bedrooms. In case we have to work late or need to keep a crew here on twenty-four-hour shifts."

"Oh." It probably didn't look like a room at the Ritz, but she had a sudden urge to see it anyway. Where would men like Gage crash after pulling an all-nighter? "Mind if I take a look? Just so I can get a feel for how you spend your downtime?"

He shrugged and gestured up the stairs. "After you."

Mac was about halfway up the stairs when it occurred to her that Gage might have asked her to go first so he could stare at her ass. She threw a quick glance over her shoulder to check and was disappointed to see he wasn't even looking. Damn. If she couldn't distract him with her feminine assets, this job might turn out to be tougher than she thought—and it was already tough to begin with.

As he'd said, some of the space upstairs was dedicated to storage, but there was also a small kitchen with a table and some chairs, as well as a large community shower, and a room with four cots that looked as if they would have fit in just fine on a military base...or a prison. Even the blankets were rough, made of uncomfortable-looking wool. The room also had a wall of gray lockers Gage explained held extra uniforms and personal gear.

Well, one thing was for sure. No one could accuse SWAT of misappropriating tax dollars for their own comfort. The place was positively Spartan.

Mac turned to say as much to Gage when she caught sight of the pile of bloody gauze bandages on the counter. Gage must have seen the direction of her gaze because he hurriedly swept them into a trash can with his arm.

"One of the men got nicked during the hostage rescue," he explained.

Martinez. She'd almost forgotten. "Is he okay?"

"Yeah, he's fine. It was just a little scratch. One of our medics patched him up."

Mac wasn't an expert on scratches, but that had certainly looked like a heck of a lot of blood for a scratch. She wished she could swipe one of those bloody bandages so she could get it tested, but there wasn't any way to do it with Gage standing there. She would have to wait until they put the trash on the curb for pickup and dig through it. Until then, the bloody bandages were just one more nugget of information to be filed away for later.

As they walked through the bedroom area, she looked

at the uncomfortable beds again, then glanced at Gage. "Do you spend much time here?"

He gave her a wry smile on the way down the stairs. "Unfortunately. I wasn't kidding when I said we have to do a lot of paperwork. I stay here two or three nights a week just trying to keep up with it."

Huh. Guess that answered the question as to whether he had a girlfriend. She already knew from his personnel file that he wasn't married, but with work hours like his it was safe to assume he wasn't seeing anyone, at least not regularly.

They ran into Diego Martinez on their way out of the building. He was carrying what looked like a footlocker on his shoulder. The thing had to weigh seventy-five pounds easy, but he held it like it was nothing. Maybe his injury hadn't been as bad as it looked—or the designer drug he might be taking made him impervious to pain as well as super strong.

As Gage made the introductions, she searched for signs that Martinez was juicing, but his eyes weren't dilated, his hands weren't shaking, and his skin wasn't cold and clammy. If he was taking drugs, it was the type that didn't have any visible side effects.

She pointed to a series of buildings as they crossed the back of the compound. "What are those?"

Gage followed her gaze. "We use those to simulate different tactical scenarios. We can practice climbing, rappelling, going through windows, breeching doors, explosive entry—pretty much anything we want."

As they got closer, Mac realized that what she'd thought were buildings were actually facades, like something on a Hollywood movie set. Gage gave her a tour, describing

the kinds of things the team used them for in more detail.
Even though she kept telling herself she was only there to
look for evidence of some wrongdoing, she couldn't help
but be fascinated by the training he and his men did. She
almost wished she *were* writing a fluff piece on them.

She found herself standing a lot closer to Gage than
necessary, too. And it had nothing to do with her trying to
play him. She might be a journalist, but she was a woman,
too. And she couldn't deny she was flat-out attracted to
Gage. Hell, she wasn't sure there were many women
in the world who wouldn't be attracted to the man. She
knew she should fight it, but she didn't. Instead, she put
her covert mission on hold and gave herself permission
to have fun.

He was one of those rare people who could talk about
anything she brought up, including local and national
politics. She was floored he knew the names and agendas
of every political mover and shaker not only in Texas but
on the national level and in Mexico, too. Before long,
they were talking about topics that had nothing to do with
SWAT, cops, or even journalism. And she was enjoying
the heck out of it.

Mac didn't even realize how much time had passed until
she noticed they'd toured at least a dozen training buildings, an obstacle course, a climbing tower that was way too
high in her opinion, two shooting ranges, and a beach volleyball court of all things. The next thing she knew, they'd
done a whole circuit of the SWAT training grounds and
were heading back toward the admin building. But instead
of taking her there, Gage led her to a one-floor building
without any windows. More storage, maybe?

"Last stop on the tour. I figured you might want to

get a look at our armory." Gage flashed her a grin. "No offense, but it's been my experience that reporters seem to have an unhealthy fascination with the weapons SWAT uses for some reason."

She smiled up at him. "No offense taken, since I'm a journalist, not a reporter."

"What's the difference?"

"About thirty thousand a year."

He chuckled, but didn't say anything as he opened the door for her. The building was a welcome relief from the blistering temperatures outside, and Mac pushed her sunglasses up on her head. A police officer behind the counter that blocked their entry into the back half of the building looked up when they entered.

"This is Senior Corporal Trevor McCall," Gage said. "Beyond his normal SWAT duties, he's also our senior armorer. He maintains and repairs all our weapons, modifying them when needed. McCall, meet Mackenzie Stone."

She shook hands with the officer, marveling that here was yet another hot, muscular guy. She didn't realize it was even statistically possible for that many attractive men to be in one place. This had to be a record or something.

"Come on back and I'll give you the grand tour," McCall said.

Gage waited for her to walk around the counter, then followed. There were actually two doors between them and the room where the weapons were kept—the first was made out of a wire material while the other was a solid metal door. Big safes and cabinets lined each wall, along with several shelves with storage bins.

The men led her around the room, pulling out weapons

and explaining what they were, how they worked, and what the SWAT team used them for. Mac had seen quite a few weapons, from the pistols the gang members in Dallas carried to the assault rifles and machine guns the cartel drug runners used, but she wasn't an expert and she quickly got lost in all the details as Gage and McCall explained the differences between this carbine and that rifle. She could barely recognize the difference. Then they showed her all the handguns they stored in the various safes and really confused her. All the numbers started spinning around her head like bees— .380, .40, .357, .38, 9mm, 10mm—and those were just the ones she caught in passing.

"Hang on," she said, holding up her hand. "Why do you need so many different sizes of guns? Are you guys hoarders or something?"

Both men laughed.

"You know, you might be onto something," McCall agreed. "We've picked up most of them over the years, but hardly ever shoot them."

"Most of us use Sig 9mms or .40 calibers for both our primary and backup weapons, but I've always thought it was a good idea to be as familiar as possible with as many different weapons as we can," Gage added. "You never know when it might come in handy."

They showed her a couple of their favorites, letting her hold them so she could get a feel for their heft and balance.

Gage eyed her curiously. "You have much experience firing a handgun?"

She shook her head. "Not really. I've only fired a gun once. My dad let me shoot his pistol when I was twelve." She pointed at the big, heavy revolver she'd just been holding. "It was about the same size as that one. Scared the hell out of me and I dropped it. That was the last time he let me try."

Gage frowned. "A gun that size isn't made for someone with small hands, much less a kid."

She couldn't argue with that. While she loved her dad, he wasn't the most patient teacher in the world, which was ironic considering it was how he made his living. If he knew how to do something, he just assumed everybody else should be smart enough to know how to do it, too. Luckily, he taught English literature and not a weapons class.

"You know," Gage said, his dark eyes softening, "if you want to try again, I could show you how to shoot a gun you'd be more comfortable with."

Mac smiled. "That sounds fun."

Gage smiled at her in return, and she realized after a bit that she was just standing there with a goofy grin on her face. She tucked a loose strand of hair behind her ear, looking away. And caught McCall looking at them expectantly.

"That does sound fun." It took her a second to remember what they'd been talking about. That's right. Target shooting. "We can get all the guys out there—it'll be a blast."

Gage scowled at him, but didn't say anything.

Mac wandered around while Gage and McCall put away the weapons they'd dragged out. That was when she saw the hard plastic cases stacked on shelves inside a heavy-duty, wire storage bin.

She smiled at Gage over her shoulder. "You guys have more guns in there? What, you run out of cabinets and safes to hold them?"

Gage glanced at her as he closed one of the safes. "Those are our night vision goggles."

Mac's Spidey senses immediately began to tingle. "Like the ones the guys used during the hostage rescue today? They sound cool. Can I see them?"

"Sure."

Gage took the set of keys McCall held out, then opened the gate. He grabbed the first box he came to and opened it, but not before she saw the name of the SWAT officer the goggles belonged to—Mike Taylor. The same Mike Taylor who'd supposedly worn them that morning. But from the layer of dust on the top of the case, it hadn't been opened in a while, much less earlier today.

"I would have thought you'd leave these on your response truck," she said as he handed her the goggles.

Gage didn't answer right away. In her experience, that usually meant whatever a person said after that would be a lie.

"They're expensive," he said. "So we keep them locked up here in the cage between incidents."

Uh-huh.

"These are PVS-14 military-grade NVGs," Gage told her. "They run about four thousand dollars a pop, but are worth every penny."

She only half listened as he explained how to wear the goggles and turn them on. Mostly because she was focused on trying to figure out what to make of this new piece of information. Obviously, they hadn't worn NVGs—as Gage called them—on the hostage rescue that morning. But why not?

Because the drug they were taking allowed them to see

so well in the dark that they didn't need NVGs? But that was too stupid for words.

"When you come by to go target shooting, you can try out a pair of these, too," Gage said as he put the goggles back in the case.

She nodded. "Sounds like a plan."

That could have come out a bit more enthusiastic, but she was still trying to wrap her mind around why a SWAT team would leave a critical piece of equipment behind when it went on a call. Maybe they'd forgotten to bring them. If so, Gage and his men weren't dirty, just stupid. And that didn't explain why they'd been able to see in a pitch-black building.

Mac gave McCall a wave as they walked out. Damn, the sun was already starting to set. She looked at her watch and saw that she and Gage had been walking around for almost four hours. And while she'd definitely enjoyed herself—maybe a lot more than she should have—she hadn't gotten anything solid to go on. She'd been so distracted by his charm, tight T-shirt, and amazing good looks, she'd barely asked any of the questions she'd planned. The SWAT commander had handled her with ease, guiding the conversation and keeping her off her game for most of the afternoon. The only thing she could say for sure was that while she didn't have a clue how all the strange tidbits of information she'd collected were connected, she was even more certain there was a story here.

But how was she going to get her hands on it? Her day with Gage and his SWAT team was about to come to an end, and she wasn't sure if a return visit was in the plans—regardless of the casual invitation to do some target shooting.

"I hope I didn't bore you too much," Gage said when they reached the gate. "I couldn't help noticing you weren't interested in what I was saying about the NVGs. Not that I blame you—it's pretty dry stuff."

Mac felt her face heat. She hadn't realized he'd seen her zone out. "I wasn't bored. I was just a little distracted, that's all."

"Distracted, huh?" His smile was so knowing that for a moment she thought he was onto her. "Why's that?"

Damn, he was making this almost too easy.

"Well..." She gave him a sheepish look. "I was thinking about the fact that I sort of fibbed to you a little before."

"Fibbed about what?"

Despite the way he crossed his arms over his chest to show off those exceptional biceps and pecs of his, he didn't seem angry. Or even mildly annoyed.

"Being here for an in-depth story about a day in the life of a SWAT officer," she said slowly.

His eyes narrowed. "Then why are you here?"

Now came the really tricky part. Straying too far from the truth could get her into trouble, but she couldn't be too honest, either. Usually, that didn't bother her if it meant getting a story. But in this case, it did.

Mac ignored her guilty conscience and pushed ahead. "My editor sent me to confirm a rumor he'd heard about the SWAT team."

"What rumor is that?"

She felt another twinge of remorse and immediately squashed it. This next part wasn't really a lie—not completely anyway. "That your team is using performance-enhancing drugs."

Gage didn't say anything. Instead, he regarded her with those beautiful dark eyes of his. Crap. What if she'd tread a little too close to the truth?

But then he smiled that gorgeous smile. "Since you're telling me this, I assume you don't believe that?"

She moved a little closer, letting her arm brush against his. The brief contact made her body tingle all the way down to her toes, and she quickly stepped back. He was supposed to be the one getting flustered, not her.

"Of course not," she said when she finally found her voice. "But my boss is going to need more to go on than my assurances. Especially since I've only spent a few hours with you."

He considered that. "I can see how that might be a problem. Any idea how you can convince him the rumors are wrong?"

She threw him a quick glance from under her lashes to see if he'd caught on to her game yet, but his face gave nothing away. "I thought I could hang around the compound for a few days, maybe watch the SWAT team train..."

"Then your editor would be more likely to believe you when you told him you thoroughly checked everything out and concluded that none of us are using PEDs?" Gage finished for her.

She grinned. "Exactly."

Gage didn't return her smile. "I wish I could okay something like that, but the department has policies against giving a journalist complete access to the unit."

Damn. "Isn't there anything we can do to get around that policy?"

He thought a moment. "I suppose I could tell the department we'd been planning this story for a while and that I'm okay with you hanging out with us while you write it."

"You'd do that for me?"

"Sure," he said. "I think we should spend a little more time talking about what you have in mind for your story before I agree, though. Say, over dinner tonight? If you're free."

Okay, she hadn't expected that. Not that she minded going out with the handsome SWAT commander. In fact, she should have thought of it herself. What better way to get Gage to open up than over an intimate dinner for two?

Mac smiled. "As a matter of fact, I am."

Gage heard two men come up behind him as he watched Mackenzie Stone walk back to her car. He didn't have to turn around to know it was Mike and Xander. And he didn't have to look at them to pick up on their disapproval.

"You know she was playing you the whole time, right?" Xander said. "She's not here because she thinks we're taking steroids. Her heart was beating too fast when she said it. She was lying."

Gage didn't answer. Instead he watched Mackenzie bend over to move something around in the backseat of the car. Damn, she had an amazing ass. He could stand there and gaze at it all day. As she straightened and closed the back door, he admitted her butt wasn't her only amazing asset—she was supermodel beautiful with long, shiny hair, curves in all the right places, and a killer smile that could make a man do stupid things. He was going to have to be extra careful around her. Mackenzie might not look it, but she was dangerous.

And it wasn't only because Xander had been right about her lying to him.

He dragged himself away from the picture of female perfection on the other side of the fence, and turned to look at Xander. "How'd it go with IA?"

He might have been occupied with Mackenzie all day, but that didn't mean he'd forgotten his senior squad leader was downtown getting grilled, or that Xander hadn't come back until thirty minutes ago. While Gage was worried about a reporter like Mackenzie Stone finding out the entire SWAT team was made up of werewolves, IA was the bigger threat. They had details on every arrest the team had made and raid they'd done. If anyone was going to connect the dots, it'd be Internal Affairs.

"It went fine," Xander said. "They just asked me to go over my story again and again. Usually that'd mean they were looking to catch me in a lie, but they didn't act as if I did anything wrong or say anything to make me think they were suspicious about something."

"Tell him about the lawyer," Mike said.

Gage frowned. "They had a lawyer there?"

"Yeah. That was definitely weird," Xander said. "They had a city lawyer there listening to everything I said. He even asked for clarification a few times. IA didn't say I could go until he gave the okay."

Gage didn't like the sound of that. "IA didn't say why he was there?"

Xander shook his head. "Not a thing. But since they didn't say anything to make me think I'm in trouble, I'm not going to worry about it. I am damn worried about that reporter, though."

"I know she was lying. But I expected that." It didn't

mean Gage liked it, though. "Whether she lied or not doesn't change anything. I'll keep an eye on her and make sure she doesn't discover anything that can cause a problem."

Mike's face looked skeptical. "You think you can honestly keep her snooping under control? She seems like a handful, if you ask me."

Understatement there. "I think so."

"You think so?" Xander repeated. "Not exactly the confident answer I was looking for."

"Confidence can be a bad thing when you're dealing with a woman like Mackenzie Stone," Gage said. "She's not only smart, she's persistent. And she has better instincts than any person I've met. She might not have a clue we're werewolves, but she knows there's something going on."

Mike frowned. "What makes you say that?"

"Because her heart sped up like crazy when she was looking at the night vision goggles in the armory."

"The NVGs?" Mike looked as confused as Gage felt. "Why would she care about those?"

Gage shrugged. "I don't know. But it's part of the reason I asked her out to dinner. I have to figure out what she knows—or thinks she knows. And to do that, I need to get her somewhere she'll relax and lower her guard. I have to get the upper hand in this situation, and fast."

"Uh-huh." That knowing grin from earlier was back on Mike's face. "And what's the other part?"

"Other part?"

"Yeah. You said finding out what she knows was only part of the reason you asked her out to dinner. Any chance the other part might have something to do with how hard you were staring at Ms. Stone's very fine ass?"

Gage opened his mouth to deny it, but it'd be useless.

Werewolves knew when one of their own found a woman attractive. They could sense it like they sensed everything else. Mike had picked up on it the moment he'd seen Gage and Mackenzie together.

"Okay, I admit Mackenzie is attractive. And that might have something to do with asking her out to dinner," he added when Mike lifted a brow. "What? You don't think I can have a good time with her and still take care of the Pack?"

"We'd like to think you can, but we'd have to be blind not to see the effect she has on you," Xander said.

Gage clenched his jaw. "What the hell is that supposed to mean?"

Xander looked to Mike for help, but he just shrugged. "I mean that it seems like she might be *The One* for you, is all."

The One, capital *T* capital *O*. Gage snorted. "You know I don't believe in that crap. Mackenzie smells great. Doesn't mean she has some psychic ability to control my mind."

"Maybe not," Mike agreed with a laugh. "But that doesn't mean she can't control the rest of you."

"Funny," Gage chuckled. "Maybe you get a hard-on anytime you're around a woman who showers more than once a week, but my standards are a little higher."

It was Mike's turn to snort. "You mean like a beautiful face, long silky hair, an awesome ass, and legs up to there? Because I couldn't help but notice that Ms. Stone has that going on, too."

Gage growled and stepped toward Mike before he even realized what he was doing. Just the thought that his squad leader had been checking out Mackenzie's ass bothered him way more than it should have. Fortunately, Xander quickly stepped between them.

"Look, Gage, we're not saying there's anything wrong with her being *The One*, if that's what she is," Xander said. "The problem is that she's a reporter who wouldn't waste a second telling the whole world if she discovered our secret."

The whole idea was ridiculous. But Xander hadn't been a werewolf as long as he and Mike had. He was still young enough to believe the urban legend that every werewolf had a single mate out there, and that once he found her, everything would be right with the world. That was bullshit made up by some desperate young werewolves as a way to make themselves feel better about the fact that they could never make things work with a human woman.

"She's not *The One*." Gage forced himself not to sound too bitter. For all he knew, Xander was one of those werewolves who hoped and prayed for the legend to be true. "And even if she was, it wouldn't matter. Protecting the Pack is my first priority."

"Even if she stumbles on our secret?" Mike asked.

That was a question Gage didn't know how to answer. When he'd convinced Mike, Xander, and the others to come to Dallas and join a team where they wouldn't have to hide their identities from each other, he promised to keep their secret. And for eight years, he'd been true to his word. The minute they thought he couldn't, they'd be gone. He couldn't let that happen, not after all he'd been through to get them to where they were now.

"She won't," he finally said.

"But if she does?" Xander insisted.

Gage met his squad leader's gaze. "Then I'll do whatever I have to do to protect the Pack."

Chapter 4

MAC WAS STILL GIDDY AS SHE STEPPED OUT OF THE elevator and weaved her way through the newsroom to her desk. Today had gone better than she could have imagined. Not only had she learned enough to know there was definitely something shady going on at the SWAT compound, but she was also pretty sure Gage Dixon was attracted to her. Even though he was supposed to be the focus of her investigation, that thrilled the hell out of her. If she was lucky, she might be able to get her story and still stay on Gage's good side. Right. Like Gage was going to forget she'd exposed whoever was using drugs and gotten them suspended…or worse. But a girl could dream. At least for tonight.

She sat down at her desk and grabbed a half-eaten bag of pita chips she'd stashed in her top drawer the previous day. She hadn't realized she was starving until she'd left the compound. There was absolutely no way she could make it to dinner without eating. She hadn't gotten more than a handful of the salty, but supposedly healthy, chips in her mouth when Zak sauntered over.

"Hey, you're back." He perched on one corner of her desk. "Ted wants to talk to you."

Mac nodded and shoved another handful of chips into her mouth.

"So, how'd things go with SWAT?" Zak asked, completely disregarding the fact she was busy with a mouthful of food.

She got enough down to answer. "They went great. I mean, I haven't learned anything definitive yet, but I discovered enough to certainly pique my curiosity, for sure."

Zak's mouth quirked. "You are talking about the story, right?"

"Very funny. Yes, I was talking about the story. What the heck did you think I meant?"

He reached into the bag to steal some of her chips. "Well, I know you have a thing for muscular men in uniform."

Mac gave him an indignant look. "I do not!"

"Right." He snorted. "So, what'd you learn?"

Mac told him about the bloody bandages and her suspicions about the night vision goggles. She left out the part about having a date with the SWAT commander. Zak was her best friend in the world and the older brother she'd never had, but he wasn't stupid.

"Okay," he said as he grabbed some more chips. "What aren't you telling me?"

She stifled the urge to groan. He should have been a journalist instead of a photographer with that nose of his. He could smell a lie a mile away. But if she told him about having dinner with Gage, he'd only disapprove. Not of flirting with Gage to get a story. She'd done that before. He wouldn't even have an issue with her being attracted to Gage. That had happened a time or two as well. The thing that'd bother Zak was this crazy idea of hers that she could have her cake and eat it, too.

"You can't work both sides of the fence," he had said more than once. *"Figure out what you want and go after it, but don't be greedy. If you do, you'll end up getting hurt. Or hurting someone you end up caring about."*

Even though she thought he was being melodramatic,

she'd always backed off. Not from going after a story she wanted, but from getting involved with whomever she was investigating. The story was always more important. But this time was different. She couldn't forget about that crazy reaction she'd had when her arm had brushed Gage's.

She popped another chip in her mouth. "Nothing. That's the whole enchilada."

Zak regarded her doubtfully. "Sure, whatever you say, Mac. But promise me you'll be careful. If you're right and these SWAT guys are crooked, you need to be careful. There are a lot of scary people in this town who piss in their boots at the idea of the DPD SWAT coming through their front door. Don't forget that."

"I won't," she promised. "Now, stop worrying. I'm going to go see Ted. Don't eat all my pita chips while I'm gone."

Ted Simms had been her editor since she'd started working at the newspaper. A big man with a serious twang and more awards than Mac could even name, Ted could be a teddy bear one minute and a grizzly the next, but she wouldn't want to work for anyone else.

He looked up from his computer when she walked in, his bushy brows coming together over his reading glasses. "Where the hell have you been all day?"

She flopped down in one of the chairs in front of his desk. "I told Zak to tell you I'd be out at the SWAT compound."

"For five hours?"

"Four, actually." But who was counting? "I got the guided tour. And starting tomorrow, I've been given a free pass to spend the next few days with them." She grinned. "No one has ever gotten this kind of access, Ted. No one!"

She didn't expect her editor to fist-bump her or

anything, but he looked as if he'd just eaten something that didn't agree with him.

He took off his glasses and set them on the desk. "I don't think it's a good idea for you to spend too much time with those SWAT guys, Mac."

What the heck? She'd just told him she got a ticket on the fifty-yard line of the biggest game in town, and now he didn't want her to go?

"Ted, I know you think these SWAT guys are squeaky clean, but I'm telling you they're up to something," she said. "I promise I won't print a word unless it's Pulitzer-worthy. If this turns out to be a simple case of cops on the take, I'll drop the whole thing."

Her editor sighed. "Do you know who was killed during the SWAT raid this morning?"

The sudden change of gear caught her off guard. "What? No, I don't know who it was. And this may sound terrible, but I saw the video of how the guy was acting—slapping women around and waving his gun everywhere—so I don't have a problem with him being dead. The SWAT team may be up to something, but they did Dallas a service by killing that thug."

"That *thug* was Ryan Hardy."

"As in the son of Walter Hardy?"

She wasn't on a first-name basis with many thugs, but she knew Walter—everyone in Dallas knew him.

"Yes." Ted's mouth tightened. "His only son. As in the kid the crazy bastard dotes on."

Now she was the one who felt as if she'd eaten something that didn't agree with her. "Oh, crap."

"Yeah—crap. Now do you understand why you need to stay away from this?"

Mac understood all right. She'd made a living out of dealing with some unsavory men, but Walter Hardy had to be at the top of the heap when it came to assholes. Drugs, stolen cars, prostitutes, sex slaves, weapons, murder—if there was an illegal way to make money and hurt people in the process, Hardy was involved in it. And in almost forty years in the business on both sides of the border, no one had ever come close to proving anything. He'd never even been taken in for questioning, much less arrested.

Part of it was because the man was more intelligent than the average criminal. He was Oxford educated and had multiple degrees to go along with a ton of street smarts. On top of that, he was rich beyond belief. And in a city of very rich men, that was saying a lot. He owned more real estate and cargo ships than anyone could count, not to mention that he sat on the board of a dozen major companies. To say he was powerful and connected was putting it mildly. He was definitely a man people didn't want to mess with.

"Rumor is he believes the federal, state, and local governments conspired to kill his son because they couldn't get to him. He's overlooking the fact that his son broke into a bank, shot several cops, then took all those hostages—all on video." Ted shook his head. "But facts never get in the way for people like Hardy."

No, they didn't. "Okay, so Hardy thinks the government is out to get him. What does any of this have to do with my investigation of SWAT?"

"Because while Hardy might not be able to go after some supposed government officials who gave the orders to kill his son, he can go after the people who pulled the trigger. He's going to make someone pay, Mac, and that someone is SWAT."

Her editor had good reason to be worried, but as sensible as it was to keep her distance from all things SWAT at the moment, she couldn't do that. It wasn't that she was crazy or reckless. She simply knew a good story when she saw one. And this story had just gotten better.

Ted must have figured that out, too, because he sighed. "I'm not going to be able to stop you, am I? Then at least promise me you'll be careful."

"I will," she said. When he lifted a brow, she added, "I promise."

———

Gage knocked on her door exactly on time. No surprise there. He'd probably gotten to her apartment building ten minutes early just so he could drive around and memorize the layout of the neighborhood.

Mac gave her reflection one more look in the bedroom's full-length mirror, wondering for about the tenth time if she should have worn jeans instead of the little black dress she had on. But somewhere between the fourth and fifth change of clothes, she'd admitted to herself that this date was about more than simply being a means to an end. She liked spending time with Gage. That wasn't such a bad thing, right?

Of course, if Gage took her to the local pizza place down the street, she was going to regret not wearing something more casual.

Her worries disappeared when she opened the door to discover the SWAT commander hadn't gone the jeans and T-shirt route, either. Instead, he was wearing a suit that showed off his impressive height and wide shoulders. Damn, he looked good enough to eat.

Gage flashed her a smile. "Hope I'm not too early."

"You're perfect." If he was any more perfect, there'd have to be a warning label on him. "Let me grab my purse."

When she turned back around, she found Gage eyeing her like she was going to be on tonight's menu. If any other man undressed her with his eyes like that, she would have been uncomfortable. But the heat from his molten eyes made her warm all over.

"You look beautiful," he said as they rode down in the elevator.

"Thank you." She smiled. "I'm just glad I picked the right one. I didn't realize until I started getting dressed that I never asked where we were going."

"I made reservations at Chambre Francaise. I hope that's okay with you?"

Whoa. Mac was so surprised she teetered a little on her high heels as she stepped out of the elevator. Chambre Francaise was one very fancy restaurant, not to mention ungodly expensive. And about as far from the pizza place down the street as you could get and still be on the same planet. It definitely wasn't the type of place she imagined Gage taking her. He seemed more like a steak-and-potatoes guy. Apparently, looks could be deceiving. She felt bad about the dent having dinner there was going to leave in Gage's wallet, though.

"You didn't have to do that," she said. "I know how difficult it can be getting into that place."

Gage opened the door of his shiny, black Dodge Charger for her—no guy had done that for her since her high school crush had taken her to the prom.

He gave her a lopsided grin. "I probably shouldn't be telling you this, but the only reason I was able to get in the place at all is because I helped out the head chef's son a while back. He promised me a table for two anytime I asked."

"Now, that sounds like a story I'd be interested in hearing. But still," she said when he'd climbed in beside her and started the engine, "Chambre Francaise is a very nice place. And expensive."

He glanced at her as he guided the car out of the parking garage and into downtown traffic. "I'm sure it'll be money well spent."

That look turned up the heat between them even more. "You think?"

"I do," he said. "Although in the interest of full disclosure, I have to tell you the table also comes with a major discount. Which is actually the only way I'm able to afford to take you there. But like they say, it's the thought that counts."

She couldn't help laughing. "You really do hang out with men all day, don't you? Little piece of advice—don't let a woman know she's getting dinner at a discount. It sort of ruins the gesture."

He chuckled. "For some reason I thought a journalist like you would be fixated on the truth."

"I am," she said. "But just because I'm a journalist, it doesn't mean I don't appreciate a little chivalry now and then."

He gave her another smoldering look. "I'll keep that in mind."

Five minutes in and they were already flirting. At this rate, she was going to have a hard time remembering this was supposed to be a fishing expedition. Because so far, it was feeling a lot more like a date to her. She needed to steer the conversation back into safer territory, and fast. So, she brought up the one subject sure to cool things down—the man his SWAT team had killed at the warehouse.

"I guess by now the department has told you who that thug at the warehouse was, huh?"

If Gage was caught off guard by the sudden shift in subject, he didn't let on. In fact, his expression didn't change at all as he took his eyes off the road to check the rearview mirror. "Actually, I didn't know who he was until I got home and saw it on the news."

She turned a little in her seat so she could see his face better. "Seriously? Isn't the fact that a member of your team just killed the son of the most powerful criminal in the northern hemisphere something your boss thought he should mention?"

"The department doesn't work like that," he said. "Internal Affairs talked to Xander and me, but their only concern is whether it was a clean shooting or not. They rarely tell us the name of the suspect in a case like that. The shrinks think it makes it too personal for the officer and can make the post-shooting counseling session even harder."

Huh. Considering their hard-core image, she hadn't thought an officer in SWAT would even attend counseling like that.

"That's all fine and good if Xander shot your average guy," she agreed. "But this was Ryan Hardy, the son of a man most people consider pretty damn scary. Word on the street is that he's already blaming your SWAT team for assassinating his son."

He shrugged. "People always stir up crap when things like this happen, but they get over it—or they don't.

What's Hardy going to do, take out a contract on the entire SWAT team?"

"That's exactly what I would think he's going to do."

Gage didn't act as if he thought that was very likely, but she noticed he spent a lot of time checking his mirrors. Dallas traffic was bad, but not that bad.

Mac opened her mouth to call him on it, but Gage asked how long she'd lived in Dallas. Guess that was his subtle way of saying he didn't want to talk about Hardy. Okay, she wouldn't push. For now.

"Since graduating from college," she said in answer to his question. "I interned at the *Dallas Daily Sun* in the summers and loved it so much, I couldn't turn them down when they offered me a full-time job."

Gage gave her a sidelong glance. "Being a journalist is in your blood, I guess."

She laughed. "I guess. I have my parents to thank for that. They're both English professors at A&M. According to them, I started writing when I was four and haven't stopped. I think they thought I'd follow in their footsteps, but I always wanted to be a journalist. What about you? Are you originally from Dallas?"

"San Antonio."

She would have asked more, but they'd already pulled up in front of the restaurant. A valet immediately came around to take Gage's keys while another opened her door. The rest of the conversation would have to wait until they were seated.

There was a line of people waiting for tables, so Mac was surprised when the hostess seated them right away. But while the chef might have promised Gage a table for two any time he requested it, the Chambre Francaise was packed seven days a week. So their booth ended up being very small and out of the way. It wasn't exactly in the kitchen, but close. Mac didn't mind, though. The short, rotund chef, however, was clearly embarrassed he only had the small booth to offer them.

"Don't worry about it, Emile." Gage stood and took the shorter man's hand in one of his, clapping him on the back with the other. "The way I see it, this is the best seat in the house. I couldn't ask for a better place to have a nice, quiet dinner, which is exactly what we're looking for. How's Kyle getting along?"

Emile beamed as only a proud parent could. "He is doing very well. Good grades, and more importantly, he's passionate about what he's learning. And once again, I owe that all to you."

"It was all Kyle," Gage insisted.

Emile looked as if he would have argued, but Gage introduced Mac before the man could say anything else.

The round chef took her hand in both of his with a smile. "A pleasure to meet you, mademoiselle." He gave Gage an approving nod. "Finally, you bring a beautiful woman with you to dinner. I was starting to worry that with your job, you would be alone forever."

Mac laughed. If she didn't know better, she'd think Gage was actually blushing.

"Sorry to disappoint you, Emile," he said as he slid into the booth. "But this is a working dinner."

The chef smiled. "It has been my experience that the best relationships start in the workplace. Look at me and my Fifi." His smile broadened. "Okay, okay. I won't embarrass you further, my friend. I will go back to the kitchen. Enjoy your dinner."

Gage shook his head as Emile disappeared through the door that led to the kitchen. "Sorry about that. He can be a bit outrageous at times. Goes along with being a head chef, I guess."

"Because he thought we were here on a date? I would have thought the same thing in his shoes, so no, I'm not embarrassed." She looked around. The brocade wallpaper, gold accents, and crystal chandeliers were even more elegant than she remembered. "Do you eat here often?"

He shook his head. "About once a month. Mostly to make Emile happy. He worries I don't have enough fat in my diet."

Mac thought about how Gage looked in his uniform pants and tight T-shirt. Emile was probably right. "Yeah, I could see why he might think that." She picked up her glass of water and took a sip. "So, what kind of favor did you do for him?"

Gage shrugged. "His son Kyle got involved in some gang stuff. Nothing too serious, but the kid was definitely heading down the wrong path. The other guys on the team and I got him out and back on the straight and narrow. Once he figured out it was okay for a man to be a pastry chef, he decided to go to culinary school. I didn't really do much except give him a little advice."

She waited until the waiter who'd appeared to pour glasses of white wine for both of them left. "Something tells me you're downplaying your part. The head chef of one of the best restaurants in Dallas doesn't offer a reserved table for life to someone who just gave some advice to his son."

Gage shrugged again in that self-deprecating way Mac was starting to like—a lot. "Maybe a little."

Mac would have pressed for more, but their waitress

placed plates of salad in front of them. Mac had a tomato halfway to her mouth before she realized they hadn't ordered anything.

"Hey," she said. "We never asked for salad."

Gage chuckled. "That's my fault. I told Emile to surprise me the first time I came here for dinner. He hasn't given me a menu since. If you don't like it, I can ask him to send out something else."

She never would have pegged Gage as the kind of man who liked surprises, but if he could trust Emile's choices, she supposed she could, too. Besides, she didn't want to insult the chef.

"No. This is perfect."

Delicious too, she thought as she took a bite. She knew she should be trying to wheedle information out of him that she could use in her exposé, but right now her story was the furthest thing from her mind. Anyway, it wasn't like she could just come out and ask him why his men didn't wear their NVGs, why they hadn't taken Martinez to the hospital, or what kind of drug his team used to help them get their job done.

So instead, she asked him why he'd joined the military straight out of high school. But while Gage willingly talked about himself, she noticed he kept bringing the conversation back around to her. By the time they'd finished their French onion soup, he probably knew more about her life growing up in College Station as she did. When he did talk about SWAT, it was about the men who worked for him and their accomplishments. He even admitted he worried about their safety.

"Sometimes, I feel more like their father than their commander," he said wryly.

Mac couldn't help but smile. Who'd have thought a big, hunky guy like Gage Dixon would have a paternal side? One more thing to like about him.

"You're definitely nowhere near old enough to be their father," she told him.

"Just listen to a conversation between Becker and me sometime," he said. "There's not a suspension bridge around that could span that generation gap."

She laughed. All her working dinners should be this much fun. They were usually spent parked in front of her laptop with a TV dinner and the television for company. She hadn't realized how dull that was until now. She could definitely get used to sitting across the table from Gage every night. Especially one this small.

It'd started with a few accidental touches as their legs brushed under the tiny table while they ate their salads. They both apologized, but when it happened again over soup, then again during the main course, she began to think maybe it wasn't accidental at all. Not that she minded. Every time his pants-covered leg pressed up against her bare one, a warm tingle spiraled through her and settled in her tummy. That was when she realized she was the one initiating the contact, not Gage. In fact, he hadn't moved at all.

She blushed, attempting to restrain herself from playing footsie as she pushed a piece of lightly breaded chicken around the creamy wine sauce it was smothered in while Gage told her why he'd become a cop after pulling a six-year hitch in the army. She didn't quite succeed, mostly because she couldn't bring herself to totally break contact with the solid form of his muscular thigh. But it was the best she could do given the limited space under the small table.

That was a lie, though. She didn't stop because touching him felt too damn good. Hell, she couldn't even remember the last time she'd been on a date. She hadn't realized how much she missed it.

She pressed her leg more firmly against his inner thigh and rubbed her knee against his as he steered the conversation back around to her again. If it bothered him, she had no doubt he'd let her know.

But Gage didn't even seem to notice. Or maybe he had noticed and simply didn't want her to stop.

"It sounds like you spend a lot of time at the office," Gage observed as he sipped his wine. "That's gotta be hell on your social life."

Her first instinct was to deny it and tell him she was getting busy every night. Not because she wanted to play hard to get, but because she didn't want to seem like the pathetic workaholic she was. She caught herself, though. It wasn't as if he was accusing her of being a loser, just busy.

She finished her chicken and set her knife and fork on her plate. "Pretty much. I spent most of my adult life getting to the top of my profession, and every minute since then working to stay there. It doesn't leave much time for anything else."

Gage smiled, and she could have sworn she felt his knee rub against hers. "Well, it's not like I can say I'm much better. I've already admitted I spend a couple nights out of every week in the office doing paperwork, so you know my social life sucks."

She let out a little snort of laughter. "We do make quite the pair, don't we?"

He gave her one of those smoldering looks of his. "Yes, we do."

His leg most definitely rubbed against hers, she was sure of it.

By the time dessert came out, she was starting to think Emile had turned up the heat in the restaurant. At least that would explain why she suddenly felt hot all over. Of course, the recent temperature spike might also have to do with the fact that she'd dropped her high heel off her right foot and begun casually running her toes up and down Gage's lower leg.

Gage leaned back comfortably in his side of the booth, watching her with smoky eyes the whole time she did it. In between, he asked her little tidbits about her life. Like whether she'd ever thought about making the jump to New York or Washington, why journalists made more money than reporters, and whether she liked to cook or order takeout.

Carrying on a completely normal first-date conversation with an extremely attractive man while caressing his leg with her foot was probably the most erotic thing she'd ever done in a nonerotic setting. That the man just so happened to be the focus of her investigation also made it one of the crazier things she'd ever done. She was putting her story and her reputation at risk, and she couldn't for the life of her say why. She couldn't help it. There was something about Gage that brought out her inner seductress. The combination of physical perfection, charming personality, and vibrant masculinity did it for her. It was all she could do not to sit in his lap and kiss the hell out of him. Damn, if she could figure out how to bottle whatever it was about him that was so alluring, she'd quit her job and start a new line of men's body spray—one that actually worked, unlike those silly commercials she saw all the time.

It took every ounce of self-control she possessed to keep her foot to those parts of his leg below the knee. The way he was leaning back it was almost as if he was inviting her to run her toes up a little higher. But she knew that if she let herself start to wander, she wasn't likely to stop until she got to his crotch. And that would be totally going too far. The thought alone was enough to make her whole body tremble.

Mac pulled her gaze away from Gage to see what kind of dessert Emile had selected for them—chocolate souf-flé, of course. She dipped her spoon into the center and tasted it. She sighed, unable to help herself.

The sound made Gage look up from his own dessert, his dark eyes almost gold in the candlelight. She smiled at him.

"When you asked me to have dinner with you earlier today, you said you needed to get to know me better so you'd feel more comfortable with me hanging around the compound." She ran her toes up and down his leg again. "Did it work?"

"Mostly," he said. "I just have one more question."

His face turned so serious that she stopped moving her foot and lowered it to the floor. Maybe she'd been wrong to try and mix business with pleasure. What if he thought her flirting was a game to get him to agree to let her hang around the compound? She wasn't above flirting to get a scoop, but that wasn't what she'd been doing with him. She was seriously attracted to Gage.

"Okay," she said. "What's your question?"

He was silent, as if he was searching for the right words. His eyes were so intense it almost took her breath away.

"Would you print the story of a lifetime if it meant that innocent people got hurt?"

She'd expected him to ask her if she was playing games with him to get what she wanted. She hadn't expected a philosophical question like that.

But looking into Gage's dark eyes, she realized it hadn't been a philosophical question about a hypothetical story. He was asking if the story she was planning to write about SWAT would hurt the people he cared about—his men.

"I would never write a story if it meant innocent people would get hurt—no matter how big it was."

He regarded her in silence for so long she thought he didn't believe her. But then the corners of his mouth curved. "Then consider me completely comfortable with you hanging around the compound."

Mac almost sagged with relief. "Are you sure the department won't mind?"

"They won't mind." He took a bite of the rich dessert. "They're always trying to get me to do more community outreach. They'll be thrilled."

Until they see the story on the front page.

He gestured with his spoon. "Eat your soufflé before it gets cold."

She spooned another scoop of the scrumptious chocolate dessert into her mouth, chewing slowly as she wondered whether she should go back to playing footsie again when she felt Gage's hand on her knee. The sigh she let out this time had nothing to do with how good Emile's soufflé was. She thought for sure the sexual thermostat had been turned down for the evening after what they'd just discussed. Guess she'd been wrong.

Mac forced herself to play it cool while they talked about her newest obsession—pita chips—and the sweet older lady who lived in the apartment next door to hers.

But it was nearly impossible not to sigh with pleasure as Gage made slow, little circles on her knee with his finger. He never ventured more than an inch or two up her thigh—even though she silently prayed he would—but it still felt heavenly. The tingling she'd felt before had disappeared, replaced by a warm rush of heat between her thighs.

She bit her lip. Damn, she really needed to get out more. All Gage did was caress her knee and she got wet. If he touched her anywhere else, she'd probably pass out.

But she was willing to risk it.

It was in that moment of bliss that Emile decided to come over and wish them a pleasurable evening. Mac had to bite her tongue to keep from telling the man that she and Gage were already in the pleasurable part of the evening—thank you and please go away. She almost groaned when Gage took his hand off her knee so he could shake the man's hand again. She pushed herself up on weak legs to do the same.

"Dinner was delicious," she told him. "I loved every bite."

"I'm so glad you enjoyed yourselves." Emile hugged her, putting his mouth to her ear. "You make Gage happy, Mackenzie. And it would make me very happy if you came with him the next time he eats here."

She laughed. "I might just do that."

Mac glanced at Gage out of the corner of her eye to see him flush beneath his tan. She didn't know how he could possibly have heard Emile's whispered words, but apparently he had.

Emile put his beefy arms around both of them as he walked them to the door. "Don't do anything foolish with this one, Gage. She's special."

They didn't talk much on the drive to her apartment,

so Mac relaxed back in the seat and used the quiet time to replay the evening. Between the fantastic food, intimate conversation, and sexy footsie under the table, she wasn't sure how the night could have been any better.

Well, that wasn't exactly true. She knew exactly how it might get better. And it'd start with inviting Gage into her apartment. Once inside, they might make it to her bedroom, but they might not. If they didn't, the floor anywhere along the way would be just fine, too.

She smiled to herself. This was turning into the most unusual story she'd ever worked. And there was a story here—she was sure of that. But there was also a hell of a man involved. One who distracted and aroused her like no one she'd ever met before.

It was almost enough to make her consider putting the story on the back burner. Maybe after tonight, she just might.

When they got to her apartment building, Gage came around to open her door for her, then rode up in the elevator so he could escort her to the door. She took out her key and slipped it into the lock, then turned to invite him in. But Gage spoke first.

"I had an amazing time tonight. I haven't had that much fun in a long time."

She smiled. "Me, too." Then she took a deep breath and jumped in the deep end. "The fun doesn't have to end yet, you know."

"I know." The hot look in his eyes almost set her on fire right there in the hallway. She wasn't sure they'd make it as far as the entryway once they got inside. But he shook his head. "We've got an early day tomorrow. PT starts at 0630. You need to get your sleep if you're going to be all bright-eyed and bushy-tailed for it."

Bright-eyed and bushy-tailed? But Gage was already heading for the elevator.

"Wait!" He turned. "What's PT, and why the hell does it start so early?"

He pushed the down button for the elevator. "It's short for physical training—exercise. We do it three days a week, and we start early so we can get it over with before it gets too hot. You said you wanted to see us train, remember? So you'll have proof that we're not using PEDs."

"But—"

Crap. After all the flirting, touching, and heated looks across the table, she'd been so sure he'd spend the night with her.

The elevator door opened and he stepped inside. "No buts, Mackenzie. See you tomorrow at 0630 hours."

The doors closed and just like that, her chance of seeing the hunky SWAT officer naked disappeared.

She stood there staring at the elevator for a long time, sure that Gage would change his mind. But he didn't. Sighing, she unlocked her door and walked into her apartment. What the hell had just happened? She'd been turned on, and so had Gage—she was sure of it. Why hadn't he stayed?

Because Gage had been playing her the whole night. The answer was so obvious she almost laughed. She should be angry, but she wasn't. She was so sure she'd been the one running the show tonight, but he'd been the one in charge the whole time. They'd spent almost the entire evening talking about her, while she knew next to nothing about Gage or the members of his team.

She kicked off her shoes, then slipped out of her dress and hung it up. If she was angry at anyone, she was angry at herself for giving up so much information. Gage knew almost everything there was to know about her—where she'd gone to school, where she'd worked, who her friends were, what kind of stories she liked to pursue. On top of all that, he'd figured out her story about the PEDs was just a front for another, more serious investigation— that was why he'd asked the question about whether she'd be willing to hurt innocent people to get a story.

All he'd had to do was gaze at her with those dark, smoldering eyes of his and she'd told him everything. The worst part was that Gage also knew how much he turned her on, and that he could use it against her.

Mac finished brushing her teeth and stripped off her underwear. Oh damn, her panties were a complete mess. She usually didn't get this wet even after an orgasm—or two. Gage had done it with nothing more than a hand on her knee.

She tried to ignore the throbbing between her thighs and climbed into bed, absently wondering if Gage could have made her come just by caressing her thigh. She groaned. Talk about safe sex.

She was going to have to be extremely careful around him. Someone with his looks, his body, his obviously clever mind, and the ability to drive her to sexual distraction with only a touch was a very dangerous man.

Chapter 5

"YOU THINK SHE'LL SHOW UP?" BECKER ASKED FOR THE third time.

Gage looked up from his email to give the young surveillance expert a frown. "I told you—she might, she might not. Either way, PT starts in"—he looked at his watch—"ten minutes. Don't you think you should get everyone out there and ready to start?"

Becker had been assigned the task of setting up and running this morning's PT session, but while the man nodded at Gage's obvious nudge, he didn't move. "Yeah, probably. But I was just wondering if maybe she might join us?"

"Why would you think that? She's not here to work out with us. She's here to write an article about us."

Becker nodded again, still lounging against the doorjamb. "Yeah, that makes sense. Still…it'd be nice if she wore yoga pants."

"What the hell are yoga pants?"

"What women wear when they do yoga. You know—those tight pants that flare at the bottom a little." Becker grinned. "I bet she'd look hot in them."

Okay, that was more than Gage wanted to hear. He growled. "Officer Becker, get outside. Now."

Becker might have been fantasizing about Mackenzie's curvy ass in a pair of yoga pants, but he was still aware enough to know when he was close to mortal danger. He gave his boss a startled look, then took off running for the back door.

Gage shook his head. Sometimes he wondered if the amount of time Becker spent playing with electricity had damaged him beyond repair. Then again, the guy had a point. Gage wasn't exactly sure what yoga pants even looked like, but he figured Mackenzie would look good in anything tight.

He felt his cock immediately harden…again.

Shit. He hadn't slept worth a damn last night because of the hard-on Mackenzie had given him during dinner. It had taken an hour in a freezing cold shower this morning to finally get the damn thing to go down. He'd been lucky to even get to work on time. And now, with a single semi-sexual thought about the dark-haired beauty, he was hard all over again. Thank God he was wearing a loose pair of shorts. It would have been damn embarrassing doing PT with the team otherwise.

He looked down at his watch. He still had a few minutes before he had to go out. Maybe he could think about something else for a while and get his erection to relax.

He tried to focus on what he needed to do that day, but that proved to be a stupid idea because he was going to be spending it with Mackenzie Stone. The purpose behind it might be serious—making sure she didn't figure out he and his men were werewolves—but all his cock cared about was that he'd get to hang out with that sexy body of hers.

He practically heard a thud as his hard shaft pressed against the underside of the desk draw.

Damn, the woman was going to be the death of him.

It had hit him like a sledgehammer when he'd gotten

in his car with Mackenzie last night. She'd smelled really nice at the compound earlier in the day, and her scent had been even more delicious when she'd opened the door of her apartment. But that all paled in comparison to what it was like to be in a small, enclosed space with her. The perfume she'd worn combined perfectly with her natural scent to create a fragrance so alluring he'd almost driven off the road he was so distracted.

And that had just been the beginning. The entire dinner with her had been one long, slow tease. The way they'd been squeezed into that tight booth, the way her knee had brushed up against his leg most of the night, the way she'd leaned in close and nibbled her dinner in that slow, sensual way she had, the way she'd answered all his questions in that sexy voice of hers. He'd been so turned on he hadn't realized he'd started caressing her leg until the thundering of her heartbeat couldn't be ignored. She'd had that distant, glassy-eyed look of a woman in some serious pleasure.

Then the smell of her arousal hit him, and he'd almost come unglued.

Thank God Emile had shown up at the table just then, or he wasn't sure what he would have done.

He'd never displayed more discipline in his life as he had when he walked away from her invitation to come inside. But he'd needed to get some space between them, get his head screwed back on right, and get his freaking lust under control. This was the safety of his pack, and he was losing it like a horny teenager.

He'd done it, but it had been damn hard.

Even now, sitting at his desk willing his hard-on to go down in the few minutes he had before PT, Gage still had no idea what the hell was going on with his out-of-control sex drive. There'd been a couple times last night while he'd laid in bed staring up at the ceiling that he wondered if maybe Xander had been right. Was Mackenzie Stone some kind of cosmically assigned perfect woman for him, genetically designed to push him over the edge with nothing more than her scent?

In the frustrating darkness, it had seemed more than possible.

Of course, an hour-long freezing shower, a lot of coffee, and the bright light of daybreak had made those thoughts seem ludicrous. Until Becker had forced the image of Mackenzie wearing skintight yoga pants into his head. Now, as he pleaded with his erection to go away, he wasn't so sure.

"Hey," Mike's voice sounded distant even though he was standing in the doorway. "We're about to get started. Stone is here, too. And she has a guy with her."

Gage growled low in his throat. Well, he'd finally found something that would make his cock relent—anger. Simple, irrational, jealousy-induced anger.

"So, why did you need me to come with you today?" Zak asked drily as he snapped pictures in what could only be called a halfhearted manner.

Mac was too distracted by the sixteen sweaty, bare-chested men running around on the obstacle course. While they all looked scrumptious, she found herself focusing mainly on Gage. *God, the man would make a Greek god feel inferior.* She had no idea if all the crawling, jumping, and climbing made for good exercise, but it sure as hell was fun to watch. She especially liked the way his muscles bunched and flexed as he scrambled up the various towers and ropes. Damn, their rippling movement was downright sensual.

And if all those bulging muscles weren't enough to make her stare like a kid in a candy store, the incredible matching ink that every one of the men had tattooed on the left side of his chest sure as heck was. She'd never been one to look twice at a man's tattoo, but the one of the wolf with its long teeth, menacing eyes, and bristling ruff of fur that each of them had in the center of his left pec was just freaking cool. Emblazoned in arching letters over the top of each wolf was the acronym *SWAT*. The work was expensive looking and had obviously taken a lot of time. She had no idea what a wolf had to do with SWAT, but she one hundred percent approved of the artwork.

Anything to provide another reason to look at a sexy man's chest was okay with her.

Zak cleared his throat, interrupting her musings. If she didn't love him like a brother, she'd smack him right now.

"I need pictures of the SWAT team training," she told him.

"So these pictures of sweaty, muscular men running around in nothing but a pair of shorts are going to be in your article?"

More likely on my personal laptop. She gave Zak an angelic smile. "It's possible."

Her effort probably would have counted for more if she'd been able to resist asking Zak to make sure to take lots of pictures of Gage flexing those beautiful muscles of his.

"I should be getting paid overtime for this," Zak groused, but he dutifully snapped more photos.

Mac leaned back against one of the telephone poles that were part of the obstacle course. She and Zak had picked out a good vantage point for this morning's PT session. Gage and his team had been going at it hard for almost an hour and didn't look like they were anywhere near wrapping it up. Muscles and stamina—what more could a woman ask for?

"So now that we're in, what's the plan?" Zak asked.

"I don't really have one," Mac admitted, again staying away from any mention of a super drug. "I'm just going to play it by ear and see where it takes me."

"What do you want me to do?" Zak asked. "Other than take pictures, I mean."

He flipped his camera to automatic mode so he could get a series of rapid-fire shots of Gage and his two squad leaders leaping from the top of a tall tower. It had to be at least twelve or fifteen feet high—sure as hell too high for her to jump from. They hit the ground hard and rolled across the sand-filled pit under the base of the tower. Sand stuck to their sweaty backs and shoulders, and it took all of her willpower not to run out there and volunteer to brush Gage off.

"See if you can make friends with Becker and Lowry," she said softly. The SWAT guys were now all the way down at the far end of the obstacle course, but she wasn't going to take any chances. "They're the newest members of the team, so they might not be involved in whatever's going on."

"Okay, I'll try," Zak said. "But they seem like a really tight group to me."

Mac didn't need Zak to tell her that. After watching

them work together on the obstacle course, it was obvious they trusted each other completely. It was unlikely any of them would rat out one of their own to an outsider, but she and Zak needed to try.

By the time Gage and the other men finished PT, Mac was worn out, and all she'd done was watch. The SWAT guys, however, looked as if they'd just woken up from a refreshing nap.

"Well, I'm out of here," Zak said. "I'll be back in about thirty minutes."

She reluctantly tore her gaze away from Gage's sweaty body to give Zak a frown. "Where are you going?"

"I saw a donut shop a couple of miles back. I thought after a workout like that these guys might appreciate some quality junk food."

Mac took in all the ripped muscles and flat abs, not to mention the tight buns as the SWAT officers loped casually up the slight hill toward the admin-slash-dorm building she'd toured with Gage.

"I hate to tell you this, but I'm pretty sure these guys don't eat donuts."

Zak laughed. "Right. You keep believing that. Just a word of advice—don't get between these guys and the boxes when I throw them down on the table or you might get run over."

She shook her head as Zak headed toward the front gate. He was going to be embarrassed when he bought a half-dozen boxes of donuts thinking it'd get him in good with the guys, only to have no one touch them.

Mac started for the admin building, wondering what she should do while Gage cleaned up, when he suddenly appeared at her side. She jumped.

"Crap, you scared me!"

"Sorry about that." He grinned. "I wanted to let you know it'll only take me about twenty minutes or so to get cleaned up. Feel free to roam around the compound if you want. Or you can watch TV over in the training building."

Mac was about to tell Gage to take his time and that she'd go watch the morning news when she got a whiff of his sweat-soaked body. The scent immediately transported her back to the lusty state she'd been in last night when he'd left her alone and unsatisfied at her front door. She'd never found men particularly sexy after a workout, but Gage was a completely different story. He smelled so scrumptious she thought she might drool.

"Thanks," she finally managed to spit out. "I'll probably walk around some, then head over and look at the news."

"Okay. I'll be quick," he said, then turned and jogged toward the admin building.

Mac didn't realize she was following him until she was halfway to the admin building. She stopped short, swearing under her breath. What the hell was she going to do in there, watch him shower and ask if he needed help getting all that sand off his back?

She shook her head. She needed to get a grip on herself, and fast.

She turned to head toward the training building, but stopped again. She'd wanted to get a look at the filing cabinets she'd seen yesterday. What better time to do it than while the entire SWAT team was showering?

She stepped into the building all prepared to give Gage some story about needing to use a computer, but he was already upstairs with the other men. Of course, this would be a waste of time if the file cabinets were locked. But they weren't. She wasn't sure if that was good or bad. Sure, she'd be able to rifle through them, but if there was something incriminating in them, would they leave them open? Only one way to find out.

The first drawer she looked in held personnel records. She skimmed through a few, including Gage's, but there was nothing in there she didn't already know. It wasn't as if they were going to maintain a list of drugs they might be taking. She closed that drawer and opened the next.

This one held more personnel records, but these were specifically related to training and weapons qualification information. Other than the fact that all the files were thick as heck—SWAT guys trained a lot—they were otherwise pretty dull.

She moved to the next cabinet and opened the top drawer. It was full of what looked like incident records for each call the team had responded to, complete with officer statements, photographs, diagrams, and procedure review documents.

Now this had potential.

She picked a folder at random and started flipping through it when she heard the sounds of laughter coming from upstairs. That was when it hit her—there were sixteen attractive, muscular, naked, and probably soap-covered men in the showers not more than a few feet above her head. The thought was almost enough to make her say the hell with these old files and sneak upstairs for a peek.

But she had a job to do—and secrets to uncover.

Mac checked the door, listening for footsteps coming down the stairs. She didn't have a lot of time to snoop around.

She tried to focus on reading between the lines of the reports, looking for any details they might have glossed over, or even left out completely. But it was hard not getting caught up in what she read.

The first report chronicled a hostage situation involving a rape victim and her brutal attacker. The next was a father who'd killed two of his own children before Gage and his men had gotten there just in time to save the mother and a newborn baby.

Murderers barricaded in their homes, thugs who'd robbed convenience stores, everyday people who'd snapped and started shooting everyone they came across, depressed people who wanted a way out and thought pointing a gun at a bunch of people might get them what they were looking for.

Mac was stunned by how many of the incidents ended with the suspects getting arrested instead of shot by SWAT. She'd always assumed SWAT only got involved when someone needed shooting.

She jumped ahead to the date Marvin Cole had been arrested. It took her a few minutes to thumb through the files, but she finally found the incident report she was looking for. She read it through quickly, not sure what she was searching for.

The report read pretty much like the story Marvin had told her, except for the part about the kidnap victim being a twelve-year-old kid and that the kidnapper—Marvin— had beaten the hell out of the kid's babysitter to get the kid away from her.

Gage's report said they'd tracked Marvin to an old hotel, where Senior Corporal Zane Kendrick, one of the SWAT team's negotiators, had tried to talk Marvin into giving himself up. Marvin had apparently threatened the kid's life, which had sent Gage and another senior corporal on the team, Trey Duncan, into the hotel room. It was impossible to tell because Gage's words lacked any emotion, but Mac wondered if he'd been concerned about going up against a three-hundred-and-fifty-pound criminal with only two officers.

The report provided the precise time the two-man team had kicked in the door, then only a simple three-sentence description of the ensuing arrest of the suspect and rescue of the hostage.

> Senior Corporal Duncan kicked in the door and covered me as I moved across the room to secure the suspect. The suspect resisted, which required me to pin him against the wall of the room for a short period of time while Corporal Duncan got the hostage to safety. My pinning technique resulted in scratches to the suspect's chest, which were treated by the EMTs on scene.

She was just flipping to the back of the report, which included pictures of Marvin and the familiar scratches on his chest, when she heard the thump of heavy boots on the stairs.

Crap.

Mac shoved the folder back in the filing cabinet and closed the drawer as softly as she could. Then she darted out the door and into the main office. Could she make it to the front door before whomever it was entered the room?

She decided against it and instead threw her butt into

one of the office chairs and grabbed the first thing to read that she could find on the adjacent desk—a magazine about handguns. She'd just crossed her legs and opened the magazine to a page advertising *Real Bleeding Zombies! Available for Target Practice Now!* when Gage walked into the room.

"I thought you'd be watching TV."

She looked up slowly, acting as if she was mesmerized by the magazine. "Oh yeah, I was going to, but then I saw this magazine and I got interested in it. I didn't realize I'd been sitting here that long until you came down."

"Really?" Gage casually made his way toward the filing room. "I never would have pegged you as someone to read a gun magazine."

Mac almost gasped out loud as he walked in the room and looked around. Oh, God. Had she left the drawer open on one of the filing cabinets?

"Hey," she practically shouted. "Did you know they make zombie targets that bleed?"

Gage looked around the filing room, then reached over and switched off the light. "Yeah, I've seen them. Unfortunately, they're not suitable for real training."

"Really?" She hadn't expected him to do more than laugh at how silly bleeding zombies were, not respond seriously to her question. But now he'd gone and made her curious. "Why not?"

He came around and plunked himself down in the chair beside her. "For one thing, they're too damn expensive. For another, it encourages bad shooting habits. Everyone wants to shoot the zombie in the head instead of the center of the chest."

She couldn't help but laugh as she envisioned the

SWAT team being pelted with bad press because they were caught preparing for the coming zombie apocalypse. "I guess I see your point. It could turn into a PR nightmare."

Gage chuckled. "Not nearly as bad as the trouble we got into when Xander brought in the fiberglass clown he found. He thought it'd be a great idea to use it as the bad guy in a live-fire hostage training scenario. The company that owns the burger franchise that uses the clown as a mascot didn't agree."

Mac laughed. "I wonder why?"

"I know, right?"

She tossed the magazine on the desk, glad she'd been able to successfully distract Gage from looking too closely at the file room. She was sure she didn't leave any of the drawers open, but she needed to be more careful. She'd have a hard time finding anything on these guys if she ended up getting caught and tossed out of the compound.

Not that she was going to learn anything worthwhile by reading through the files. The only thing she'd gained by going in there was to verify that Gage had been the one who'd pinned Marvin up against the wall and put those scratches on him. He'd come right out and confessed to it in his report. Then had the EMTs take pictures of the scratches for the police records.

Not exactly the act of a cop whacked out on drugs. And Marvin's assertion that only someone on drugs could pick him up and pin him against a wall? That seemed more than a little dubious now that she'd met Gage and seen all those rippling muscles. She got the feeling Gage might weight-lift criminals like Marvin for fun.

She almost screamed in frustration. Right now she felt more than a little stupid. She'd practically begged Ted to let her go after these guys, and other than the mysterious issue of the dusty NVG cases and at least one team member who was too stupid to get his injuries checked out by a hospital, she had nothing. Even the injury angle was looking like a bust. She'd done some serious eyeballing of every member of Gage's team during PT—considering that none of them had been wearing much more than socks, sneakers, and shorts, there'd been a lot to eyeball—and she couldn't find a wound on any of them, Martinez included. Apparently, Gage had been right about that scratch thing.

For the first time that she could remember, Mac doubted her instincts. She'd sworn there was something going on here, but now she wasn't as sure.

She was still musing about how she could have been so wrong when she realized with a start that Gage wasn't talking anymore. She looked up to see him regarding her with mild amusement. How long had she zoned out? Oh crap, she was completely losing it on this case.

"So, what's on the agenda for today?" she asked.

"Mike and Xander have some squad-level training they'll be doing. We can go watch that." He gestured to the magazine on the table beside her. "Or since you seem to have taken a sudden interest in handguns, I can take you out for that shooting lesson we talked about yesterday."

Mac's heart beat faster. She knew she shouldn't do it. Her best chance to learn something—if there was even something to learn—was to stay with the largest number of team members. You never knew who'd slip up and say something, so the more people you were around, the higher the probability.

But that was logic talking. And right then for some reason, logic wasn't making decisions for her. Her rapidly increasing heart rate was. Besides, she'd just been thinking this story was looking more and more like a bust anyway.

"Just the two of us, you mean?"

He gave her a sinful smile, as if he knew that was exactly what she was hoping he meant. "Well, yeah. Unless you'd prefer to have a few other people come along with us?"

She didn't.

It turned out that Zak had been right about the donuts. The SWAT guys did indeed eat donuts—voraciously.

She'd been shocked when her friend had walked into the training classroom with six boxes of assorted death-by-sugar bribes. It was one thing trying to get on someone's good side, but it was another to do it so blatantly or with that many donuts. That was crazy.

But it was kind of scary the way the men ripped into the boxes. They'd cleaned out three boxes before she'd even picked through them, looking for something with sprinkles on it.

Zak looked at her smugly. She ignored him.

After the donuts were gone, Xander and Mike gave the training briefing. She and Gage sat in the back of the classroom so he could explain what was going on.

"This is a standard hostage training scenario for us," Gage said softly into her ear. His breath felt deliciously warm against her neck. "Xander's team will play the part of the bad guys, while your photographer will play the part of the hostage."

Mac almost laughed. Zak wasn't going to like that. Then again, he might. He seemed psyched about the idea. Probably all those video games he played.

"I thought maybe Ms. Stone could be the hostage," Becker said, half turning in his seat to give her an expectant look. "You know—give her a better perspective on how we operate."

The rest of the men nodded in agreement.

"Ms. Stone won't be taking part in the training exercise," Xander said firmly. "But she will be sticking her head in occasionally to watch, so you might want to pay attention to the briefing. That way, you won't make idiots of yourselves when she happens to look your way."

A few of the men laughed, but Becker looked positively glum. It was enough to make Mac feel bad. She leaned over to whisper in Gage's ear. "I guess we could put off our shooting lesson for a little while, if it would help. I can play a very convincing hostage."

The muscle in Gage's jaw flexed. "Zak will work fine as the hostage. Besides, Becker just wants to see you tied to a chair, squirming to get loose. I think he has a thing for you."

Mac laughed, until she caught Becker studying her. And he wasn't the only one. She wouldn't go so far as to say their looks were predatory, but she could have sworn the temperature in the training room jumped up three or four degrees. She didn't mind being the center of attention in a room full of hot guys, but this was a little more than she might be ready for.

She looked at Gage. "Maybe it's time for that shooting lesson?"

"Good idea." He swept the room with his gaze. "Ms.

Stone and I will be down at the lower shooting range. You probably should stay well clear of that part of the compound. I wouldn't want an errant shot going wide and putting a hole through any of you."

As they left the training building and headed for the armory, Mac gave Gage a sidelong look. "Your guys really need to spend some more time around the opposite sex. You ever thought about getting a few women on the team? Maybe mellow them out a little bit?"

She'd meant it as a joke, but Gage must have thought she was serious. "I've considered it, but it's damn hard finding women who can fit the specific requirements I've put in place for the team. I'm always looking, though."

When they got to the armory, Mac leaned back against the counter and watched as Gage took several pistols and boxes of ammo from one of the safes and packed them in a soft-sided bag about the size of a carry-on.

"Are you really that worried I'm a bad shot?" she asked, enjoying the view as he bent over to pull out some hearing protection. Damn, what she wouldn't give to see him do that naked.

He turned to give her a curious look. "No. Why?"

"Well, you warned everyone to stay away from the shooting range. I figured you were worried I'd miss the target and accidently hit someone."

She tried to sound casual about it, but honestly, she was a little concerned about the possibility of screwing up.

Gage picked up the bag, then held open the door for her. "I never said you'd be the one shooting them."

She glanced at him out of the corner of her eye as they walked along the sandy path to the shooting range he'd pointed out the day before. "So, you were just making sure we had some privacy?"

He grinned. "I thought you might be more relaxed if it was just the two of us."

She smiled back at him, keenly aware of the familiar heat swirling in her tummy again. Target shooting as a form of foreplay—who knew?

—⁂—

Gage stood behind Mackenzie, steadying her arms as she aimed the small .22 automatic he'd started her on. She was actually better at this than she'd given herself credit for, especially when she realized that not every handgun was so powerful it'd put her on her ass to fire it. The .22 was the perfect gun for her because it wasn't too loud, didn't have much recoil, and was easy to aim. And now that she'd figured it out, she was starting to enjoy herself.

He knew he sure as hell was. Mostly because Mackenzie had a bad habit of leaning forward when she pulled the trigger. It helped her line up the sights, but made for an unstable shooting base. On the bright side, her unorthodox stance did cause her butt to stick out nicely. And as close as he was standing, that ass of hers was doing some interesting things to his focus as well. At first he tried to keep his rapidly hardening cock from grazing her bottom, but that quickly became impossible—he was simply standing too close to her.

He would have felt bad about getting hard during a shooting lesson if it wasn't for the fact that Mackenzie was just as turned on as he was, maybe more so. He knew because he could smell her arousal. That uniquely feminine scent was so heady and overwhelming that it was almost hard to see straight, much less instruct her in the finer points of handgun use.

Worse, his mind kept slipping to the idea of how much better she'd smell if she was naked. It'd probably bring him to his knees.

He swallowed a groan and tried not to think about it. Yeah, like that was going to work. His hard-on was threatening to rip through the front of his uniform pants to get closer to her. He wasn't doing a good job of thinking about anything but how tempting Mackenzie smelled.

After coming downstairs and finding Mackenzie's scent all over the filing room, he'd realized that last's night's dinner had done nothing to dissuade her from pursuing her story. He'd known right then that he'd be spending the next several days working his ass off to keep her distracted. Of course, he'd assumed he'd spend the time distracting her the old-fashioned way, not the sexual way. But hey, this way was much better anyhow.

"I don't think I'm doing this right," Mackenzie complained. "I've only hit the target a few times."

She fired the last bullet in the clip, missing again.

He reluctantly moved away from her to reload the magazine. He would reload the four others she'd already fired while he was at it. She loved the little .22 and had gone through the first fifty rounds in nothing flat.

"You're doing better than you think. It's just that the bullet holes are so small, you can't see the holes in the target."

"You can?"

She squinted at the target. God, her face was so cute when she scrunched it up like that.

"Yeah," he said. "But it's just because I've been doing

this for a while. Trust me, you're putting almost all your shots on the paper."

She picked up one of the magazines and loaded it, her hands moving more confidently than they had the first time. "Yeah, but I was aiming for the center of the target. What am I doing wrong?"

He watched as she slid the magazine back in the pistol and released the receiver. Damn, she was getting good at that. "Let's see how you shoot this magazine. Then I'll give you some ideas on how you can improve."

Gage took up the guide position behind her that he'd been in before. Mackenzie didn't complain. Hell, if anything, she pushed her jean-clad ass back a little more than necessary, just so they'd be in close contact. Man, this woman was dangerous. She could turn him to mush with no effort at all. The scary part was that he could actually feel that tingling in his gums that told him his fangs were trying to slip out. Her mind-numbing scent practically had him on the edge of losing control.

Damn, he hadn't experienced control issues like this since he'd first turned years ago. And if her rapidly beating heart was any indication, this attraction wasn't all one-sided—she was feeling the same way. He'd thought so last night, but he hadn't been sure of anything until they'd gotten on the range.

He had to admit, he'd been jealous as hell when Mike told him Mackenzie had brought some guy with her that morning. For some stupid reason, that had pissed him off. He'd been out of his seat and headed for the gate before he even knew what he was doing. The moment he'd laid eyes on Zak, though, his anger had disappeared. In a way only a werewolf could know, Zak had *friend* written all over him.

That was also when Gage knew Mackenzie Stone had gotten to him.

"Okay," he said loud enough for her to hear over the sound of the pistol. "Stop for a minute. I know what you're doing wrong." He reached around and put his hands under hers, supporting the lightweight weapon. "First of all, you're not breathing like I told you to. Take a deep breath and let it half out. Pause. Then shoot."

Mackenzie practiced breathing deep like that a few times, which made for an enjoyable view of her expanding T-shirt. He barely stifled the groan this time. God save him.

"This next part is critical." He moved his mouth closer to her muff-covered ears so he wouldn't have to shout. "You're jerking too hard."

She turned her head to give him a teasing smile. "Jerking too hard? Is that even possible?"

Okay, maybe picking a word that had such a sexual connotation hadn't been the best idea. "Oh yeah, it's possible. And you're doing it."

"Huh. So, can you show me the proper way I should be jerking it?"

Gage groaned. Thank God none of the guys were close enough to hear this little exchange. He'd never live it down.

He repositioned her fingers around the grip, then moved her left hand into a better position to support the weapon. "Remember to squeeze it firmly, but not hard. You want your grip to be tight enough that it won't pop out when it bucks, but not so tight that your fingers get tired."

"Wouldn't want my fingers to get tired," she agreed. "Okay, now what? Just shoot?"

"No, not yet. You've got the breathing and the grip down. Now I have to make sure you know how to stroke the trigger."

That flirty smile of hers was back. "You're making this up, right?"

"Absolutely not. These are time-honored shooting tips that everyone in SWAT learns."

"Uh-uh." She looked down the barrel of the .22 again. "So, are you going to share these tips or do I just have to guess?"

"You can't rush these things." He pressed himself more tightly against her and put his mouth close to her ear. He was about to tell her to tighten her grip on the pistol when he felt her bottom moving slightly side to side, like she was shifting her weight from foot to foot. It might have been a completely subconscious effort to get more comfortable, but it sure as hell seemed like she was purposely rubbing her ass against his hard-on.

He immediately went from really frigging hard to painfully stiff in the span of a few heartbeats, which only seemed to encourage Mackenzie more. Damn, it was all he could do to not drop his hands down to her hips and pull her ass tightly against him.

Then he realized that Mackenzie's breath was coming faster. For a moment he wondered if she was going to start panting.

It was the tips of his fangs pressing into his tongue that jerked him out of his trance and forced him to get control of himself and the situation. Yeah, Mackenzie was amazing, but he had to remember what was at stake here. His pack was depending on him to deal with this woman.

He backed off an inch or two, enough to break the

contact between her butt and his groin. That also broke the almost hypnotic hold she seemed to have on him. He ignored what could have been a moan of disappointment and leaned his mouth close to her ear again, ready to get back to the task they were supposed to be here for. It was tough, but controlling emotions was part of being a werewolf.

"Get a firm grip on the weapon, then take a breath and let it out halfway." He waited until he felt her breath hitch. "Now, slowly caress the trigger. Don't squeeze it. You should be completely surprised when it goes off."

The gun still jumped in her hand, but she had a better grip this time, so it didn't move nearly as much as before.

Mackenzie laughed. "I hit the target dead center."

He couldn't help but smile with her. "Yes, you did. Now do it again."

She breathed deep, took her time, and put every shot through the nine ring. When she'd emptied the magazine, she set the pistol down on the counter and spun around in his arms, hugging him with a breathless laugh.

"I did it!"

Even though he knew he shouldn't, Gage found himself automatically wrapping his arms around her. Her breasts were soft against his chest, her hips enticing. And her lips… The way they were parted, it was like they were begging to be kissed. God, he could almost taste them. Something told him one kiss wouldn't be enough. But he was willing to take the risk. He might have done it too, but luckily she pulled away.

"I want to do it again," she said excitedly.

"Okay," he laughed. "Unless you want to…"

"Unless I want to…?"

The way she was looking at him almost made him forget again that she was here looking for a story that could destroy his life and the lives of his pack members. And just like that Gage felt the stirrings of a foolish emotion he shouldn't be feeling right now—definitely not this fast, and definitely not for this woman.

He reached around her, picking up the 9mm he'd brought. "Or we could try something a little bigger?"

Her lips curved. "You think I can handle something bigger?"

He turned her around so that her ass was pressed snugly against him, then placed the 9mm in her hands and aimed it at the target. "Something tells me you can handle just about anything."

~

Mac had no idea target shooting could be so much fun, but she was hooked. She was already thinking about what kind of handgun she wanted to buy for herself. She adored the .22 she fired first, but the 9mm had been so fun. And Gage had told her that most of the well-known manufacturers even had model lines specifically for women, with accessories like pink handgrips. She was definitely getting one of those.

She wanted to tell Zak about her shooting lessons, but everyone around the handful of tables the restaurant staff had pushed together for the SWAT team in the large back room of the steak house had a story to tell. And Zak was talking louder than any of them. It turned out that in order to escape the horrible villains holding him hostage, Zak had to take a more active role than expected of an average hostage.

Mac couldn't stop laughing as Zak described how he'd been cut loose by some of the guys on Mike's squad, then crawled out of the dark building on his hands and knees, only to find himself on the roof. Then he'd been taught enough about rappelling to lower himself down to the ground.

Unfortunately, just when it seemed that he'd get away safely, Xander's squad had reappeared and started shooting at him with paintball guns. Zak—who was covered from head to toe in orange paint—had picked up a weapon when one of Mike's team had gone down and helped the team fight their way to freedom.

"I have to admit I didn't think you had it in you," Mike said to Zak. "But you did good."

Everyone around the table applauded, including Mac. She wasn't sure how much training the guys had accomplished that morning considering that paintball was involved, but it sounded like they had fun.

"Did you know they were going to do that to Zak?" she whispered to Gage.

"I figured they'd do something to have a little fun with him, but I didn't think they'd break out the paintball guns," he said. "They only do that when they think a person can handle it. Your photographer must have a little action hero in him."

She laughed. "I wouldn't have figured that in a hundred years, but I guess so."

Two waitresses came to take their orders, which reduced the noise around the table to a mild roar. When Gage leaned in to tell her about something on the menu, he still had to put his mouth close to her ear. The feel of his warm breath on her skin made her shiver, and she closed her eyes until it passed. When she opened them,

Mac saw that Zak was smiling at her from the other side of the table. She stuck out her tongue at him.

"What was that about?" Gage asked.

She turned and leaned in close again, enjoying the feeling of heat coming off his skin. If it were anyone else, she'd think he had a fever, but instinct told her Gage ran hot. "Nothing. You know, I was just thinking that I really owe you one for that shooting lesson."

"You don't owe me anything." He grinned. "I'm glad you enjoyed yourself."

Oh, she had enjoyed herself. If she thought he'd gotten her hot and bothered last night, that was nothing in comparison to what it was like to have Gage's big arms around her and his hard-on pressing into her ass as she practiced shooting targets. Thank God she had to keep both hands wrapped around the pistol or she might have been tempted to touch herself. Or him.

It was official, Gage Dixon could arouse her just by being near her.

Something else was official, too. She was seriously close to tanking this story idea. She was so crazy about Gage that she was ready to ignore anything he'd ever done wrong short of a felony. And from the way Zak was laughing and joking with the SWAT officers at the table, he'd agree with her. Maybe she'd do a story on the day-in-the-life of the men who made up the SWAT unit and leave it at that.

The men tore into their meals with the same gusto they'd attacked the donuts that morning. Mac didn't know whether to laugh or shake her head. They ate like a pack of wild animals.

She was still cutting her baked chicken and steamed

vegetables when the whole table suddenly fell silent. She looked up, watching as each of the men set their forks and knives down, as if they were done eating. Which didn't make sense, not with that much food left on their plates. What was going on?

She gave Zak a questioning look, but he seemed as confused as she did.

Mac turned to ask Gage, but the words died on her lips as eight men strode into the room. She wasn't sure how it was possible, but something told her they were the reason the SWAT guys suddenly went on high alert. Despite their expensive suits and clean-cut looks, the men were trouble. She'd seen enough men like them in her line of work to be sure of that.

They spread out along the wall behind her, surrounding the table while at the same time blocking the doorway. Mac's heart kicked into high gear as she caught a glimpse of the pistol underneath the coat of the man closest to her.

"I'm looking for Gage Dixon," the man with the gun said.

Gage was on his feet before Mac even saw him move. A single step put him inches away from the man, making their difference in height immediately apparent. The guy in the suit backed up almost involuntarily.

"It's your lucky day then," Gage said in a much calmer voice than she could have managed. "You've found him."

"I need you to come with me," the man said.

"I'm in the middle of lunch."

The man's lip curled. "That's too damn bad. The man I work for wants to talk to you." When Gage didn't say anything, the man opened his jacket to show him the large handgun in an underarm holster. "Now."

Crap.

Mac knew she'd seen the man somewhere, but couldn't remember where until now. His name was Roscoe Patterson and he was Walter Hardy's enforcer. She had to warn Gage.

She started to get to her feet, but Xander pulled her back down and shook his head. What the hell? How could he and the rest of the SWAT team just sit there while Hardy's thugs dragged Gage out of the restaurant?

She whirled around in her seat just in time to see Patterson put his hand on Gage's shoulder and shove him toward the door.

But Gage didn't go anywhere, he didn't move at all. "I said I'm in the middle of lunch. If you give me a name and an address, I'll stop by and see your boss when I get a chance."

Patterson's eyes narrowed. "Are you stupid? I have a gun."

"Yeah, I noticed that," Gage said. "Funny thing about guns, they don't work if they're shoved up your ass."

Mac was glad she hadn't eaten anything yet because her stomach was one big knot. She didn't know Patterson very well, but he looked like the kind of guy who wouldn't be afraid to pull his gun and shoot Gage right there in front of fifteen other cops.

But Gage didn't give him the chance. He grabbed Patterson by the front of his suit jacket and shoved him against the wall. The rest of Hardy's thugs scrambled for their guns only to freeze when every cop at the table drew their weapons and aimed in their direction.

Mac did a double take. How had the SWAT guys moved so fast?

She couldn't see Gage's face because his back was to her now, but the look he gave Patterson must have scared the hell out of him because the man went white.

"That's the problem with guns these days," Gage said softly. "Everybody's got one."

Holding Patterson still with one hand, he reached under the man's jacket with the other and came out with a flashy automatic. It looked a little like the 9mm she'd fired that morning, only bigger.

"You should probably leave now." Gage released Patterson. "If you feel like getting this back, you can come by the compound for it. I'm sure you know where it is."

Patterson swallowed hard. His eyes darted around the room, a frown creasing his brow as if he couldn't understand how the tables had turned so quickly on him and his men. He gave them a nod and jerked his head toward the door. They hesitated, but then slowly filed out.

Patterson made a show of straightening his jacket, then headed for the door. Once there, though, he stopped to fix Gage with a glare.

"Yeah, I know," Gage said before the other man could speak. "I'll regret this. I'll be sorry. This isn't over. Whatever. Get out."

He didn't wait to see if Patterson followed orders, but instead walked back to the table and sat down beside Mac. She watched over her shoulder as Hardy's enforcer stormed out of the room. When she turned around, it was to find Gage reaching for the bottle of steak sauce.

He gave Xander an accusing look as he took off the cap. "Did you drink this or something? It was full just a second ago."

"Wasn't me." Xander grabbed the bottle in front of Delaney and reached across her to hand it to Gage. "It was empty before I got it."

And just like that, everyone started arguing, one side talking about who'd hogged all the steak sauce while the other debated why anyone would ruin a perfectly good steak with the stuff to begin with.

Mac stared at them. How could they sit there and debate the merits of steak sauce as if nothing had happened? Didn't they realize that any one of them could have been shot a minute ago?

"Aren't you going to do something?" she asked Gage.

He stopped cutting his steak to look at her. "What do you think I should do—arrest them?"

"Well... Yeah." She would have thought that was obvious. "They had guns and they threatened you."

He went back to cutting his steak. "This is Texas. Everyone has guns. But they never actually pulled their weapons or even said they were going to hurt me. They simply said their boss wanted to talk to me. That's all. Nothing there to warrant an arrest."

Nothing there? "Those men work for Hardy."

His hand stilled on the knife, the muscle in his jaw flexing. At least he wasn't taking this as lightly as it seemed. "It doesn't change anything."

How the heck could he be so calm about this? There was a rich, powerful, violent man out there who blamed SWAT for the death of his son—and Gage was the face of SWAT.

"They'll come after you again," she said quietly. "You know that, right?"

"Then I'll be ready for them."

He sounded so casual about the whole thing it made her want to scream. Mac pushed her plate away. She'd lost her appetite.

Gage might have dealt with Patterson, but that wouldn't be the end of it. Hardy was coming for him, and now he'd be even more determined than before.

And for some reason, that scared her more than if the man had been after her.

Chapter 6

GAGE DROVE MACKENZIE HOME THAT NIGHT. SHE'D told him she was fine catching a ride with Zak, but after that episode at the restaurant, he felt better doing it himself. He didn't have to try too hard to convince her. Just another indication of how upset she still was after the run-in with Hardy's men.

It wasn't just her, either. Regardless of how relaxed the team had seemed after Hardy's thugs left the restaurant, they'd been anything but. Even after Mackenzie had allowed them to cajole her into taking Zak's place as the hostage in the afternoon training session, his guys were on edge. They knew Hardy wasn't someone to take lightly. If he wanted to come after any of them, he could do some damage.

"You don't have to walk me all the way to my door, you know," Mackenzie said as they stepped off the elevator on her floor. "Hardy's not after me."

"This has nothing to do with Hardy." He sounded so sincere even he almost believed it. "I was just hoping that if I walked you to your door, you might invite me in again. I felt bad about turning down your offer last night."

At least that part wasn't a lie. He had felt bad about bailing on her last night, and had been thinking about rectifying that mistake during the drive over to her place.

Mackenzie laughed. "I'm not sure I believe that, but you're welcome to come in if you want. I can even fix you something to eat, as long as you don't expect me to cook like Emile."

Gage hadn't actually given dinner much thought, but if it gave him an excuse to hang around Mackenzie's place for a while, he was all for it. Because regardless of how calm he'd been about Hardy's thugs showing up at the restaurant, he really was worried—just not for himself.

He'd been expecting Hardy's men, if not the man himself, to show up at some point. The thing that pissed off Gage—and scared him, too—was that Mackenzie was with him when they'd done it. What if they went after her to get to him?

He had no idea why he was even thinking that. It wasn't as if Hardy's goons had even noticed Mackenzie. And if they had, they wouldn't know who she was or have any reason to go after her. But he still couldn't shake the feeling Mackenzie was in danger and that he had to keep her safe.

"Come on. I'll give you the nickel tour of the place," Mackenzie said as he followed her inside. "Then I'm going to get cleaned up real quick. That last rescue your guys put me through would have been a lot more fun if I hadn't been forced to low crawl halfway across the compound in order to get away."

Gage laughed as he looked around the small apartment. It had a casual, eclectic vibe with a touch of class. "They didn't want you to get your butt shot off with paintball pellets."

She opened the fridge and took out a beer. "I'm pretty sure it had more to do with Becker and Cooper watching my butt than protecting it."

His mouth quirked. "That's a possibility as well. Though I can't say I blame them."

She gave him a heated look as she handed him the bottle of beer. "Two bedrooms that way, though I've turned one into my office." She motioned toward a closed door on the far side of the living room. "The guest bathroom is through there." She spun around in the tight space between the kitchen and living room. "And that concludes the tour. Impressive, huh?"

"It's nice." He took a swallow of beer. "This is good, by the way. Wouldn't have pegged you as a beer drinker."

"I'm not. In fact I never touch the stuff. I keep it in there for Zak. He's over here a couple times a week."

Gage felt the same twinge of jealousy he'd felt earlier when he thought about Mackenzie spending time alone with Zak—or any other man for that matter. The reaction was as unexpected as it was nerve-wracking. He'd known this woman for all of two days and she was provoking gut-level responses like he'd never experienced before.

The crazy part of it was that when he'd watched them interact this morning, his wolf instincts had told him she and Zak weren't physically attracted to each other. Attraction was chemical and you couldn't hide that from a werewolf. But that didn't seem to matter to his inner lycan-influenced caveman. When it came right down to it, Gage didn't like any man getting too close to Mackenzie.

He caged the animal inside and forced a smile to his lips. "Tell him that he has good taste in beer then."

"You tell him. If I do it, he'll never let me forget it." She grinned. "The remote is on the table there. You can watch TV if you want while I clean up. I promise I won't take too long."

He opened his mouth to tell her to take her time, but she'd already walked into the bedroom. She yanked off her shirt just before disappearing inside. The barest flash of tanned skin and silky white bra was enough to make his cock go hard. He took a big gulp of beer, then exhaled slowly. Damn, he had it bad for her.

It was all he could do not to strip off his clothes and join her when he heard the shower turn on. He needed a distraction—fast.

But instead of grabbing the remote and turning on the TV, he wandered around the apartment looking at the various knickknacks, photos, and awards she had. Most of the awards were for her journalism work, but it was more than just a bunch of I-love-me stuff. Sure, there were some personal awards lined up neatly along the wall of the hallway, but more of the space was dedicated to the everyday people she ran into and the amazing places she'd been. A grin tugged at the corner of his mouth.

He was still looking at her collage of news articles she'd written—arranged to look like a silhouette of Mickey Mouse—when he heard her coming down the hall. He glanced at his watch. Twelve minutes? Had she even gotten wet?

But Mackenzie's long hair was still moist after a quick towel dry and her skin still blushed from the hot water. She wore a simple pair of workout shorts and a worn tank top with a picture of Snoopy on it. And she looked completely amazing.

His cock got hard all over again, and he had to turn away from her so he could adjust himself into a better position.

She came up next to him just as he got his hard-on pointed in a direction that wouldn't totally cut off the flow of blood. "Sorry. Didn't mean to startle you."

"Nah, you didn't." He tried to act like he'd just had his

hand in his pocket for the hell of it, but wasn't sure if he succeeded. "I was just looking at your collage. What's the Mickey Mouse thing about?"

"It's just something I put together to remind me to never take myself too seriously. No matter how big the stories are that I write, every kid on the planet would rather meet Mickey Mouse than me."

He chuckled. "You know, that's not a bad way to look at the world."

She walked into the kitchen. "Want another beer?"

"I'm good, thanks."

Gage moved closer to the island separating the kitchen from the living room just in time to see her lean over to get something out of one of the lower cabinets. Her slightly wet hair fell forward over her face, and she casually flipped it over her shoulder as she reached in to get whatever she was after.

That's when her scent hit him.

He couldn't say why he hadn't picked it up before—maybe it was the battle he'd been having with his hard-on—but he hadn't. He inhaled even deeper. That wasn't perfume or shampoo he was picking up. That was how Mackenzie smelled after a shower, with every scent but hers washed clean. It was so overwhelming that he had to grab the counter to keep from climbing over it to ravish the hell out of her.

Maybe all the crap Xander and the other young were-wolves said about *The One* might be true. Because no other woman had ever made him feel anything like this.

Mackenzie popped up with a big spaghetti pot in her hands. "Chicken nuggets over angel hair pasta good for you?"

"Huh?"

She held up the pot, completely unaware that he couldn't focus on a damn thing she was saying or doing at the moment. "Angel hair pasta with spaghetti sauce, topped with store-bought chicken nuggets. Like I said, it won't measure up to Emile's food, but it's one of my specialties."

"Um, sure. Sounds good."

Gage watched in silent appreciation as she moved around the kitchen with practiced ease. She might have put on the shorts and tank top purely for comfort, but they let him drink in a serious amount of skin. Enough to get drunk from. He put down the beer so she wouldn't see his hand shaking. He took a deep breath, getting himself back under control as she filled the pot with water and started chatting about the day's training. He noticed she carefully avoided any mention of lunch.

She threw him a smile as she opened the fridge and pulled out a bag of frozen chicken nuggets. "These things are awesome."

She dumped some into a glass bowl, looked at him, then dumped even more in the bowl. She filled a second glass bowl with an entire jar of premade spaghetti sauce that she took from an upper cabinet. Both bowls went in the microwave and Gage watched in awe as her fingers literally flew across the touch pad. By the time everything was ready, Gage had his wits back in order and was able to help her carry the food to the table. He even did a pretty good job of maintaining an intelligent conversation. He had to admit, the nuggets tasted good with the pasta, like bite-sized pieces of chicken parmesan.

In reality, it didn't matter what they ate. He just enjoyed talking about the day's SWAT training, and what they'd do tomorrow. He was looking forward to spending another day doing nothing more than distracting her.

But after the food was gone, and they'd discussed everything Mackenzie could possibly want to know about training, the subject they both wanted to avoid sat there staring them in the face.

"What are you going to do when Hardy sends his men after you again?" she asked softly.

She was really worried—he knew because he could hear her heart speed up. He was worried, too.

"If that happens—and I'm not necessarily sure it will—I'll deal with them," he said.

Gage was very sure Hardy would come at him again, but he wanted Mackenzie to at least think there might be a possibility it wouldn't happen.

"Just like that? You'll deal with them?" He didn't miss the twinge of sarcasm in her voice. "That doesn't seem like much of a plan."

His mouth quirked. "Coming from a woman who's made her living walking into dangerous situations when most rational people wouldn't, you should appreciate when someone doesn't overthink things. If they show up, I'll let my instincts and training dictate how I react. Thinking too much about things like that ahead of time would just slow my reaction time."

She picked up the plates and carried them over to the sink. "I usually don't have much of a plan when I walk into those situations because I'm lousy at thinking too far ahead."

"Maybe I don't like to think too far ahead myself. Perhaps there are times I prefer to just be in the moment."

She came over and leaned her hip against the edge of

the table. She was so close they were nearly touching.
"And is right now one of those times?"

He moved one hand over until his forefinger was able
to gently caress her hand where it rested on the table.
"Yeah, I think now might be one of those times."

Her lips curved. "Then maybe you'd like to be in the
moment over on the couch?"

"The couch would be nice."

He followed her over to the sectional piled high with
a crazy amount of pillows. Mackenzie shoved a bunch
of them aside, making room for them both. When he sat
down next to her, she immediately turned to face him,
pulling her knees up so she was sitting cross-legged. The
move was so casual it was hard to understand why he
found it so sexual. Maybe because it was such a confident
and relaxed pose.

Or maybe it was because the position provided a view
of a tantalizing expanse of inner thigh.

"What should we talk about, now that we're in the
moment?" she breathed.

There was some tiny part of him—the part that agreed
with Mike and Xander about his needing to be on guard
around her—that warned him he was on dangerous ground.
But he ignored that part and instead listened to the one
that'd known this moment was coming from the second
Mackenzie Stone had stepped into the operations vehicle.

"I'm fine with not talking at all."

She smiled. "Works for me."

Gage leaned forward at the exact moment Mackenzie
did. He absently wondered how that could be comfortable
with her legs crossed like that, but she was clearly very
flexible. He was still pondering the potential benefits of

being that flexible when their lips met. There weren't any fireworks or sparks, or any of that silly stuff young werewolves insisted happened when you kissed *The One*.

But that didn't mean kissing her wasn't amazing.

Gage slipped his tongue into her mouth, teasing hers to come out and play. Mackenzie was more than willing, even moaning a little as their tongues tangled. He slid his hand into her hair, growling as he pulled her closer. She tasted so damn good. Like strawberries on a hot summer day, only sweeter.

Mackenzie pulled away with a husky laugh. "Never had a man growl while he kissed me before. I think I like it."

Reminding himself to keep his inner wolf in check, Gage tugged her close, trailing kisses from her mouth all the way down her neck and back up again. Mackenzie's heart was beating out of control, thudding in his ears. Her pheromones filled his nose, evidence of her arousal.

Mackenzie slowly and sensually uncoiled from her cross-legged position and straddled his lap. His hands slid down her back to rest on her hips. He could barely think, much less maintain control. And it only got worse when she started grinding against his hard-on. He swore he could feel the warmth of her pussy through his uniform pants. He couldn't believe how badly he wanted to let his claws slip out so he could rip off her tank top and shorts and eat her up.

Gage didn't know how he managed to keep it together. But he had to—he had to protect his pack. He wanted to think Mackenzie was focused more on him than the story she was chasing, but he couldn't be sure. Until he knew for certain his pack wasn't in danger of being exposed, he couldn't afford to let himself be distracted by her searing-hot kisses, soft skin, or enticing curves.

That was easier said than done. Resisting her would have been hard as hell if he'd been a normal man, but he was a werewolf, which meant he had to battle the added temptation of her arousal, too. The scent engulfed him, making it hard to remember the reason he couldn't lose himself in her.

It took everything he had to stop her when she reached down to grab the hem of her tank top. He couldn't go that far and still stay in control.

She blinked liked she was confused. He knew the feeling. "Don't you want to?"

Gage stifled a groan. "More than you know."

He really should get a medal for this much willpower. Grasping her ass in both hands, he picked her up and got to his feet. She wrapped her legs more tightly around his waist and draped her arms behind his neck. Her smile faded when she realized where he was heading.

"You're leaving?"

He helped her slide gently down to the floor. While her legs weren't wrapped around him anymore, her arms were still around his neck, which meant her body was still pressed up against his. Forget a medal. He deserved a freaking street named after him.

"If I don't leave now, I might not get out of here at all," he told her.

She grinned. "Would that be such a bad thing?"

The sultry look she gave him almost weakened his resolve. But he forced himself to stay steady. This was for his pack. "No. But I think we both know we have something good going on between us. We don't need to rush it."

She slid one hand down to place it on his chest, right

over his heart. He doubted she needed werewolf senses to feel the pounding going on under her palm.

"I don't want to rush it, either." She laughed. "Well, maybe rush it a little."

He put a finger under her chin and tilted her face up for a slow, lingering kiss. Maybe he was being too cautious. But while his body told him to sweep her into his arms and carry her to bed, his head was telling him to get out of there...while he still had the strength.

"The first time we're together, I want to make sure we have all the time we need. I don't want to get interrupted halfway into making love because the alarm clock went off in the morning."

Her eyes opened wide as his words slowly sunk in. "Halfway?"

He kissed her again, then leaned over to whisper in her ear. "Halfway."

He felt a shiver pass through her body. "I suppose a promise like that is something worth waiting for then."

He brushed her silky hair back from her face. "See you bright and early at the compound tomorrow?"

She nodded, but then frowned. "Well, maybe not too early. About nine?"

"Nine o'clock is fine."

He opened the door, but Mackenzie yanked him in for another hard kiss before he could leave. He buried his hand in her hair, returning the kiss with an intensity that confused him. Why the hell was he so out of control around her?

Thank God she was the one who broke the kiss this time. He wasn't sure he would have had the fortitude. "There's more where that came from," she whispered. "Don't make me wait too long, okay?"

Gage felt Mackenzie's eyes on him as he walked down the hall to the elevator. Risking a glance in her direction was dangerous, but he pushed the button and did it anyway. She was standing in the doorway, her face flushed, her eyes full of desire. How could he walk away from her?

He was on the verge of telling his conscience to go to hell when the elevator doors opened. He stepped inside and pushed the button for the lobby, then leaned back against the wall and closed his eyes. He only prayed Mackenzie Stone, the journalist, would drop her story and be content to be Mackenzie Stone, the woman. And soon. Because he didn't think he could hold out much longer.

Chapter 7

"Did you even hear a word I just said?" Zak asked as they drove to the SWAT compound the next morning.

Mac gave herself a shake. "Yeah, of course I did."

Zak raised a brow.

She felt her face color. Damn it. He could always tell when she was lying. "Okay, not all of it. Sorry. I was thinking."

He gave her a sideways glance as he turned the news van onto the road that led to the SWAT compound. "About what?"

Gage. Or more precisely, the handsome SWAT commander's promise—the one about the two of them making love all night. But she wasn't going to tell Zak that.

She'd hardly slept a wink after Gage left. How could any woman expect to fall asleep when they were fantasizing about a man like that? She'd been so turned on she finally pulled out her vibrator for some relief. But unfortunately, the bunny didn't keep going and going, and she was still unsatisfied. When she finally fell asleep, she'd alternated between dreams of making love with Gage and wondering why the hell she was so crazy for him. She'd never had it this bad for a guy in her life.

"Let me guess," Zak said when she didn't answer. "You're not sure you want to keep investigating Gage and the SWAT team, right?"

Mac didn't say anything. Besides the fact that

investigating SWAT would probably end up being a waste of time, there was the bigger, ethical issue of writing a story about a man while she was desperately trying to get him into her bed.

People in her line of work called that a conflict of interest. She just called it stupid.

"Yeah," she finally said. "I've been thinking that maybe there isn't as much going on here as I thought."

She waited for Zak to question where this sudden case of self-doubt was coming from. But he surprised her.

"I know I'm just your photographer, but for what it's worth, I think you're right. These guys seem clean to me."

Mac stared at him. Who was this guy and what had he done with the real Zak? Because the Zak she knew never hesitated to call it like he saw it. Besides, he was more than her photographer.

"O-kay," she said slowly. "I agree with you, but why do you think so?"

"I spent a lot of time with them yesterday while you were out shooting with Gage. And then I went out to some clubs and stuff with them last night."

It was her turn to lift a brow. Zak didn't usually go clubbing. And he especially didn't go clubbing during Shark Week. "That must have been interesting."

"Hey, I get out sometimes, you know. But I was just saying, they were really cool to hang with. They didn't get drunk. Or stupid. We just sat around, had a few beers, and talked."

"You're telling me those guys went clubbing and all they did was hang out with you?"

"Well, they danced some, too. Actually, they danced a lot." He frowned. "Women seem to gravitate to them for some reason. But the important thing is that we talked long enough for me to get a good feel for them. I really think they're stand-up guys."

She could have ragged Zak about his legendary instincts when it came to telling the difference between good guys and bad guys. But she didn't because she knew he was right this time.

"Yeah, I think so, too."

"So, what are you going to do?" he asked.

That was a damn good question. "I don't know. I guess I'll just let the next few days play out. If you're right and we don't find anything, I'll drop the story."

His mouth edged up into a smile. "I'm guessing the fact that you're attracted to Dixon sort of makes your decision a bit more complicated than it should be?"

Zak didn't miss much. "When did you know?"

"The moment you walked out of the operations vehicle on Belmont the other day."

She laughed. "Now you're just making crap up. Even I didn't realize I liked him at that point."

Zak shook his head with a sigh. "You always were a little slow about that kind of stuff."

Mac opened her mouth to tell him she wasn't slow, thank you very much, but the two SUVs heading out the gate just as they were pulling in stopped her. The big operations vehicle was right behind the first two vehicles. Gage leaned out of the window just long enough to tell her he was going on a call at a shopping mall in Arlington.

"Xander's inside. He's arranged for you to sit down and talk to some of the other guys." Gage flashed her a smile. "I figured you'd want to get some background on someone besides me."

Not really. But he was gone before she could even consider telling him that out loud, or try and invite herself along.

Mac climbed out of the news van and fell into step beside Zak. Maybe it would be a good idea to talk to a few of the other guys. Just to get a different perspective on her theoretical story. God knew she couldn't focus on anything when Gage was around.

The rest of the team was waiting for her and Zak in the classroom in the training building. While they greeted her warmly—and fist-bumped Zak for bringing more donuts—there seemed to be a weird vibe in the room. Kind of like walking in a friend's house after she and her husband had a fight. Did it have something to do with the incident Gage had gone on?

Then again, considering that several of the men were going out of their way not to look at her, maybe not. And every time she caught them checking her out, they quickly looked away. All the men except Cooper. He held her gaze for a long time before he finally grabbed a donut at random and walked off without a word. What the hell was that about?

Mac wandered over to the desk at the front of the room to see if there were any donuts with sprinkles left when Xander walked in.

"Ms. Stone."

"Corporal Riggs." She smiled. "Donut?"

He shook his head. "I saw you talking to Sergeant Dixon before he left. He asked me to keep you occupied while he was gone."

What was she, a puppy? "Keep me occupied?"

Xander winced. "Not exactly the way Sergeant Dixon

put it. Now you see why he does all the talking when it comes to the press."

She might have laughed if she thought Xander'd been joking. But he looked even more intense and serious than usual. "Is something wrong?"

Surprise flickered across his face, but it was gone just as quickly, replaced with the same austere expression. He glanced over at the other men. They were leaning back in their chairs, laughing at something Zak had said. The tension she'd picked up earlier seemed to have faded.

She turned her attention back to Xander and found him regarding her with a suspicious look. "What?"

"Nothing," he said.

There was definitely something going on behind those dark eyes, but damned if she could figure out what it was. "You didn't answer my question."

"We just kind of got into it about something before you got here." His smile didn't quite reach his eyes. "It wasn't a big deal. Just guy stuff."

Uh-huh. "And by something, do you mean me?"

"No, of course not."

Xander was lying his ass off and not doing a very good job of it. Why had they been arguing about her? She wanted to ask, but Xander probably wouldn't tell her anyway. Time to change the subject.

"Gage said something about me interviewing the men while I waited for him to come back," she said.

The muscle in Xander's jaw jumped. She was going to have to be careful trying to manipulate him. He had a suspicious streak a mile wide, and he definitely didn't trust her.

"Yeah," he said. "He mentioned that."

"Would you like to be first?"

Xander didn't look any more thrilled about the idea than she was, but he nodded. "We can talk in the weight room."

The couches out by the television would be more comfortable, but Xander had already headed in that direction, giving her no choice but to follow. The senior corporal was standing in the middle of the room, arms folded across his chest, his expression guarded. Oh yeah, this was going to be fun.

Mac sat down on one of the weight benches and took out her notebook. At least they'd gotten new mirrors put in since the last time she was here.

Xander was polite, but evasive. Okay, maybe that wasn't fair. He answered all her questions. He simply didn't elaborate on any of his answers. She didn't get much more than the boring stuff she'd already read in his file. He'd worked for the Kansas City Police Department for several years before Gage recruited him to join the Dallas SWAT team. Yes, he was single. No, he wasn't seeing anyone.

She spent the next few hours interviewing the rest of the guys on Xander's squad. Trevino and McCall were reserved like Xander, but Lowry, Delaney, and Becker were more forthcoming. Not only did they have more stories than a boatload of sailors, they were charming as hell and knew how to make a woman laugh. She took a lot of notes. If she ever wrote a human interest piece about the SWAT team, she'd have enough to write a dozen articles.

Mac skimmed her notes while she waited for Cooper to come in and noticed that none of the guys were married. Huh. How was it possible for a group of cops this hunky to all be single? That had to some kind of statistical anomaly.

Something else was odd, too. Most of them had transferred from other police departments around the country. She didn't know enough about the subject to say for sure, but it was hard to believe no one in the Dallas PD had measured up.

While that was certainly strange, it also indicated Gage and his team were clean. If he'd schemed to fill the unit with his people so they could get away with something dirty, wouldn't he have gotten other cops from his own department, cops he knew were dirty, too? There was no way Gage could have known officers from other departments well enough to know they were crooked.

She was investigating SWAT because she thought they were dirty, but if anything, Gage had almost gone out of his way to make it the cleanest unit possible.

Mac was scribbling some notes when Cooper walked in. He still wore that half-angry expression he'd had earlier. But then he smiled and she wondered if she hadn't imagined things.

"I saved a donut for you," he said as he sat down on the weight bench opposite her. "I noticed you didn't grab one before you left and figured you'd be starving after listening to all the BS the guys were probably trying to sell you."

She set down her notebook to take the sprinkle-covered donut he'd wrapped in a napkin. He'd even been thoughtful enough to bring her a cup of coffee with the right amount of cream. She took a sip. Artificial sweeter, too? Damn, he was good.

"Okay, bringing me a donut with sprinkles is impressive enough, but how did you know how I take my coffee?"

He chuckled. "Four years in the Army Bomb Squad,

two tours in Afghanistan, one in Iraq. You learn to notice everything or you get blown into a pink mist real quick."

Something in his tone told her he wasn't joking. "I see. Well, thanks for thinking about me. I was getting hungry."

He nodded and crossed his arms over his chest, emphasizing his biceps. His arms weren't as big as Gage's, but they were close. The perturbed look was back on his face now. What the hell was going on with him? Just yesterday, this cute guy was staring at her butt like he was in love with it. Today, he looked at her like he wanted her the hell out of here.

"Mind if I ask you a question, Ms. Stone?"

She set her coffee down on the bench and picked up her notepad. "Not at all. And call me Mac."

"Okay then, Mac. Are you screwing with my boss's head just to get a story?"

Mac was pretty sure her jaw dropped. And people said she was direct. "I don't know what you mean."

God, that sounded horribly lame.

He snorted. "Sure you do. It's a simple question. Do you honestly care about Gage or are you planning to screw him over to get the story you're after?"

If anyone else on the team had asked her that question, she probably would have BS'd her way through it. But she didn't think she could do that with Cooper.

"Does it matter how I answer?" she asked. "You have no reason to believe me even if I tell you the truth."

"Just answer the question. I'll know if you're telling the truth."

Mac wasn't sure how he could tell, but she believed him. "Yes, I honestly care about Gage."

"So, he's important to you?"

"Yes."

Why the heck was she answering like she was on a witness stand? She was supposed to be the one asking questions.

"Are you in love with him?"

She didn't know why she even hesitated. How could you fall in love with any man that you'd just met a few days ago? Even if he was as hunky, sexy, arousing, and tempting as Gage. Hell, she hadn't even slept with him yet.

She opened her mouth to tell Cooper she wasn't in love with his boss, not that it was any of his business, but she couldn't get the words out. She might not know if she loved him—she was a practical woman, and practical women didn't fall in love in three days—but she felt something for him. Something stronger than she'd ever felt for any other man.

She was still trying to figure out exactly what the hell she felt when Cooper stood. "I think I have the answer I was looking for."

Mac frowned up at him. "But I didn't say anything."

His mouth curved. "You said plenty."

She watched in confusion as he headed for the door. "Hey. Aren't you going to let me interview you?"

He stopped in the doorway to look back at her. "I'm boring. Nobody wants to know anything about me."

Mac gazed down at the blank page on her notepad. If she didn't know better, she'd think that Cooper had just Dr. Phil'd her butt. Because as crazy as it sounded, things seemed a whole lot clearer than they'd been a little while ago.

―――∽∽∽―――

Mac was snooping around the upstairs bedroom a few hours later, and finding nothing, when a pair of strong arms wrapped around her waist. Even though she knew it had to be Gage, she let out a little gasp of surprise anyway. He chuckled softly, his warm breath brushing her ear and making her shiver.

"Sorry. Didn't mean to scare you," he said. "I thought you would have left already. Find anything interesting up here?"

She wrapped her arms around him, leaning back against the hard wall of his chest. "I was hoping to find a stash of needles and steroid bottles under the mattress, but no luck."

Since finishing the one-on-one interviews, she'd spent hours covering just about every inch of the compound—with Xander's complete knowledge and permission. She'd skimmed through the rest of the files, then pawed through every storage space and equipment room she could find before coming up here to do a detailed search. Nothing. No drugs or anything indicating that anything inappropriate was going on.

"Sorry to disappoint you," Gage said. "I could go buy some if it'd help. I'll need a prescription first, though, so it might take a while."

She turned in his arms, surprised at how relieved she was to see him back safe and sound. She hadn't even realized she'd been worried. "How'd it go at the mall?"

He stepped back with a heavy sigh, and she immediately missed the warmth of his arms. "Better than I thought it would. There was a teen with a gun holding hostages in a sporting goods store. He was upset that some girl had made fun of him and wanted to kill her and everyone she worked with. It was tense for a while there, but Kendrick finally talked him down. It took almost four hours to convince the kid to walk away."

Wow. "I'm glad no one got hurt."

"Me too."

She followed Gage into the small kitchen, watching as he rifled through the cabinets. He opened just about every one of them, but came up empty-handed.

"Looking for anything in particular?" she asked.

"Not really. Just had an urge for something."

"Like what?"

The teasing look he gave her made her pulse skip a beat. "Now I know what I wanted to eat." He took her hand and pulled her against him with a low, sexy growl. "You."

His mouth came down on hers with a possessiveness that made her knees go weak. She clutched his shoulders to keep from melting to the floor. How could she go all gooey from a simple kiss?

Because there wasn't anything simple about it. The kiss was amazing.

"I've been thinking about doing that all day," he rasped.

She smiled. "Good thing I didn't leave then."

He chuckled and bent his head to kiss her again, but a loud cough from the top of the stairs made them both freeze. Damn, she'd completely forgotten where they were. Apparently, so had Gage. He stepped away from her.

"Sorry to interrupt, Sergeant," Mike said. "But we have another one."

~~~~~

Mac sat in the operations vehicle, her eyes glued to the monitors as Gage and the entire SWAT team finished their sweep of the first floor of the fleabag motel and headed up the stairs at both ends of the building. Despite being worried to death about what came next, she was glad they were finally done with the ground floor because what she'd seen there was going to haunt her for a very long time.

From what Mac had been able to piece together, a local gang had been having some kind of initiation party on the first floor when a rival gang had shown up and started shooting. Gang Number One had returned fire and what had started out as a party had quickly turned into a bloodbath.

The cops had gotten there in time to force the gun-wielding survivors of both gangs up to the second floor of the motel, where they'd barricaded themselves in several rooms. Unfortunately, each gang had taken the people staying at the motel hostage, and were ready to kill all of them—if they hadn't already.

When she, Gage, and the rest of the SWAT team had arrived, the uniformed officers were still trading fire with the gangs on the second floor. It had been like a warzone, with the gangs taking shots at each other as well as the cops and anyone else who came within sight of the motel.

After making her promise to stay in the operations vehicle parked four blocks away, Gage and the rest of the SWAT team immediately headed into the fray—not to take out the thugs, but to try to rescue any of the hotel guests still inside. She'd almost turned off the monitors when she'd seen all the carnage there. Any remaining thought that the SWAT team was crooked, dirty, or anything other than the biggest bunch of heroic, dedicated cops she'd ever seen in her life was gone now. Gage and his men had gone into the motel over and over, carrying out the wounded while being shot at the whole time.

Mac held her breath as Gage reached the second floor.

The two gangs had knocked out windows and piled up furniture to barricade themselves behind while they used up what seemed like an unlimited supply of ammunition. She knew Gage and his team were good at their jobs, but she didn't see how this was going to end well.

Her hands were freaking shaking, she was so scared. Gage was going in there, and she suddenly realized she didn't want him to.

The audio system in the operations vehicle was tied into the headsets every SWAT officer wore, so why the hell couldn't she hear anything? She darted from one monitor to the next, but the men moved so fast it was making her dizzy. She wasn't even sure where everyone was. A minute ago, Gage had been on the stairwell, but now he looked as if he was on some kind of gravel surface. Where the hell was he, on the ground behind the building? That made no sense at all.

Several men suddenly kneeled down in front of Gage's camera, and she had only a second to identify one of them as Cooper before they scattered again. She almost screamed in frustration.

Gage's voice came over the speaker. "Three…two…one…go!"

There was a thunderous boom and a flash of light, then…chaos.

Mac's heart pounded harder, almost drowning out the sound coming over the speakers. What the hell good were cameras if everything on the monitors was too fast and jarring to comprehend? There were bright flashes of light, then the pop of gunshots followed by the ear-shattering cacophony of automatic weapons being fired. Screams and shouts turned into cries of pain, but they were barely audible over the low, angry growls the SWAT team made. She'd heard the same thing when Mike and Xander had led their squads into the pitch-black office building that first day. Only this time, it was much louder.

She closed her eyes, unable to look at the monitors any longer. Why the hell was she so terrified? She'd been in situations like this before. Heck she'd been shot at half a dozen times in the course of her career and even been near an explosion once. But she'd never been this scared.

Because she wasn't the one in danger. The man she cared about was. And that made it worse. She prayed Gage and his men made it through this safely.

Mac didn't know how long she sat there with her eyes closed. But when she opened them again, an eerie kind of quiet had descended upon the motel. She could still hear moans, whimpers, and the occasional sob, but no gunfire.

Then Mike's voice came over the speaker. "One clear."

"Two clear," said Xander.

"Three clear," reported Cooper.

The SWAT team was calling in by some kind of number pattern, letting Gage and everyone else know they were alive and that their area of responsibility had been cleared. She held her breath as fifteen numbers were announced.

"All clear," Gage said. "Get the EMTs in here."

Mac slumped down in the seat, more exhausted than if she'd run a marathon.

Behind her, the doors of the operations vehicle opened. She jerked around to see Zak stick in his head.

"Everyone's running inside. What happened?"

Mac had completely forgotten Zak had been outside taking pictures of the scene. "I'm not sure, but I think everyone's okay," she said. "I heard all of them over the radio at least, and they sounded okay. I don't have a clue what happened, though."

Zak climbed in the truck and shut the door. "I think they blew their way in through the roof, both ends of the building at exactly the same time. There was gravel and flaming tar flying everywhere."

That explained the gravel she'd seen. They'd been on the roof.

She and Zak sat in silence, watching the monitors and trying to figure out what was going on, but it was too dark and chaotic. A lot of people had gotten hurt in the little gang war, so the monitors were filled with EMTs, uniformed officers, and SWAT team members rendering first aid. The motel looked like a scene out of a *M*A*S*H* episode as an endless stream of ambulance gurneys rolled in and right back out.

She was going to get sick if she kept trying to watch the crazy scene. But she couldn't tear herself away until she knew Gage was okay. When she finally caught a quick flash of his tall, broad-shouldered form in one of the other men's cameras, she let out the breath she didn't even realize she'd been holding. He was safe. She could breathe again.

Twenty minutes later, Becker and one of the team's medics, Senior Corporal Trey Duncan, came out to give them an update.

"Cooper and Nelson—our demo guys—blew entry points through the roof in four different places." Becker said it so casually, as if they did stuff like this every day. Which she supposed they did. "Then the whole team dropped through, right into the middle of each gang."

"Are the hostages okay?" Mac asked. "Is everyone okay?"

"Everyone in the unit is fine. A few minor nicks and scratches, but that's about it." Duncan frowned. "Some of the hostages are in pretty bad shape, though. At least three were shot before we even went in, and two more were hit during the rescue. The gangbangers seemed pretty intent on taking as many people with them as possible. They're on the way to the hospital now, but we don't know if they're all going make it."

Mac shook her head.

"Sergeant Dixon asked me to tell you that he's going to be here for a few more hours," Becker said. "He thought you might want to call it a night."

Then he and Duncan left to go back to the motel.

Zak glanced at her after the two cops stepped out of the operations vehicle. "Silly question, but I'm guessing you're going to stay?"

"Yeah. I want to hang around and make sure they're all okay."

He grinned. "I thought so. You gonna need me at the compound tomorrow?"

She shook her head. "I don't think so. I'll see you at the paper."

After Zak left, Mac turned her attention back to the monitors, patiently waiting to catch another glimpse of Gage.

Gage was so tired he could barely keep his eyes open. All he wanted to do was go home, fall into bed, and pass out for a few hours until the alarm went off and he had to get up and do it all over again. But Mackenzie insisted he needed to eat, and kept telling him that until he stopped at the next fast-food drive-through they came to.

"Don't stare at the burrito," she scolded gently. "Eat it."

He forced himself to take a bite, closing his eyes for a moment as the spicy beef filling hit his tongue. Maybe he wasn't too tired to eat after all. Next to him, Mackenzie bit into her own burrito.

Gage had been surprised to find her waiting for him when he'd climbed into the operations vehicle. He thought she'd left hours ago. But she told him she'd wanted to wait. It might be selfish, but he was glad she had. Seeing her beautiful face after the long-ass day he'd had made him feel a little less exhausted.

The two incidents he'd gone on weren't the only reason he was dragging. The other was the argument he'd gotten into with his pack that morning after PT. He'd thought that after yesterday, his guys wouldn't mind sitting down with Mackenzie for a one-on-one interview, but they'd been flat-out pissed off at the idea.

"That's too damn bad because you're doing it anyway," he'd told them. "If it's any consolation, you won't have to put up with Ms. Stone snooping around much longer."

"How do you know that?" McCall asked.

"Yeah." Kendrick's eyes narrowed. "Just how involved with this reporter are you? Is there something going on that you haven't told us?"

Gage bit back a snarl. "What the hell is that supposed to mean?"

Cooper looked up from the graphic novel he was thumbing through. "He means, are you sleeping with her?"

Gage had been so shocked he'd just stood there staring at his explosives expert like a damn pig with a Rolex.

"Well, are you?" Cooper demanded.

Gage had to clench his hands into fists to keep from slugging the man. Getting into a brawl with Cooper might be satisfying as hell, but it would only confirm what he and the rest of the men feared—that he was letting his attraction to Mackenzie cloud his judgment and it was putting the Pack at risk. He understood where their concern was coming from, even if it was misplaced.

"No," he said as evenly as he could manage. "We're not sleeping together."

"Bullshit," Xander snarled. "We can smell her all over you."

Gage didn't even realize he'd moved toward his senior squad leader until Mike stepped in front of him and put a hand on his chest.

Brooks moved to stand next to Xander. "Sergeant, how do we know she isn't playing you?"

"She's not playing me," he growled.

"How can you be sure?" Mike asked.

"I just know, damn it!" he snapped.

That probably wouldn't be good enough for them, but he didn't know how to put it into words. Mackenzie might have come here looking for a story that first day, but something in his gut told him that wasn't the reason she kept coming back.

Xander swore under his breath. "It's not just about her finding out about us, Gage. Having her around is dangerous."

Gage frowned. "What the hell are you talking about?"

"For one thing, you're not thinking clearly," Xander said. "Hardy sent his goons to rough you up and you don't seem to give a damn."

"Like hell I don't."

"Yeah? Well, you haven't mentioned what you're going to do about it." Xander shook his head. "Anyway, it's not just that. She's putting off pheromones all of us are picking up, and it's affecting some of the younger wolves. To say it's a distraction is an understatement. It's going to get someone killed."

That's when things had gotten really ugly. Not everyone in the Pack agreed with Xander, and the guys had taken sides. And the ones who went against Gage weren't only pissed about Mackenzie, they were calling him out as Pack leader. There'd been a few stare downs over the years, but it'd never gone further than that, and certainly never with any of the more senior werewolves. But this fight was going to make the scuffle in the weight room the other day look like child's play. Blood would definitely be shed.

Or it would have been if Cooper hadn't defused the situation with one simple question.

"Mac's *The One*, isn't she?"

Gage didn't answer. He didn't have to. The rest of the Pack retracted their claws, suddenly more interested in debating whether the myth was real—and what that meant for the Pack. If Mackenzie Stone was really *The One* for him, would it keep her from spilling their secret if and when she discovered it? Did the intense attraction have the same effect on her, too?

Gage hoped to God it did, but he didn't know much about it. Unfortunately, neither did Cooper. But before Gage could say anything, dispatch had called about the hostage situation at the mall.

"Should we drive through again and get you another burrito?"

Mackenzie's soft voice interrupted his thoughts and he looked down to see he'd not only eaten the entire burrito, but had practically licked the wrapper clean, too.

He grinned and crumpled the wrapper. "Nah, I think I'm good."

She didn't look convinced. "You can have some of mine, if you want."

"Thanks, but I think it's time we get you home. It's late."

She didn't protest as he started the car. It was well after midnight and she looked as exhausted as he did. She finished the rest of her burrito in silence, then leaned back in the seat.

Gage had to resist the urge to pull over just so he could see if her lips were as sweet as he remembered from that afternoon. He tightened his grip on the wheel and forced his attention back to the road. Xander had been right. He didn't think clearly when he was around her.

Xander was right about something else, too. Mackenzie was a distraction to the team. Gage had thought they were tense because they were worried she'd stumble on their secret, but now he realized it was because her pheromones were making them crazy. Mackenzie was jonesing bad for him and his pack knew it.

Gage thought again about what Cooper said. He'd never believed the myth about every werewolf having one perfect soul mate waiting somewhere out there for him. He'd always thought it was something werewolves came up with to explain why they had such shitty luck with women. They had shitty luck with women because werewolves were moody, secretive, aggressive, and just plain crappy at connecting on a human level. Or so he'd

thought. But maybe Cooper was onto something. Maybe
Mackenzie was *The One*.

What else explained why he couldn't think clearly
when he was with her? Because he'd dated a lot of
women, and none of them had ever had this kind of effect
on him.

And how do you know she's not just playing you?

Brooks's words echoed in his head. What if he was so
blinded by Mackenzie that he couldn't see what was right
in front of him?

Gage glanced at her as he pulled into the parking garage. She could barely keep her eyes open, she was so
tired. Looking at her right then, he was ashamed for even
thinking she might be using him.

"Do you want to come in for a while?" Mackenzie
asked when they got to her door.

Man, he wanted to. But he needed to put some space
between them if he was ever going to sort out the jumbled
mess of emotions he was feeling.

"It's late and we're both beat." He brushed her hair
back from her face. "Rain check?"

"Of course," she said, then frowned. "Are you sure
you're not too tired to drive home? Maybe you should
stay and sleep on the couch."

He chuckled. "If I stay, something tells me neither one
of us will be getting any sleep. I think it's better if I go."

"Okay." She gave him a stern look. "But you have to
promise to text me and let me know you got home, okay?"

"I will." He tilted her face up to gently kiss her on the
mouth. The feel of her lips under his was enough to make
him say the hell with it and take her up on her offer. He
needed to get out of here. Now. "I'll see you tomorrow."

She smiled and went up on tiptoe to press her lips to his once more. "Count on it."

Damn, she was making it hard to believe she wasn't *The One*. Why else would it be so hard to turn and walk away from her?

Chapter 8

MAC USUALLY NEEDED FOUR ALARM CLOCKS SET FIVE minutes apart and positioned in different places around the room to force herself to get out of bed in the morning. And that was when she got up at a reasonable time like eight o'clock. But last night, she'd set all four clocks for 6:00 a.m. so she could get to the SWAT compound before Gage had to run off and save the world like he'd done yesterday.

But he and half the team were already loaded up and ready to roll by the time she pulled into the parking lot. Not about to let him leave without her this time, Mac jumped in the passenger seat of the SUV Gage was driving.

"You're perky this morning." Gage gave her a side-long glance as he followed the big operations vehicle out the gate. "Guess you slept well."

After everything she'd seen yesterday at the hotel, it wouldn't have been a leap to think sleep would be a long time coming last night. But she'd gone to bed with only one thing on her mind—Gage. And thoughts of him had brought her the best night sleep she'd had in… well…forever.

Mac's smile quickly turned into a frown when she noticed the tight lines etched around Gage's mouth. He looked more exhausted than he had when he'd dropped her off at her place.

"Did you get any sleep last night?" she asked.

"Yeah, I got a few hours. But unfortunately for me,

I don't look as good as you this early in the morning, especially when I haven't had my coffee yet."

Gage must have noticed her concern, because he chuckled. "Don't worry. I'm off duty for the next two days, so I'll be able to catch up on my rest." The look he gave her made her breath hitch. "Unless I have something better to do, of course."

"Like have dinner together?"

The words sounded casual enough, but her pulse was going a mile a minute. All she could think about was what had happened between them the last time they'd had dinner together.

A grin tugged at one corner of his mouth. "You feel like Chambre Francaise again?"

She licked her lips. "I thought maybe I could make dinner for you again. Say tonight?"

His grin broadened. "Sounds good to me."

Mac opened her mouth to ask what he wanted for dinner, but the radio squawked with a bunch of static, then all those codes and police jargon Zak always translated for her. Gage picked up the hand mic and spoke a few terse sentences into it. Something about maintaining the perimeter and not using any sirens.

"So, what do we have?" she asked.

"Drug lab…meth probably." He glanced at her, all business now. "An anonymous caller reported all of the typical telltale signs of a meth lab. They also reported seeing automatic weapons, so the on-scene commander asked us to go in first."

Where just a few moments ago, a warm, pleasurable sensation had been, now a cold, stomach-clenching fear existed. She'd almost forgotten what Gage did for a living.

"Isn't that dangerous?"

Gage shook his head. "They won't even know we're coming until we kick in the door. That's why I told them to maintain the perimeter at four blocks. Plus, half the people in those labs are usually drugged out of their minds. We'll be in and out of there in ten minutes."

He sounded so confident and sure of himself Mac almost found herself believing him. Then she remembered all the shooting and blood from the day before, and her stomach clenched even more tightly.

Mac promised Gage she'd stay in the operations vehicle, but right after he left, the signals on the monitors kept going in and out. She supposed it was because they were parked so far away. Regardless, she couldn't see or hear anything. She wished Zak were there. He'd know how to fix the darn things.

She pulled her small camera from her back pocket and climbed out of the operations vehicle. She still couldn't see Gage, but at least she could see the house. Plus, she could take photos. There were a half dozen uniformed officers and detectives behind the big vehicle with her, so she was safe.

After she and Gage had arrived, he'd had a short conversation with Lieutenant Weaver, the lead officer from the narcotics division, then instructed Trevino to take up a sniper position on the roof of a nearby building. Gage, Cooper, and Delaney had immediately disappeared around the left side of the suspected meth lab, while Xander and the other three members of his squad had gone around the right. Mac kept her ear glued to the radio in Weaver's hand, waiting for the signal that SWAT was about to enter the building. Gage had told her that as soon as they took the automatic weapons out of play, the rest of the cops would go in.

Mac chewed on her lip as she clicked a few pictures of the house. The place didn't look like much. While it was dilapidated, there wasn't anything about the two-story structure that made her think it was a drug lab. Granted, the paint on the casement window was a little suspicious, but a lot of homeowners did that so people on the sidewalk wouldn't be able to see into their basement. Obviously the person who'd reported it to the cops knew more than she did.

"We're in position." Gage's voice was soft and sure as it came through the radio. "Breaching the doors in ten. Over."

Mac jumped when she heard the battering rams strike the doors. It was immediately followed by the sound of flashbang grenades exploding. She braced herself for the weapon fire she knew was coming next, but there wasn't any. Ten seconds passed, then fifteen, but the inside of the house was quiet. That was a good thing, right?

Next to her, Weaver thumbed the button on the side of his radio. "Dixon, what the hell's happening in there?"

Gage didn't answer.

Weaver swore under his breath and thumbed the button again. But whatever he was about to say was lost as a deafening boom echoed in the air. Pieces of wood, metal, and concrete sailed over the operations vehicle, raining down on Mac and the cops with her.

She ducked, covering her head with her arms. What the hell?

It took a minute for Mac to make sense of the smoking debris around her. It was Weaver shouting into his radio, ordering dispatch to send as many ambulances as they had, that finally broke through the fog enveloping her.

She scrambled to her hands and knees to see around the operations vehicle. The dilapidated-house-turned-meth-lab was gone, leveled to the ground, and in its place, was a heap of rubble.

Gage.

Mac was up and running across the street toward what was left of the house as fast as her legs could move. She was halfway there when someone grabbed her arm and dragged her to a halt. She fought against the grip, but it was as strong as steel and wouldn't give an inch.

"Mac, stop!"

The hand on her arm spun her around and she found herself looking up at Alex Trevino. Where the hell had he come from? "I have to get to Gage," she told him. "He and the other guys were in there."

Trevino transferred his grip to her shoulders, holding her still as he looked deep into her eyes. "I know. And I'm going to get them out. But I can't do that and worry about you, too. I need you to stay here. Can you do that?"

She thought she nodded, but she wasn't sure. It must have been good enough for Trevino because he ran toward the house.

Mac followed despite her promise, but stumbled to a halt within a few feet. Trevino was right. She couldn't help Gage or the other men by climbing into the smoldering wreckage of the house. She'd only get in the way.

So, she stood there, feeling useless as the other police officers caught up and passed her. She watched as they joined Trevino in the remains of the building, shouting for the SWAT officers by name.

While smoke was rising steadily from the remains of the house, there wasn't a lot of fire. That had to be good.

But there was still so much damage. Most of the walls were gone, along with the roof and a good portion of the second floor. Jagged pieces of beams and steel pipes stood up in crazy angles, a testament to the force of the blast that had destroyed the place. She'd seen photos of meth labs that had blown up, but in person, the aftermath was a hundred times worse.

Mac was almost afraid to move closer, but she couldn't hang back anymore, either. As the minutes slowly ticked by, she lost more and more hope. There was just so much damage. No one could survive a blast like that, no matter how much training they had or protective gear they wore.

She couldn't explain why, but it felt as if she'd lost something that would have been very important in her life. Not something—*someone*.

Mac didn't realize she was crying until she tasted tears on her tongue. She choked back a sob. She couldn't stand here and watch while they pulled Gage's body from the rubble.

"Over here!"

She spun around, her heart pounding. Trevino was clawing at the chunks of concrete and pieces of brick like he was possessed.

Mac hurried over, trying to see around the cops who'd stopped searching other parts of the house and moved to help. She was afraid to hope, afraid to believe.

Alex grabbed a section of what used to be part of a brick wall and tossed it aside like it weighed nothing.

Underneath, there was a set of steps leading under the house and into the basement. Mac's heart beat even faster. Just because some of the SWAT officers might have made it to safety and survived the explosion didn't mean Gage had been one of them. But as Trevino reached down into the blackness, she couldn't stop hope from surging through her.

A bloody hand grasped Alex's. The team's sniper pulled, yanking a man from the rubble. He was covered in black soot and bloody scrapes, but there was no mistaking Xander. A uniformed cop tried to throw a thermal blanket around the squad leader, but Xander shrugged it off, instead turning to help pull someone else out of the basement.

Men climbed out one by one. First Cooper, then Delaney. And after them, Becker, Lowry, and McCall. Mac hadn't realized she'd climbed into the wreckage of the house until Trevino and Xander had dragged the last man out of the basement.

When she saw Gage, Mac's tears flowed even harder and faster than before. He was covered in soot from head to toe, but he was alive.

Thank you, God.

Mac heard Weaver ask Xander if there was anyone else in the house, but she didn't hear his answer as she stumbled through the rubble at a run and threw herself into Gage's arms. She almost knocked him back down into the basement, but he didn't seem to care. He hugged her to his dirty uniform as she buried her face in the curve of his neck and cried.

She completely forgot they weren't alone until she pulled away and saw Cooper standing there with a knowing grin on his face. Embarrassed, she lifted her hand to wipe the last traces of tears from her cheeks when she caught sight of Xander's arm. He was bleeding. So were Lowry and Becker.

"Oh God, I'm sorry," she said. "I didn't know you guys were hurt. I saw Gage and I..."

Xander's mouth edged up in what looked like a smile, though it was difficult to tell under all the soot. "Don't worry about it. We're fine."

"Like hell you are," Weaver said. "You're all a bunch of bleeding pincushions and everyone is getting a free ride to the hospital."

None of the SWAT guys looked too happy about that. Remembering how Martinez had declined medical attention when he'd been shot, Mac wouldn't be surprised if they got in their vehicles and went back to the compound to treat their cuts, scrapes, and abrasions themselves.

But Gage squashed that idea. "He's right. Everyone's getting checked out—no exceptions." He grinned at her, and suddenly she felt like a weight had been lifted from her shoulders. "You ever ride in an ambulance before?"

Gage knew he wasn't the only one who was steaming mad. His entire pack would walk out of the hospital with him if he gave the word. Unfortunately, the doctors and nurses weren't going to let them out of here anytime soon. Which meant he had to lie in this damn hospital bed and stew. He wasn't really mad at the medical staff. They were just doing their jobs, even if they were a pain in the ass with all their stupid tests. No, he was pissed because that freaking meth lab they'd been lured into had been a trap, and he knew exactly who was behind it.

Walter Hardy had tried to kill them, and if they'd been regular cops, he would have succeeded. The only reason they weren't dead was because werewolves were damn hard to kill.

That said, they were still beat up. Of all of them, Xander and Becker had gotten the worst of it, which meant they'd probably be staying in the hospital overnight for observation. But as soon as Gage could leave, he was going to pay Walter Hardy a visit and let him know exactly how SWAT took care of its own.

Gage dropped his head back on the pillow and stared up at the ceiling. Werewolves or not, he and his men had been lucky. They'd all sensed something was wrong the second they'd breached the doors and entered the house. Instead of coming face-to-face with people wielding automatic weapons, the place had been empty. It had smelled wrong, too. Gage hadn't been able to place the odor, but Cooper recognized it. Gage and the others had already begun to spread throughout the first floor with weapons at the ready when the explosives expert had shouted out one word—*bomb*.

Gage knew in his gut that there was no time to get everyone out of the house before the device detonated, especially since whoever had set it was probably somewhere nearby with his finger on the remote. Even if they managed to escape, they would never have survived the blast and frag that went with it. That was when he'd ordered everyone into the basement.

Unfortunately, he, Cooper, and Delaney had been too far away from the stairs leading under the house to even consider them. So, he'd done something he rarely ever did anymore and let the beast inside free, allowing most of his upper body to shift more than it had in years. His shoulders, arms, and chest had bulked and twisted so quickly it was painful, but the temporary agony was worth it as he crouched down and drove his fist into the cheap linoleum floor in the kitchen. Two savage punches later, the floor caved in, leaving a ragged hole barely large enough for him and the other two men to fit through.

He'd shoved Cooper and Delaney ahead of him, then followed. He hadn't even hit the basement floor when the explosion came. It smashed him into the concrete of the basement floor like a jackhammer, knocking him senseless. When he came to, Cooper and Delaney were dragging him toward the far side of the basement as the floors above rained down on top of them. Thick black smoke filled the air, making it hard to breathe, and he feared he'd saved his men from the blast only so they could burn to death in the fire. But luckily, the fire only smoldered after the blast and the smoke cleared. In the dark of the partially collapsed basement, he, Cooper, and Delaney had crawled around until they found the rest of the Pack.

Becker and Xander had been trapped under hundreds of pounds of rubble, but not before they'd gotten skewered by jagged pieces of wood. While Cooper and Delaney worked quickly to free them, he'd searched for Lowry and found him pulling a piece of metal from his leg. Werewolves were tough and hard to kill, but they still needed oxygen like every other living thing on the planet—which was in short supply underneath the collapsed house.

Gage had just been looking for a way out when a shaft of sunlight penetrated the darkness of the basement. Even though he and the other guys had only been trapped down there for a few minutes, it seemed like a hell of a lot longer. Probably because he'd hurt like a son of a bitch all over. But all the aches and pains had disappeared when he climbed out of the basement to see Mackenzie running toward him.

She'd been crying so hard she was shaking all over. But that was nothing compared to how fast her heart had been beating. That made him hurt worse than anything. He'd wrapped her in his arms, wanting to protect her from every pain in the world. But of course, he couldn't do that because she wasn't crying over her pain—she was crying over his.

As dumb as it sounded, the ride to the hospital together in the ambulance had been one of the most pleasant times he'd spent with a woman. Mackenzie had simply sat beside him and held his hand, leaning down to kiss him whenever the EMT wasn't fussing over him. That was when he'd finally decided to accept Cooper's silly-ass theory that she was *The One* because as far as he could tell, she was.

Apparently, the rest of the Pack had come to the same conclusion. After seeing the way she'd reacted, it was obvious she wasn't playing him. Even Xander couldn't dispute that.

Gage turned his head on the pillow, looking for her. She'd been in and out of his room several times over the past two hours, but kept getting chased out by the nurses and their damn tests. He smiled when he saw her. She was sitting in the hallway with Mike and Zak. His senior squad leader had gotten to the hospital minutes after Gage and the rest of the guys had been brought in.

The photographer showed up fifteen minutes later, telling Mackenzie he'd heard about the blast on the scanner.

Gage was just about to get out of bed and go join them—screw the nurses—but then he saw Mackenzie, Mike, and Zak stand up quickly. That could only mean the doctor had finally come back. About damn time. They'd been taking X-rays, running a dozen tests, and re-checking his vitals to cover their asses. He couldn't blame them, he supposed, but he needed to get out of here. He had someplace to be.

The doctor walked in with Mackenzie on his heels. She looked concerned and more than a little scared. *Shit.* Gage hoped that look meant the good doc hadn't told her much of anything. Zak and Mike followed, but stayed near the door.

"What's the word, Doc?" Gage asked.

He smiled at Mackenzie. She smiled back, and some of the aches and pains that still lingered magically felt better.

"You're damn lucky, that's the word." The gray-haired man gave him a surprisingly stern look. "You came through the explosion surprisingly intact, but whatever accident you had recently caused a lot of damage. You have stress fractures to half a dozen bones, including two ribs and both bones of your right forearm. You shouldn't even be on duty, much less raiding a meth lab."

Mackenzie's eyes went wide. "You were in an accident? When? What happened?"

Gage swore under his breath. Between punching his way through the kitchen floor and getting smashed into the basement, he'd done more damage than he thought. Of course his X-rays wouldn't show much. Just a couple of two-week-old stress fractures—werewolves healed fast.

If the doctor took X-rays again in a couple of days, they wouldn't show anything at all. But Gage would make sure that didn't happen.

"It was nothing. Just a training accident while rappelling. I didn't even realize I'd hurt myself," he told Mackenzie.

The doctor's eyes narrowed suspiciously behind his glasses. He was probably wondering how a cop with all those stress fractures had walked around for two weeks without major painkillers.

"I'll get some rest, Doc. Promise," he added. "What about my team?"

"They're doing as well as can be expected considering they almost got blown up. I'll be keeping three of them..." He glanced down at the clipboard in his hand. "Becker, Lowry, and Riggs. They're fine, but I want to keep them overnight to watch for signs of concussion. They should be able to leave in the morning."

All three men would hate staying here, but it was actually a good thing. Cooling his heels for the night would give Xander time to calm down, not to mention keep him from doing something stupid, like inviting himself along when Gage confronted Walter Hardy.

After putting on the spare uniform Mike had brought him, Gage stopped in to see Xander, Becker, and Lowry before meeting up with the other guys. Mackenzie hovered beside him the whole time as if she was worried she'd have to catch him any second when he fainted from exhaustion. He had to admit, it was kind of cute.

When they reached the parking lot, he automatically followed Mike and the others, but Mackenzie darted in front of him and put a hand on his chest.

"Where do you think you're going?"

"To the compound for a few hours to catch up on some paperwork," he told her.

It wasn't entirely a lie. He did have to write up the incident report for the raid on the meth lab that wasn't a meth lab. But his main purpose was to find out where Hardy lived, then go scope out the place. One look at Mackenzie told him she wasn't going to cooperate with that plan.

"No way," she said. "You just promised the doctor you'd get some rest, and I'm going to make sure you do. Your paperwork can wait."

He'd known Mackenzie Stone was strong willed, but he didn't know she could be so fierce, too. But damn, she looked as if she could make a grizzly bear back down. He knew where she was coming from—he really did. She'd watched someone drop a house on him, and it had scared the hell out of her. But he needed to send a message to Hardy that the shit that'd happened today would never be allowed to happen again, and he needed to do it fast.

But as he stood there gazing down at Mackenzie, he realized something. If Cooper was right about them being cosmically connected—a possibility that was looking more and more likely by the minute—then he needed to make decisions based on what was important to her, too.

That was a big leap for him.

"Okay," he agreed. "But I do have to brief the deputy chief on what happened today."

She opened her mouth to protest, but Mike cut her off.

"I'll brief the deputy chief," he said. "Go home and get some rest. Don't worry. I know what to say to Mason."

Which was Mike's way of telling him that he wouldn't say anything about the bomb to the deputy chief. If Mason knew it was an assassination attempt, he'd want to put the entire SWAT team in protective custody until they could bring Hardy up on charges. Luckily, it would take a while for the arson investigators to piece everything together.

But Gage still hesitated anyway. Then he noticed that Mike and the other men were all grinning at him. Gage shook his head. He was outnumbered.

He turned his attention back to Mackenzie. She still had her hand on his chest as if she could hold him back with nothing more than her willpower. He was starting to think she could probably do it, too.

"So, Ms. Stone, what do you have in mind?" he asked. "To make sure I get my rest, I mean."

She gave him that devastating smile. "Well, I did offer to make you dinner, so how about we start with that?"

"I don't suppose we're invited, too?" Cooper asked.

"No," Gage said before Mackenzie could answer. "But since you're being nice and filling out the reports on the explosion at the meth lab for me, I'll make sure Emile gets you a table at Chambre Francaise the next time you want to impress a woman."

That seemed to satisfy them. After a reminder to take it easy, they headed across the parking lot, leaving Gage and Mackenzie with his senior squad leader and her photographer.

"Mind if I talk to Mike for a second?" he said. "If I'm going to blow off work early, I need to make sure a few things are taken care of."

Mackenzie regarded him suspiciously. "Okay, but don't be too long. You need to get some rest."

Gage wasn't sure how much rest he was going to get if he went home with her, but he nodded anyway. As soon as Mackenzie and Zak were out of earshot, Gage turned to Mike.

"I need you to find out where Hardy's going to be tonight."

Mike lifted a brow. "We're moving on him tonight?"

"Not we, just me. I'm going to deliver a message to him—one he'll be sure to understand."

Mike's brows drew together. "You sure you want to do this on your own? A man like Hardy is going to have a lot of muscle protecting him, especially after what he pulled today."

"I know, but that'll make the message that much more effective. I walk in there all by myself and show him I can get to him anytime I want," Gage said. "I want him focused on me. I don't want him targeting the entire team like he did today."

Hardy might have sent his goons to the restaurant yesterday to pick Gage up, but there was no way for the bastard to know Gage would be in that house today. He'd kill everyone on the SWAT team to get to Gage if he had to.

Mike glanced at Mackenzie and Zak. They were standing beside the photographer's car, talking. "I'll text you the information," he said. "But how the hell are you going to slip away from Mac? She's not stupid. If you say you're running to the store for a carton of milk, she's going to know what you're up to. And I don't think she's the kind to let you do it."

No kidding. She was already looking at him impatiently. "Then I guess I'll have to make sure she's so exhausted when I leave that she won't know I'm gone."

And he knew exactly how to do it.

Mac knew what Gage had been talking to Mike about before they'd left the hospital parking lot and it sure as hell hadn't been paperwork and duty rosters. They were discussing what they were going to do about Walter Hardy and the assassination attempt he'd made on Gage and his team. While she'd been waiting in the hallway outside his room, she'd overheard Cooper tell Mike there'd been a bomb in the house. She'd been terrified Gage was going to make up a reason to leave so he could go to Hardy's place and beat the hell out of him, at the very least.

But that had been an hour ago, and since they'd arrived at her place and she'd started throwing together another simple pasta meal, he hadn't indicated he was going to bail. So maybe she'd been wrong. Or more likely, he simply knew how worried and upset she'd be if he left. And there was really only one reason she could think of that Gage wouldn't want to worry her. Somehow in the last few days, he'd come to care for her.

She'd realized Gage had feelings for her earlier today, while she'd been waiting for the doctors to come out and tell her how badly hurt he was. When he'd climbed out of the rubble left by the explosion, she'd been the first one he'd looked for. And when he'd found her, the emotion on his face had been real. She'd seen it, and so had his men. That certainly explained why they'd been so tense around her yesterday, and why Cooper had asked all those strange questions. They knew their boss was falling for her and were worried she was playing with his heart just to get a story.

The horrible part was that she had been playing him, at least in the beginning. She felt even worse because she'd secretly accused him of doing the same to her. It was obvious now that he hadn't. His friends wouldn't be worried about him getting hurt if he had. And after this morning, she was ready to admit she was seriously attracted to Gage, too.

When that house had exploded, her heart had exploded with it. The whole bottom had dropped out of her world, and all she could think about was running into the smoking rubble to pull him out. Waiting while Alex and the other cops had dug through the wreckage had been like holding her breath underwater, drowning second by second. When they'd finally pulled Gage out, she could breathe again. Suddenly, her whole world had seemed a lot different. And a lot clearer.

Gage gestured at her plate with his fork. "Aren't you going to eat any more?"

She looked down to see that she'd barely touched her food. "I'm full."

She expected Gage to point out that she'd hardly eaten anything and that she couldn't be full, but instead he put down his fork and picked up hers, then twirled some angel hair pasta on it and held it out to her.

"Don't stare at it," he prompted gently. "Eat it."

Mac couldn't help but smile. She'd said the same thing to him in the parking lot of the fast-food place last night. The gesture was so endearing that she opened her mouth and let him feed her even though she wasn't hungry.

As she chewed, he loaded the fork again. "I know what you saw today bothered you. But I want you to know that I'm okay. Really okay."

When she opened her mouth to respond, he slipped the forkful of pasta right in. She frowned at him, but finished chewing before she answered.

"I know you're okay, but it still scared the hell out of me. I didn't realize seeing you in danger would affect me the way it did."

Gage gave her a piece of chicken, then more pasta. He was really good at feeding her—he didn't even make a mess. Plus, it was kind of sexy.

"I'm sorry I scared you," he said softly.

"It's not your fault," she told him equally softly. "I'm just glad you're safe."

He kept feeding her, and she kept eating for him. There was something so fascinating about such a big man using her fork so carefully. It made her wonder what he'd be like in bed. Just as slow and considerate as he was at the table, she was sure.

"I think I really am getting full now," she said with a smile.

He speared another piece of chicken. "Eat a little more. You're going to need your energy for later."

She raised an eyebrow. "I thought the plan was for you to get your rest?"

He grinned as he fed her the piece of chicken. "There'll be plenty of time for rest. I'm off for the next two days, remember?"

Mac laughed. "I remember. But if we're not going to be resting, what are we going to be doing?"

He put down her fork and pushed his chair away from the table, then stood and moved around behind her. He leaned down so his mouth was right near her ear. "I thought we might burn off all those calories from dinner."

Mac couldn't suppress the shiver that ran through her. After the last few days of playing the sexual equivalent of hide-and-seek, she was so ready to burn some calories.

She laughed as Gage tugged her to her feet. She put both her arms around his neck and pulled him in for a kiss as his hands slid down to her waist and lifted her easily off her feet. She wrapped her legs around him as he carried her to the bedroom.

When Gage draped her across the queen-sized bed, then joined her, she discovered it wasn't quite as roomy as she'd thought. With Gage's broad shoulders and long legs, the two of them were going to have a hard time fitting.

"I think we're going to need a bigger bed," she said.

Gage let out a throaty chuckle. "Don't worry, we'll make do. Just stay close."

As if demonstrating, he leaned over and trailed scorching kisses along the curve of her jaw and down her neck. *God, that feels amazing.*

"I can do close… Close is good," she whispered, letting her head fall back on the pillow as he nibbled his way along the V-neck of her shirt toward her cleavage.

She twined her fingers in Gage's short hair and urged him lower. That earned her another chuckle.

"Thanks for the guidance, but trust me, I know where I'm headed."

"Just wanted to make sure," she said as he kissed his way to the first button of her shirt. "I know how men hate to ask for directions."

That got her a growl and a little nip. "Okay, you asked for it."

He reached up and yanked her blouse open, sending buttons flying. Then his hot mouth was on her again, moving over the exposed parts of her breasts. She couldn't stifle the moan that escaped her lips, but whether it was from the feel of his mouth on her or the animalistic way he'd torn her blouse, she couldn't say. She'd never had a man tear her clothes before, but decided she definitely liked it—as long as Gage was the one doing the tearing. She wondered if her other clothes might end up in a similar condition.

Gage kissed his way down to her belly button before moving back up to tease her nipples through the silky fabric of her bra. She couldn't resist grabbing at his hair again, silently begging for him to stay right there for a while.

"God, that feels good," she whispered. "Please keep doing that."

He didn't complain at her additional guidance and direction this time. Instead, he ran his hands up her torso to squeeze her breasts together while he suckled on her nipples. *Mmm*, she'd always appreciated a man who knew how to take his time.

He slid one hand under her back and popped the clasp on her bra. And he had nimble fingers, too. That boded well.

Then his mouth was back on her nipple, this time without the nuisance of the intervening fabric. She arched with a whimper, pushing her breast more firmly into his mouth. *Damn, did he have a talented tongue or what?* And there were so many other places he had yet to visit with it.

She was so lost in what he was doing to her nipples she didn't even notice when he undid the buttons on her jeans. He stopped feasting on her breast to yank off her jeans. When the hell had he taken off her shoes? She seriously didn't remember that.

As Gage continued to work his magic on her nipples, she realized she was completely naked—okay, she still had her panties on—but Gage hadn't taken a single stitch of his uniform off yet.

That just seemed unfair—and kind of hot.

Especially when he stopped nibbling and sat back to gaze at her with eyes positively brimming with yearning. Talk about a boost to her self-esteem. Every woman wanted to be lusted after, and that was definitely what Gage was doing right then.

She laid there trembling as his eyes wandered up and down her body, devouring every inch of her. If all that nibbling and suckling hadn't made her wet, the heat in those eyes sure as hell did.

Mac sat up on her elbows, looking at him. "I couldn't help noticing that I'm almost naked and you're still completely dressed. Are you planning on doing anything about that?"

The smolder in his eyes as he grinned was almost enough to make her moan. "There is one thing I could do."

Holding her captive with nothing more than his eyes, he tucked his fingers in the waistband of her panties and slipped them off as smooth as silk. She was left gasping by the heart-thudding sexiness of the move.

Gage moved off the bed to stand there gazing at her— all of her—in absolute hunger. All she could do was lean back on her elbows and enjoy the pleasure of being his object of adoration. She could definitely get used to this.

"That's better." His gaze lingered on the triangle of downy curls between her legs. "Completely naked suits you. In fact, you should stay that way all the time."

She parted her legs just enough for him to get a glimpse of the wetness there. "Something tells me I'm going to be this way a lot when you're around."

His mouth edged up. "Probably."

Gage seemed more than satisfied to stand there and

devour her with his eyes for the rest of the night. But if he did it much longer, she was going to start touching herself. He must have sensed her desperation because he smiled and unbuttoned his uniform shirt. Once that hit the floor, he shed his black T-shirt in that casual way guys did—just whipped it over his head like it was nothing.

Her gaze immediately locked on the epic display of perfect muscles. Broad shoulders, pecs that looked like they could bench-press a car, and abs so tight they almost made her want to get down on her knees and worship him.

And there was more where that came from.

She watched in fascination as he took off the ankle holster holding his backup pistol and placed it on the bedside table. His boots and uniform pants joined the T-shirt on the floor, letting her get a good, long look at his tanned, muscular legs. But as mouthwatering as his chiseled body was, she was almost more captivated by the part of him she couldn't see—the blatant bulge in his tight, black boxer briefs.

She was done with passively lying back and watching. Time for her to be in charge of the final reveal. Sitting up, she wiggled to the edge of the bed. Gage chuckled as she hooked her fingers in the waistband of his underwear and tugged him closer until he was positioned comfortably between her legs.

She was tempted to simply yank down his briefs—there was a big part of her that yearned to see what he was hiding in there—but she controlled herself. She ran her hand over the bulge, teasing herself, and him, a little first. His shaft felt so hard through the fabric of his underwear. Slipping her fingers in the waistband of his briefs again, she carefully hauled them over his erection.

Mac tried to act nonchalant as his hard, thick cock came into view, but she was pretty sure she failed. He was just so…perfect.

Giving in to the overwhelming desire to taste him, she dipped her head and wrapped her lips around him. The growl he let loose was almost as rewarding as the flavor that awaited her—almost. She told herself she'd only take a little taste. No need to go too crazy. But once she started, she couldn't control herself. He tasted like heaven.

Gage slid his hand in her hair, encouraging her to keep doing what she was doing. She let herself go, licking and nibbling up and down the shaft, swirling her tongue around and around the head, moaning as his essence filled her mouth and coated her tongue.

She didn't know whether to be thankful or annoyed when Gage took charge and gently nudged her back on the bed. She suspected her lover had other plans.

Her pulse quickened as he spread her legs and kissed his way up the inside of her right leg. For such a big man, he had the gentlest touch. Her body quivered as he moved higher and higher. By the time he reached her inner thigh, she was practically squirming.

He lifted his head, a smile tugging playfully at his mouth. "Is this too much? I can stop if you want."

She shook her head. "No. I'm fine. Keep going."

He chuckled and spread her legs even more, then pressed his very warm lips to the sensitive skin of her inner thigh. But whereas he'd moved quickly before, now he practically went at a snail's pace, which just about drove her crazy. When he got to the tender flesh just inches from her sex, he lingered there, teasing her. She bit back a scream of frustration and got her fingers in his hair, tugging him right where she needed him.

He didn't fight her, and she almost let out a cheer as that talented mouth of his finally settled onto her very wet pussy. His tongue moved up and down the folds, swirling around her clit every time it reached the apex.

"Oh yeah," she breathed. "Just like that."

He probably didn't need the directions—in fact, he was doing just fine without them—but she couldn't stop herself from babbling. Talking soon became impossible as Gage spent more time focusing on her sensitive nub. Moaning was still an option, though. She did a lot of that.

Mac ran her hands over his scalp, loving the feel of his short hair under her fingers as he ravaged her with his mouth. She especially liked the way he slipped his big hands under her ass and lifted her up to devour like she was a juicy slice of watermelon.

It didn't take long before she felt the familiar tingles that told her an orgasm was on the way. She clenched her fingers into the hair on the back of Gage's head and wiggled her hips in tight, little circles. He must have picked up on her signals because he pulled her tighter to his mouth and focused solely on her clit.

Mac tensed, her breathing coming faster and faster as the tingles got stronger. This was going to be a strong one—she could feel it.

"Please don't stop," she begged, not thinking for a second that he would.

Gage continued moving his tongue in that perfect rhythm, pushing her higher and higher until it was hard to breathe. The pressure of her orgasm building was like a flood that was barely being held back. When the dam finally broke, she screamed loud enough for the whole apartment building to hear. And when the wave crashed over her, it swept her up and carried her out with the tide until her whole body spasmed.

The first wave receded, only to be followed by a second one that was almost as strong. The third, fourth, and fifth waves weren't nearly as intense but they were just as pleasurable. Gage kept licking her, using the perfect amount of pressure to make her body tremble for a long time. Damn, even the aftershocks were better than a lot of the orgasms she'd had.

When she finally surfaced and figured out which way was up, she lifted her head to see Gage regarding her with a very satisfied smile.

"You look beautiful when you come, did you know that?"

She felt her face heat. Or maybe her face was still flushed from orgasm. "Thank you," she said softly. "Though I must admit, I'm impressed with your multitasking—making me come and watching me at the same time? I didn't think guys could do two things at once."

Gage nipped her inner thigh. Not hard, but enough to make her jump. While she was still recovering from that surprise, he smoothly climbed up her body until his eyes were level with hers. Wow, he was really nimble for a guy his size.

He gave her a wolfish grin. "I'm going to enjoy showing you how many things I can do all at the same time."

His erection pressed against the inner thigh he'd just bitten, as if he was kissing it to make it feel better. "I look forward to it." She reached down between her legs to wrap her hand around him. "But maybe we should start with this first."

He sucked in a breath. "Condoms. Do you have any?"

Mac felt a moment of panic. She still had some from when she'd gone out with that guy from the mayor's office a few months ago, didn't she?

"In the top drawer of the nightstand."

She hoped.

She was forced to let go of his cock so he could get the condom. Thankfully, he moved quickly, and was soon kneeling between her legs again. She caught her lower lip between her teeth as he rolled the thin latex down his shaft.

He braced himself with a strong, muscular arm on either side of her head and nudged her wet opening with the tip of his erection. "Where were we?"

"I think you were about to impress me with your multitasking skills," she said.

He grinned. "Oh yeah, I remember now."

Gage dipped his head, capturing her mouth with his at the same time he slowly eased himself inside her. She was wet and oh-so-ready for him, but it still made her catch her breath. He was just as built below the belt as he was everywhere else.

But he moved carefully, waiting for her to relax before going deeper. Mac was more than a little eager for him to pick up the pace, but he refused no matter how much she lifted her hips. Even when she wrapped her legs around him and urged him to giddyap with her heels, he continued his leisurely thrusts.

He definitely had the multitasking thing down, too. He kept up a perfect steady rhythm with his hips while kissing her so thoroughly she was almost dizzy from it.

She slipped her hands up his powerful arms, their muscles bulging from the exertion of holding himself perched above her, to his broad shoulders, and finally around the back of his head, where she got a firm grip so she could kiss him hard. Their tongues tangled, and she moaned at how delicious he tasted.

Letting out a sound that was half growl, half groan, Gage pumped his hips faster. With him pounding deep inside her like that, she found it impossible to keep kissing him, and she tore her mouth away from his.

"Who's the one with problems multitasking now?" Gage asked huskily.

Mac would have answered with a snappy comeback, but her mind was a complete blank at the moment. Every time his cock bottomed out, little shocks of lightning shot through her body. She mumbled something unintelligible and squeezed him tighter with her legs, silently begging for more.

He gazed down at her, his eyes almost gold in the soft light coming through the bedroom window. "Do you need me to do it harder and faster?"

She nodded.

But instead of going harder and faster, Gage *slowed down*, hesitating when he pulled out, then sliding back in inch by glorious inch. She whimpered.

"What's wrong?" Gage asked softly.

She shook her head, unable to do more than mutter incoherently.

He kissed her again, sucking gently on her lower lip before trailing his mouth over to her ear. "Tell me exactly what you need, Mackenzie."

She had no idea why, but the way he whispered her name—her full name—in her ear that way, demanding that she communicate exactly what she wanted him to do turned her on like mad. She probably wouldn't have been able to say it, not if he'd been looking at her. But with his mouth by her ear like it was, that wasn't a problem.

"I need you to take me hard and fast, Gage."

He gave her exactly what she asked for, pounding into her with a powerful rhythm that threatened to break the bed.

On either side of her head, Gage's arms were tense as he balanced above her in an effort to keep his weight from crushing her. She wrapped her arms around him, pulling him down even as she lifted her hips to meet his. Instead of feeling smothered by his big, muscular body, she felt protected by it. And that only made the orgasm rolling through her even more powerful.

She buried her face in the curve of his neck and dug her nails into the rippling muscles of his shoulders. She didn't mean to hurt him, but she was too far gone to do anything about it. She cried out, squeezing him so tightly with her legs she had no idea how he could even keep thrusting. But he did, and it transported her to a world of pleasure she hadn't known existed until tonight.

When she felt him stiffen above her, felt every muscle in that spectacular body of his contracting at once, she knew he was coming with her.

It was amazing. It was beautiful. It was perfect.

Gage rolled onto his side and pulled her into his arms. Mac snuggled up to him, throwing her arm possessively over his chest. This felt so completely right—like she'd won the boyfriend lottery. Gage was the guy she'd been looking for without even knowing she was looking.

She laughed at how crazy that was.

"What's so funny?" Gage asked softly.

Since it might be a little early to confess she might be falling in love with him, she decided to fib. Men could get so squirrely about stuff like that.

"Nothing." She traced her fingers over the perfectly

sculpted muscle of his chest. "It's just that was the best sex of my life."

That hadn't been a fib, though. Sex like that was probably illegal in some states.

It was his turn to laugh.

She tilted her head to look at him. "What?"

"Nothing," he mimicked. "It's just that you're talking like the night's over when it's only just getting started."

"Seriously?"

He rolled her onto her back, balancing above her. His eyes had taken on that smolder she was getting to be familiar with. "Seriously."

That was when she realized the cock pressing against her was well on its way to getting hard again. She sucked in her breath as he slid his shaft up and down her pussy like a sex toy.

"Mmm." She sighed. "And what do you have in mind this time?"

He gave her a lazy grin. "I don't know. Maybe we'll try out a half dozen different positions or so until you find one that's your favorite. Then we'll just stay in that one until you tell me you can't come anymore."

Fresh heat pooled between her thighs, and she bit her lip. "I think I can come a lot before calling it quits."

"Then I guess we're in for a really long night."

Gage rolled off her and repositioned her on her hands and knees. His breath was warm on the skin of her lower back as he pressed a kiss to her bottom.

She buried her face into the bedding and moaned. "The longer the better."

Chapter 9

GAGE SAT ON THE EDGE OF THE BED, WATCHING Mackenzie sleep. He could tell from her slow, steady heart rate and even breathing that she was well on her way to dreamland. Not surprising. They'd gone at it for hours. She was sleeping the deep sleep of a well-satisfied woman. He only wished he could stay in bed with her. She'd worn him out, too.

After spending hours with her, rolling around in bed, on the floor, and up against the wall, he knew she was *The One*—period. He believed to his very core she was the woman he was supposed to spend the rest of his life with.

He glanced at the clock—0400 hours. He needed to move. Even though every fiber of his being demanded he climb into bed with Mackenzie, wrap his body protectively around her, and never let her go.

Perversely, that was part of the reason he had to leave. Mackenzie was in his life now and that meant she was in danger, unless he dealt with Hardy. Putting it off would only endanger Mackenzie even more.

He scribbled a quick note on a scrap of paper he found in her nightstand. Something about needing to get more condoms—and donuts. He didn't think she'd wake up before he got back, but if she did, he didn't want her freaking out and leaving the apartment looking for him. Or thinking he'd left her.

Gage dressed quickly and silently, then grabbed a copy

of the apartment key Mackenzie had hanging on a hook in the kitchen. He checked his phone as he waited for the elevator and found that Mike had left a text with Hardy's address. There were also notes about the layout of the place, like the number of guards and existing perimeter security systems. Efficient as always.

At that early hour, it took less than thirty minutes to get to Hardy's residence just outside Southlake on a wooded section of Grapevine Lake. Gage stopped his car along a quiet lane near the shore. If anyone saw it, they'd assume it was a couple of kids making out down by the water. Few people, even cops, would get suspicious. Southlake wasn't the kind of place where lowlifes hung out.

He weaved through the trees, letting his superior night vision guide him. Thank God Hardy liked his privacy. There were very few houses along this section of the lake. Not that Gage gave a damn. He would have found a way onto Hardy's property without being seen if the man lived in the middle of a mall food court.

Gage found the perimeter fence quickly enough. It was an eight-foot high chain-link deal with a few sections filled in with older mortared stone. He prowled the length of it, checking for guards, cameras, and motion sensors. He found the only two cameras that covered this side of the property without even trying. They weren't well hidden. It wasn't difficult to stand out of their field of view since they seemed to be aimed to catch people on the narrow, paved pathway that ran just inside the fence. Apparently, security wasn't too worried about someone hopping over the fence. But then again, who'd be dumb enough to trespass on property owned by Walter Hardy?

Next, Gage confirmed there were no passive infrared

or microwave motion sensors, active infrared beams, or pressure pad sensors. He could have bypassed them, but it said a hell of a lot about Hardy's arrogance. There was nothing to keep a person from slipping onto his property except a reputation for brutality and ruthlessness.

Gage had downplayed it for Mackenzie's benefit, but he'd been worried about Hardy and what the man might do from the moment he'd learned his identity. Gage knew he was a powerful and dangerous man who wouldn't hesitate to come after them if he believed they were responsible for his son's death. By standing up to his thugs, Gage had hoped Hardy might back off. But from the bomb at the fake meth lab, it was obvious that plan hadn't worked. Hardy was coming for Gage, and he didn't mind killing the rest of the SWAT team to get him. For all Gage knew, the man intended to kill all of them anyway. Gage wasn't going to let that happen.

There was a single light on in the back of the house. Probably where the security guard, or guards, stayed. Gage would hit that first. He'd do anything to protect his pack—and now Mackenzie. He didn't want to kill Hardy in cold blood, but if that was the only way to stop the man and keep the people close to him safe, he'd do it without hesitation.

He only hoped it wouldn't come to that.

Gage moved along the fence until he was in a dead spot between the cameras. He still didn't see any guards, but he could pick up their scent. It was blanketed by the stronger smell of gasoline, which made him think they probably patrolled the property in a golf cart at night. Since both odors lingered heavily in the air, that meant they'd been through here recently.

He found a place where the fence was screened by the low-hanging limbs of a big tree and placed his hand close to the chain link, but not quite touching. He didn't feel anything that indicated it was electrified.

Gage looked around one more time, then let the claws on his right hand extend to their full length. *God, that felt good*. He hadn't done it in a while. There wasn't a lot of call for it in his day-to-day work. But he missed being able to let go and shift like that.

He slashed at the fence, sending pieces of chain link flying and opening a gap large enough for him to step through. Once he was on the other side, he listened carefully, but there still weren't any sounds coming from the house.

As he crept slowly through the trees along the rear of the property, he considered what he knew about Walter Hardy.

He owned three different houses in the Dallas area, the other two being penthouse apartments downtown. He used one mostly for business meetings and for those times he stayed in the city. He'd given the other to his twenty-six-year-old son, Ryan, the presumptive heir to the Hardy name, fortune, and business.

There was no Mrs. Hardy so Gage didn't have to worry about that. Ryan's mother had divorced Walter and disappeared back to someplace in Eastern Europe years ago.

Gage kept moving toward the back door of the house, pulling on gloves as he went. He still had no idea what he was going to do once he got inside, but he didn't want to leave fingerprints regardless.

He was about fifteen feet away from the back door of the house when it opened and a big man in dress pants, a white shirt, and a military buzz cut walked out.

Shit.

Gage thought for sure the guy had seen him, but one look at the man's face changed his mind. He had that sleepy-eyed look of someone who'd just gotten out of bed. Probably a guard starting his shift.

Gage closed the distance between them, landing a solid right cross to the man's jaw before he even knew what hit him. Gage caught the man and lowered him to the ground, then dragged him into the shadows of the trees. It wasn't until he checked for a pulse that he realized the guy was one of the goons who'd come to the restaurant the other day. He didn't bother zip-tying the man or stuffing something in his mouth. He'd be in and out of the house before the guy even woke up.

Gage darted a quick look around, then jogged over to the house. He tried the doorknob just to see if he'd get lucky. Well, damn, it was unlocked.

He quietly closed the door behind him, then soundlessly made his way through the darkened kitchen and down the hallway toward the room he'd seen with the light on—the one where the security guards hung out.

Their scent hit him before he even reached the partially opened door. Gage paused outside the room to do a quick recon. Two men sat on the couch, their backs to the door, their attention focused on the video game they were playing. They were so busy annihilating pretend monsters with their pretend weapons that Gage could have shot both of them and they never would have seen it coming.

Instead, he moved up behind them and punched one in the temple, bouncing his head off the other guard's. Before the second guy could figure out what the hell happened, Gage hit him with a ridge hand strike to the side of the neck that knocked him as unconscious as his buddy.

This might take even less time than he thought.

Gage was heading for the steps when he almost walked into someone coming out of the bathroom. He recognized Roscoe Patterson's ugly mug at the same time Hardy's enforcer recognized him.

Patterson reacted faster than the other goons. Instead of reaching for a weapon he had no prayer of getting a hand on, he lashed out with a quick jab straight at Gage's face.

If Gage hadn't been a werewolf, the punch would have landed and probably made him see stars long enough for Patterson to go for his weapon. But Gage brought up his forearm, blocking the blow and connecting with the other man's wrist hard enough to break something. Patterson didn't even flinch. He merely shifted his stance and whipped out a knife with his other hand.

Gage jerked back, easily avoiding the blade, then caught Patterson's arm just as he went in for another strike. The man's eyes widened. *That's right, asshole. I'm faster, stronger, and a hell of a lot more dangerous than you are.*

Gage delivered a jab to Patterson's chin, following it up with an uppercut under the jaw, then a roundhouse kick that sent the man tumbling back ten feet to crash against the wall. Patterson slid to the floor, the knife slipping from his hand to land on the wood with a horrendous clatter. If the noise hadn't been enough to wake up Hardy, nothing would.

Shit.

Gage bounded for the stairs, taking them four at a time. Hardy was probably on the phone to the cops even now. Wouldn't that be ironic? A murdering scumbag calling the cops to protect him from another cop.

But when he reached the top of the stairs, it was to find Hardy bursting out of his bedroom, a gold-finished automatic in his hands. Before Hardy could pull the trigger, Gage closed the distance between them and wrapped his hand around the pistol, ripping it out of the man's grasp. He shoved Hardy back into the bedroom with a growl.

Gage followed as the man stumbled back, continuing to push and shove until he'd moved Hardy all the way back to his bed and knocked him across it.

"You!" Hardy shouted. "I'll have your fucking badge for this."

He tried to get to his feet, but Gage pushed him back down. "That might be a bit difficult since I'm not wearing a badge at the moment."

Hardy's heart sped up as he suddenly realized there weren't any other cops there shouting orders or waving warrants. There was just Gage—and the gun he'd taken from Hardy.

The fastest way to make his problems go away was to kill Hardy. And if Gage was smart, that's what he'd do.

Hardy slowly inched toward the head of the bed. Did he have another gun in the nightstand? Gage hoped so. Because he couldn't kill a defenseless man in cold blood. It just wasn't in him.

He only hoped Hardy didn't know that.

Gage found a chair and moved it closer to the bed, positioning it so that he could look Hardy in the eye while pointing the man's own gun at him. Damn, a Desert Eagle

Mark XIX, in titanium gold no less. He really hated it when scumbags carried such nice weapons.

"You tried to kill me and my team yesterday."

Hardy eyed the gun as he shook his head. "I have no idea what you're talking about. I was at a meeting with the mayor all day yesterday. As a matter of fact, we spent some of that time talking about your out-of-control SWAT team. And about how you killed my son."

Gage leveled the gun at the space right between the man's eyes. "Do you think I care that you had one of your people set that bomb, or make the call to lure us there? You made it happen, which is all that matters."

Hardy's gaze nervously darted to the gun again.

"And as for your son, you know as well as I do that he signed his own execution order the moment he decided to kill innocent people."

Hardy didn't respond to Gage's statement, but he didn't deny it, either.

"You won't shoot me," he finally said.

Gage could tell by the man's erratic heartbeat Hardy didn't really believe that.

"I just walked into your house all by myself, put down four guards like they weren't even there, then took this thing away from you like you were a two-year-old." Gage gestured with the Desert Eagle. "Tell me again why I won't do exactly anything I want?"

Clearly, Hardy had been under the assumption that if he held out long enough and kept the conversation going just a little longer, his men would come running to the rescue. The man had spent most of his adult life scaring the hell out of people, but Gage wasn't scared, and Hardy knew it.

"What do you want?" Hardy demanded. "If you wanted me dead, you would have done it already. So, what is it? Money?"

Typical. The bastard thought all he had to do was wave a wad of cash in someone's face and all his problems would go away. Gage bit back a snarl. "I don't want your money."

"What then?"

Gage stood up and moved closer to the bed, keeping the pistol trained on the bull's-eye he'd mentally painted on Hardy's forehead. He didn't want to kill Hardy. Even after what the man had tried to do to his pack, Gage couldn't just execute him in cold blood. That would make him no better than Hardy. But he had to make Hardy believe he would kill him, so the man would be scared so shitless he'd back off.

"It's simple really," he said. "If you ever make a move against me or anyone close to me again, I'll track you down, kill every one of your guards, then rip out your fucking heart."

To make sure Hardy knew he meant every word, Gage jammed the bolt carrier back so hard he ripped it off the rails.

He tossed both pieces of the weapon on the bed beside Hardy. "Is that easy enough for you to understand?"

Hardy didn't answer. He was too busy staring at the Desert Eagle Gage had just destroyed as easily as if it had been made of plastic.

Gage let out the same low-throated growl he used when he wanted to force a member of his pack to pay attention or behave. It had the same effect on Hardy.

"Do I make myself clear?" he asked.

Hardy swallowed hard. "Yes."

"Then we're done here."

With that, Gage turned and walked out.

Gage walked back into Mackenzie's apartment just before six a.m. Including the stop at the store for donuts and condoms—a purchase that had earned him one hell of a strange look from the cashier—he'd been gone for an hour and thirty-five minutes.

He didn't hear any movement coming from the bedroom, so he left the donuts on the kitchen counter and silently made his way in that direction. The sun was peeking in the window at Mackenzie, who was huddled under the blanket fast asleep. She looked so beautiful it made his chest hurt.

Gage stripped off his clothes and set the economy-sized box of condoms on the nightstand, then climbed into bed. He pulled her into his arms and buried his face in her silky hair, breathing in her scent. God, she was like heaven.

Mackenzie mumbled something unintelligible and pressed herself back against him. He tightened his arm around her, holding her close. He hadn't intended to do anything more than fall asleep with her, but she wiggled her bottom against his crotch, making his cock harden.

He stifled a groan and tried to put a little space between his hard-on and her very warm, very soft ass, but it was impossible. Even though she seemed to be completely zonked out, she scooted back even more and rotated her hips in a very sexy dance that made his cock poke her in certain places completely on its own.

Mackenzie stirred.

Ah, hell. He might be dead tired, but apparently certain parts of his anatomy weren't. Reaching for the box of condoms, he couldn't think of a better way to start the day.

―∾―

Mac snuggled into the pillow with a sigh. Was that bacon and eggs she smelled? She inhaled deeply. Damn, it was. Gage was making breakfast for her. Which meant he must have run to the store because she hadn't bought bacon and eggs in…forever. Normally, she didn't eat stuff like that, but she was starving. Not surprising. She and Gage had worked up quite an appetite last night. Not to mention this morning. She smiled at the memory.

She had been awakened at an insanely early hour by Gage's very hard cock slowly sliding into her very wet pussy. He'd made slow, teasing love to her as they spooned together in bed. He had moved in and out of her from behind while one hand caressed every inch of her body—her face, her neck, her breasts, her stomach, her thighs, her clit…oh yes, her clit. It was, without a doubt, the most romantic sex she'd ever had in her life. And afterward, all she could do was pull his arm around her and go back to sleep.

Now he was making breakfast for her? What had she done to deserve this man?

It was hard to leave the cozy nest of blankets, but she forced herself to climb out of bed. She washed her face and brushed her teeth, then pulled on the first piece of clothing at hand—Gage's uniform T-shirt. But if she was wearing his T-shirt, what was Gage wearing? Eager to find out, she ran a brush through her hair and hurried out of the bedroom.

The sight that met her as she walked into the kitchen was even better than she'd imagined. Her big, strapping lover was at the stove wearing nothing but those really tight boxer briefs of his. Wow, he had a great butt.

Mac went up behind him and wrapped her arms around his stomach, pressing herself against him as she kissed the warm skin of his back.

He smiled over his shoulder at her. "You could have stayed in bed. I was planning to bring this in to you."

She ran her hands over the muscles of his chest and abs as she rested her cheek against his back. "As much as I like the idea of breakfast in bed, I don't think we would have gotten to the bacon and eggs part if you served them to me dressed like this."

He chuckled as he finished cooking the eggs—half a dozen over medium by the looks of them—and transferred them to plates where the bacon and toast were already waiting. She couldn't help but shake her head as she watched him work. He moved with the quick grace of a person who'd been working a grill for years. She couldn't flip an egg to save her life, which was why she always made scrambled, when she had them at all.

"I can go put some more clothes on, if you think you'll be distracted," he said as he carried the plates to the table. The coffee was already poured and steaming.

She shook her head as she sat down. "I don't want to put you to any trouble. I'll just have to control myself."

He slanted her a sexy grin. "You can always give me back my T-shirt."

"I could, but I prefer you the way you are."

Gage attacked his food. It took her a little longer to get her eggs and bacon cut up, but when she finally took her first bite, she found herself eating almost as fast as he was.

"This is really good."

"It's just bacon and eggs."

She took another forkful of both, then followed it with a bite of the toast he'd already buttered for her. "It's better than anything I could make."

Gage took a swallow of coffee. "I could give you a few lessons if you're interested."

She wouldn't mind getting some lessons from him in the kitchen, just not the kind he was talking about. "I have a better idea. If you keep making breakfast for us, I'll make sure you always wake up hungry. How's that?"

The heat in his eyes almost made her swoon. "Deal."

She took another bite of toast. "So, what's on the agenda today? If we assume that you're planning to follow your doctor's order and get some rest?"

He wiped up his plate with the rest of his toast, then popped it in his mouth, devouring her with his eyes as he chewed. She wondered if he was envisioning all the different ways they could have sex together for the next two days.

If so, she liked the way he thought.

"I thought we might just hang out together. If that's okay with you?" he said when he was done chewing. "Though I guess I need to run by my place and grab some clothes and stuff."

She eyed him over the rim of her mug. "Seems like you have all the clothes you need, if you ask me."

He chuckled. "While I don't have a problem with that, I think we'll have to leave your apartment at least once. You don't have enough food in here to keep us both going for a whole weekend."

Mac thought about how much he'd eaten last night, and this morning. He'd consumed about three days' worth of food in less than twenty-four hours. Yeah, maybe they'd need to go out and shop some.

"Okay," she agreed. "But I'm coming with you. I want to see where you live."

"Sounds good. Just don't hold what you see there against me. I don't spend a lot of time at my place, so it's not as nice as yours."

She steeled herself. When a guy said something like that, it usually meant he hadn't cleaned in a month.

It turned out that Gage's place was nothing like what he'd described and a lot cleaner than she'd expected. It was a first-floor, one-bedroom apartment with a tiny eat-in kitchen, an equally small living room, and a guest bathroom. It was probably less than eight hundred square feet total. But while there wasn't much in the place, what was there was neat, organized, and dust-free. She couldn't say the same for her apartment.

"I'm going to pack a bag," Gage said as he headed for the bedroom. "There's some soda in the fridge if you want it."

She didn't really want a soda, but she did want to check out the fridge. You could learn a lot about a man from what he had in there.

Like the rest of his place, Gage's refrigerator was clean and organized, and way better stocked than hers. In addition to soda, beer, and bottled water, there were a variety of lunch meats, cheeses, and condiments. Gage was obviously big into sandwiches. But a look in the freezer showed a distinct lack of TV dinners. There was plenty of meat, though. Maybe the two of them should hang out over here—they'd definitely eat better.

She grabbed one of the bottles of water and wandered into the living room. Gage's apartment lacked that cozy feminine touch. It was sparely furnished with a utilitarian-looking sofa and matching chair. It was also sparsely decorated, with the exception of one wall that held a dozen framed photographs and a few military-themed knickknacks sitting on a shelf in the bookcase. She found herself smiling at the pictures of Gage in various military and police settings.

He was younger in the military ones, but she still recognized him. Most of them were of Gage with eight other men, usually hamming it up for the photo, with their arms around each other or with their various weapons held casually in their hands. Gage looked really happy in all the pictures.

The clothing had obviously changed in the more recent pictures, with Gage wearing the standard police uniform in some, civilian clothes in others, and his SWAT gear in the most recent. She couldn't help noticing that while the poses were very similar in all the recent photos, Gage wasn't smiling in any of them. It made her feel as if she was witnessing a loss of innocence one frame at a time.

She noticed something else, too. While Gage was easily the biggest man in any of the military photos, it didn't compare to how much larger he seemed in the more recent pictures. She moved back and forth, comparing him over the years. It looked like he'd not only put on muscle after leaving the Army, but grown a few inches as well.

Running out of stuff to see in the living room, she meandered toward the bedroom. Gage was standing naked in front of a tall dresser, going through a drawer of underwear.

Mac stopped and let herself enjoy the view. Out of the corner of her eye, she took in several other facets of the room—a big bed, another dresser with its drawers hanging half-open, a wall closet holding mostly uniforms, and a black duffel bag sitting on the floor half-full of clothes and toiletries.

But mostly, she looked at Gage and that amazing naked body of his.

She bit her lip as heat pooled between her thighs. It shouldn't be possible to be aroused. They'd made love so many times last night she should have been satisfied for the next month. But that wasn't the case at all. As she enjoyed the play of muscles over his tight ass and broad back, she felt herself getting wet. She was definitely going to have to change her panties when they got back to her place.

How the hell did Gage do this to her?

He stopped, his head coming up sharply. Then he turned to her with a smoldering smile. The hungry expression only served to make her wetter, and left her wondering if he'd picked up on her arousal.

"I'm almost ready."

Against her will, her eyes drifted down to the perfect, thick cock at the junction of his muscular thighs. His shaft pulsed slightly, then slowly hardened.

"You most certainly are," she murmured, only realizing after the fact that she'd said it out loud.

He closed the distance between them in two strides, yanking her fully clothed body against his completely naked one and kissing her hard. It felt so wicked and so perfect, and it took her breath away. He tasted so good, and felt even better. Damn, she was practically vibrating with need. This must be what they meant when they said two people were sexually compatible because right now, she couldn't imagine another man in the world who could make her feel like this.

The sensation of his now rock-hard cock pressing against her stomach was enough to almost drive her crazy, and she would have dropped to her knees in worship to it, but he wouldn't let her. Instead he picked her up and carried her over to his bed. He yanked off her flip-flops and jeans and yet it still wasn't fast enough to suit her.

A tiny part of her—the part that had nothing to do with helping Gage strip off her panties so he could flip her over on her hands and knees—wondered how she could possibly go from not even thinking about sex to wanting it so badly she didn't care if he ripped her clothes to tatters. But one look at him as he took a condom packet out of the bedside table and rolled it on told her everything she needed to know.

Gage made it possible for her to act like this. She wanted him so badly because that was exactly the same way he wanted her. Like she was the only thing he could think about. Like she was as important to his survival as air.

When he pulled her ass closer toward the edge of the bed and plunged into her wetness, they both released groans of pure pleasure. His was a deeper—almost possessive—growl, but hers wasn't any less animalistic. She wanted him to possess her completely, make her his in every way possible.

His hands firmly grasped her hips as he slowly moved inside her. With each thrust, he pumped harder and harder until he buried himself all the way to her very core. She was panting so hard she was almost dizzy.

The rush of her approaching orgasm didn't surprise her. She'd learned last night that Gage could make her come almost anytime he wanted—and right now he wanted her to come right away.

Her teeth clamped down on the blanket covering his bed and she swore she could taste him on it. That thought, however crazy, only brought her climax on faster. She screamed into the bed, clutching the covers as her whole body shuddered violently. And when the first waves of orgasm passed, she got an even firmer grip. Because there was something else last night had taught her. Gage wouldn't stop with making her come only once. He would take her like this until she was sure she'd pass out—then he'd make her come even harder.

Mac cuddled against Gage's chest, running her fingers over the muscles and lightly tracing his tattoos. She'd never been into guys with tats, but he made them work. She'd seen the wolf-head SWAT tattoo during PT and when they'd made love the previous night. But she hadn't gotten a good look at the other tattoo—the one he called his Ranger Scroll—until now. She traced her fingers along the black ribbon outline with its red inner line. Inside both lines were letters and numbers.

"Second Ranger, I get," she said softly. "What's *BN* stand for?"

It took Gage a minute to answer—he was pretty much comatose beneath her in his own post-orgasmic bliss. "Battalion. I was in the 2nd Ranger Battalion out of Fort Lewis."

He said the words so quietly she wasn't sure if she

should ask him anything else about it. She remembered how he'd smiled in all the military pictures out on the wall, but looked almost somber in every photo after that. She wanted to know more about Gage, though. Hell, she wanted to know everything about him there was to know.

"I remember seeing in your public relations bio that you spent six years in the Army. Was all of it with the 2nd?"

"Not counting Basic and initial schooling, yeah, I was in the 2nd the whole time. I came in right after Desert Storm kicked off and was out by the middle of '97."

"I saw the pictures out on the wall. Were they your friends in the 2nd?"

Of course they'd been his friends—he'd taken pictures with them. But he seemed to understand what she was asking.

"They were more than that. They were like my family," he said quietly. "First Platoon, First Rifle Squad. My brothers."

Mac realized then that he'd never said a word about family until now, and when he did, it was in terms of the soldiers he'd served with.

"They sound like amazing guys. Do you stay in touch with them?"

Gage didn't answer, and the silence stretched out until she lifted her head off his chest to look at him. His eyes were closed, and when they opened, she couldn't miss the sadness in them.

"No," he said. "They're all dead."

Crap. Why the hell had she asked that question? Couldn't she have just left well enough alone?

"I'm so sorry. I didn't mean to bring up a painful subject."

He gently twirled a lock of her hair around his finger. "It's okay. You couldn't have known. It was a long time ago anyway. It hurts to think about, but not like it used to."

She rested her head on his chest again, furiously trying to think of something that would help change the topic of the conversation. But her mind was completely blank.

"It was back in August, 1996."

Gage's voice was soft and so full of sadness that she almost stopped him, but she didn't. If he wanted to talk, she'd shut up and listen.

"We were supposed to be on a simple training rotation in Kuwait. You know, run around, shoot some blanks, cross-train with the Kuwaitis and Saudis. But for some reason, somebody with a star on his shoulder decided to send First Platoon up to the northern part of Iraq—the part that's called Iraqi Kurdistan now—to conduct some goodwill development with the regional Kurd forces. My squad leader tried to point out it wasn't even a Ranger job, but nobody really cared about that, so we were sent up there anyway."

He fell silent for so long that Mac thought he was finished. But then she realized she could hear his heart beating fast beneath her ear.

"It wasn't so bad at first. Kind of fun, actually," he continued. "The platoon leader had each of the squads farmed out, working with a different part of the Kurdish militia. They certainly needed our help, so none of us minded. Then on the thirty-first, Saddam got a hair up his ass and decided to send his forces up to the town of Irbil for a little ethnic cleansing. Right where our squad was set up. Nine of us, stuck right in the middle of a place we really weren't supposed to be, with no support and almost no ammo."

Mac held her breath, waiting.

"As you can imagine it didn't go well for us. We were fighting side by side with the Kurds, and we put up one hell of a defense, but they didn't have much in the way of heavy equipment, and we didn't have any. A whole lot of people died in a really short period of time, including every member of my squad but me. My squad leader died in my arms as I tried to drag him out."

Mac was crying, and didn't have a clue why. She hadn't known those men. But Gage had, and their deaths had hurt him, so she hurt, too. "August of 1996," she murmured. "Isn't that what they called Desert Strike? I remember reading about it somewhere, but I don't remember seeing anything about any US ground casualties. We just dropped a bunch of bombs and fired off some cruise missiles."

He snorted. "Yeah, that's what they called it. But the bombing and cruise missiles happened in the days after the initial attack. Didn't do us or the Kurds any good. My squad was wiped out by then and I just barely dragged my shot-up ass back to the extraction point in time to hook up with the rest of the platoon. They'd been pretty beat up, too, but nothing like my squad. The worst part? The official report reads that my squad members all died in a training accident down in Kuwait. No one wanted to admit the US even had ground forces up in the Kurdish region."

Crap. "Is that why you decided to get out?"

He hesitated for a long time before answering. "That had a lot to do with it. I just couldn't be part of the big machine anymore. They didn't even care about us."

Mac understood Gage a little better now than she had before. How he'd risen so fast through the Dallas PD ranks, why he'd taken over the SWAT team and rebuilt it in his image. They were an organization that took care of their own above all else.

His arm tightened around her. "Sorry I unloaded on you like that. I'm not sure why I did. It definitely doesn't qualify as romantic pillow talk."

"I don't mind," she said. "I get the feeling you've needed to tell somebody that story for a long time. I'm just glad it was me."

"I guess you're right." He sighed. "I try not to think too much about that part of my past. I didn't even realize it was weighing on me until I told you about it."

She tilted her face up to kiss him. It was amazing how close she felt to him after that little peek into his past. It made her want to learn everything about him. "You can tell me anything."

He gazed at her so deeply and thoughtfully she almost teared up again. "I might just take you up on that offer sometime."

She rested her head on his chest again, smiling as she realized his heart was now beating in the strong, slow rhythm she was used to. "Anytime you're ready."

Chapter 10

GAGE COULDN'T HELP RETURNING MACKENZIE'S SMILE as he held open the door to the restaurant. "After you."

He would have been quite happy hanging around her apartment again tonight, watching TV, talking, and making love like a couple of minks, which was what they'd been doing for the past two days, but she'd wanted to go out to dinner. And whatever Mackenzie wanted, Gage was ready to give her. She'd picked this place way out toward Bonham. He'd never heard of it, but she promised him it'd be worth the hour-plus drive to get out here. He didn't care where she wanted to eat. As long as it was with him, he was game.

Across from him, Mackenzie scrunched up her nose as she studied the menu. He smiled. She looked so cute when she did that. He still couldn't believe how well things had worked out. Last night—sometime between dinner at her place and making love on the couch in the living room—Mackenzie had told him she was dropping the whole SWAT-team-on-PEDs story. They both knew there'd never been a PED story, but that had been her way of saying she was done snooping around. His pack was safe.

But while he'd started out hoping to keep a nosy journalist from finding out his pack's secret, somehow, he'd wound up falling for Mackenzie and finding the one woman in this crazy world he clicked with. It was way too soon to say he was in love, but he was more serious about her than he'd ever been about any woman. And he liked to think she felt the same way about him.

"So, what do you feel like eating?" Mackenzie asked, still studying the menu.

When he didn't answer, she gave him a quizzical look. She must have read his mind because she grinned. "On the menu, Gage. On the menu."

He chuckled. "I'm feeling like a big cheeseburger with a huge pile of fries."

"Sounds good to me. Make it two." Mackenzie closed her menu and placed it on the table. "So, what were you asking me as we pulled in the parking lot?"

She was looking at him expectantly, her blue eyes dancing. Apparently, this was a test, and if he didn't remember what they'd been talking about, she was going to seriously start thinking he was some kind of deviant who constantly thought about sex when he looked at her. Which was actually true, but he forced his mind back to their previous conversation. They'd been talking about his work schedule, then her schedule, then what she'd be working on next week. Yeah, that was it.

"I asked you what story you were going to work on next. Since the SWAT piece didn't pan out."

That sounded so smooth he almost patted himself on the back, but then he noticed she was grinning at him like she knew exactly how hard it'd been for him to remember. She didn't call him on it, though.

"I wouldn't say it was a complete waste of time." She gave him a sultry look that made him wish they'd stayed at her place. "I'm not really sure what I'm going to work on. I haven't given it a lot of thought."

Gage let the waiter set down their drinks and take their order before asking her something he'd wondered about more than once.

"How do you decide what story to go after? I know you mentioned your boss gives you a lot of leeway, but how do you even start? I mean, do you look at the news and wait until something grabs your attention?"

She stirred artificial sweetener into her iced tea. "Most of the time, yeah. I see something that's just wrong—a person getting away with something everyone knows they did, someone lying about something important with a perfectly straight face, a group of bad people using the system to get away with hurting people over and over. I see things like that and I just have to do something about it."

"You want to right wrongs then."

She sipped her drink. "Unfortunately, I rarely get to right the things that are wrong. The most I can usually do is make sure the truth comes out."

In his experience, truth could be one hell of a four-letter word. It was frequently held up as this amazing tonic that cured all ills, but it didn't always work out that way.

The funny thing was, he'd been wondering all weekend—in between romps in the bedroom and intimate conversations on the sofa—if he should tell her that he was a werewolf. Not right away, but soon. There was just something about her that made him want to be completely, one hundred percent honest with her.

But this wasn't just his secret, and that was what held him back every time he thought about opening his mouth.

"What about those situations where the truth coming out will only lead to more problems?" he asked.

She regarded him thoughtfully, as if she was wondering if he was just making conversation or whether this was one of those other secrets he had.

"It might cause some pain and suffering at first, but I tend to believe the world is a better place when all the secrets are out in the open," she said.

Damn, sometimes it was hard not looking at her and assuming she could see right through him. But with that question, he'd just exposed the biggest difference between them. She'd seen the real world, but she was still an idealist. She lived in a place where honesty and truth always led to the best outcome. He'd seen the same real world, but lived in a place where lies and cover-ups kept people safe.

"What about secrets the world isn't ready to handle yet?" he asked.

"Give the world more credit than that. People can handle more than you think." She gave him a pointed look. "Besides, no one has the right to decide what secrets another person can and can't handle."

Yeah, Mackenzie had definitely figured out this wasn't a theoretical discussion. Not surprising. She was a journalist after all.

But when the burgers showed up, she changed the subject and started talking about the last time she had a burger this big and how much she loved them.

Great. Now Gage felt like shit. She probably thought he was trying to work the courage up to tell her about something else that had happened when he was in the Army, and that he'd tell her when he was ready. She'd freak if he told her his biggest secret—that he hadn't gotten out of the Army because he couldn't deal with the

death of his friends, but because he couldn't deal with
becoming a werewolf. No matter how well Mackenzie
thought she could handle things, she wasn't ready for
that kind of secret. He wasn't sure she'd ever be ready
for that.

He shoved those thoughts aside and focused on his
burger. At least that wouldn't make him feel depressed.

He'd just drowned his fries in ketchup and taken the
first bite of his burger when his phone rang.

Mackenzie looked at him, a French fry poised halfway to her mouth. "Guess you have to answer that,
don't you?"

He reached in his pocket and pulled out his damn
phone. One weekend, that was all he'd been looking for.
"Yeah, they wouldn't call if it wasn't important."

Of course, it might not be work... Gage glanced at the
call display. It was Mike's cell, not the main line at the
compound. He thumbed the accept button.

"Yeah, Mike, what's up?"

"Damn, I'm glad you picked up. I was worried you'd
let it go to voice mail."

The tone in Mike's voice immediately made his inner
werewolf go on alert, and all kinds of bad shit start running through his head. "What's wrong?"

"I just got a call from a guy I know over in Customs and
Border Protection at Dallas/Fort Worth International,"
Mike said. "We've got trouble."

"What kind of trouble?"

"Red flags have been coming in on nearly every flight
inbound from Mexico and South America since 0900 this
morning. We're talking more than a dozen guys. All cartel connected and all well-known killers."

That sinking feeling in his stomach just got worse. "Why are we only hearing about it now?"

"Federal district attorneys have a couple major drug cases going on right now and thought the guys were in town for a hit on one of their witnesses," Mike said. "My guy called me from the freaking bathroom because he knew they weren't coming in for any witness. Not when they figured out who brought these guys in."

Gage swore. "Hardy."

"Yeah, and he's not even trying to cover his tracks. The son of a bitch had limos waiting for every one of these guys. According to cops and informants I know back from my days undercover, the word on the street is that these guys are here to take you and your girlfriend out. Soon."

"Shit."

On the other side of the table, Mackenzie had put down her burger and was looking at him with concern.

"Gage, the deputy chief is going to want to put the two of you in protective custody, you know that, right?" Mike asked.

"That sure as hell isn't going to happen," Gage growled.

"No shit," Mike agreed. "Hardy has men on the inside. He'd know where you were going before you got there. What do you want to do?"

Gage hesitated. His first instinct was to protect Mackenzie. His second was to protect his pack. But the Pack could take care of themselves—and Mackenzie—if they were warned. And if they were together.

"Call everyone in and get loaded up and ready. Mackenzie and I will be there within the hour. We'll go from there."

Mike didn't argue. He didn't comment about the fact that Gage's visit to Hardy's residence hadn't had the desired effect, either. Damn it, he should have killed Hardy when he had the chance, badge be damned.

"What's wrong?" Mackenzie asked when Gage hung up.

Gage didn't have a clue what dinner cost, but he pulled fifty dollars out of his wallet and tossed it on the table. Then he stood and held out his hand to Mackenzie. "I'll tell you on the way to the compound."

Mackenzie didn't demand answers, but just took his hand and let him lead her out of the restaurant. Even though she was the poster girl for calm, he could hear her heart pounding.

"Gage, you're scaring me," she said when he made her wait while he scanned the parking lot. "What's going on?"

He hurried her across the lot, his nose taking in a hundred different scents, his eyes shifting just enough to sharpen his night vision without giving off that telltale glow. The sun was just going down, so it wasn't completely dark out, but he still focused as he peered into the deepening shadows.

The parking lot was clear and he hustled Mackenzie in the car before he'd even thought about how to answer her question.

He seriously considered making something up. But he wouldn't make her any safer by lying to her. In fact, he'd probably do the opposite. If she didn't know the danger she was in, she might take a careless risk without even realizing it. So, as he spun out of the parking lot, he told her the truth.

"Hardy's brought in a bunch of heavy cartel muscle from outside the country. They started arriving earlier today. And everyone who knows anyone has it on good authority that they're here to kill me." He slanted her a glance. "And my girlfriend."

He sped down the road, checking every mirror in quick rotation as he waited for her to say something.

"Girlfriend, huh?"

He glanced at her out of the corner of his eye. Mackenzie had always struck him as a pretty cool character, but of all the things he'd expected her to say, that wasn't one of them. "That's the word on the street, according to Mike."

"I wonder how Hardy found out about us so quickly."

Gage shook his head. "You did hear the part about them planning to kill us, right?"

"Yeah, but I could have told you that. In fact, I'm pretty sure I did," she said. "He must have had someone watching you for the past few days and they saw us together. I wonder why he's making such an aggressive move now, though. I thought someone like Hardy would have taken a more calculated approach."

Gage took the opportunity to check his mirrors again. He knew exactly why Hardy had hired those hit men—because Gage had miscalculated and poked the man with a stick.

"I know there was a bomb in that meth lab the other day." When Gage did a double take at that, she added, "I overheard Cooper tell Mike at the hospital."

He swore under his breath.

"Hardy was behind it, wasn't he?"

Gage nodded, his gaze going to the mirrors.

Mackenzie looked over her shoulder, out the back window. "You think those hit men are going to come at us while we're driving, don't you?"

He forced himself to stop looking in the mirror every five seconds. "Not really. I doubt anyone could have followed us all the way out here along these back roads without me noticing them. And no one could have guessed this is where we'd go. I don't think many people in Dallas even know that place is out here."

She sat back in the seat, looking surprisingly relaxed. Well, as relaxed as a person could look knowing that a rich, powerful man wanted you dead.

"So, what's the plan?" she asked. "Are they going to put us in protective custody?"

Gage couldn't believe how well she was taking this. Most women—hell most people—would have been freaking out by now.

"I'm sure Mason is talking to the chief of police right now about putting together a protective detail, but I trust my own people a whole lot more," Gage told her. "We're heading straight to the compound."

"Okay. But then what?"

Gage was trying to figure out how to answer that question when the glare of headlights reflecting sharply off the rearview mirror caught his attention. He had just enough time to punch the accelerator to the floor and tighten his grip on the wheel when the car coming up behind them smashed into his bumper.

If the Charger had been any lighter—or if he hadn't lucked out and seen the asshole coming—the collision would have knocked his car completely out of control. As it was, he and Mackenzie nearly slid sideways into a ditch. Tires squealed as the sports car threatened to roll on him. He fought for control of the wheel as he tried to figure out where the psycho behind them had gone.

"Watch out!" Mackenzie screamed.

Gage snapped his head around just in time to see two cars pull across the road in a classic roadblock position. There was no way he could bull his way through, and he sure as hell didn't want to stop. He slammed on the brake, trying to steer toward the side of the road. He had to get around them.

His werewolf reflexes were good enough to pull it off, but whoever was in the cars blocking the road started peppering the Charger with rounds from what sounded like an automatic weapon. Bullets smashed into the front of the car and Mackenzie screamed as the windshield shattered. Gage threw as much of his body in front of hers as he could, considering he was wearing his seat belt and needed to keep one hand on the wheel.

He was still moving fast when he clipped the rear of one of the blocking cars, smashing it to pieces and sending him and Mackenzie hurtling off the road and into the ditch. He gripped the wheel tightly as they bottomed out in the ravine, then bounced up the far side. Mackenzie screamed again as they ran into a line of small trees at the top of the embankment.

There were so many bullets hitting the car that Gage couldn't believe neither of them had been hit yet. That wouldn't last long.

He needed to get them out of here, and fast. With all the trees, he had no choice but to put the Charger into a sideways slide and bring the car to a halt the hard way—by smashing it broadside into a thick hardwood.

He grabbed Mackenzie and tried to protect her from the impact as best he could, but she still slammed against the inside of the door pretty hard. He reached over to unbuckle her seat belt. They had to get out of the car now.

He dragged her off her seat and across the center console, slipping one hand down to his ankle holster to pull out his gun. Mackenzie was so woozy she could barely stand on her own, and he held on to her with one hand while he scanned the area. He could hear the sound of feet pounding on the dirt, could smell the sweat coming off the men as they ran.

Gage put a bullet through the head of the first man to crest the embankment, sending him tumbling backward. That would sure as hell slow them down some. Nobody was going to feel like poking their head up for a few seconds at least.

Not waiting to see if he was right, he turned and scooped Mackenzie off her feet, then ran into the forest as fast as he could—and he could run pretty damn fast.

They'd gotten maybe two hundred feet into the woods before bullets started tearing up the sparse forest around them. Apparently the bad guys hadn't waited as long as he'd hoped.

Shit.

There were at least six of them crashing through the woods after him, spread out in a ragged line in an effort to make sure he didn't slip past them in the gathering dark. If he'd been by himself, he would have shifted into his half-werewolf form so he could go on the offensive. The assholes would have never even seen him coming.

But he had Mackenzie to worry about. There was no way to keep her safe and go after the men at the same time.

So he kept running. Bullets buzzed past them like

angry bees, and Gage was forced to zig and zag erratically. That only allowed the men behind them to gain on them.

"They're catching up," Mackenzie said.

Gage glanced down at her. "You okay?"

He ran faster. He needed a better plan. He wasn't going to be able to stay ahead of these guys forever while carrying Mackenzie. All it would take was one lucky shot.

"Yeah, I bounced my head against the window, but I'm okay," she said. "Put me down. We'll be able to run faster."

Gage wasn't so sure of that. But what he was doing sure as hell wasn't working.

He caught sight of a barbwire fence up ahead. He sprinted to it and set her down on the other side, then vaulted over it while she was facing away from him. Their pursuers were only about sixty feet behind them and closing fast. Gage aimed at the man closest to them, but held his fire. He only had one magazine in the Sig, which only carried eight rounds. He might be good with a gun, but he didn't have ammo to waste on a low-percentage shot.

Unfortunately, the bad guys didn't have that issue. Every one of them was carrying an MP5 submachine gun and had lots of spare ammo. The moment they realized he and Mackenzie had stopped, they painted the area with 9mm ball rounds.

Gage turned to grab Mackenzie's hand and was shocked to see her holding that damn camera of hers. She was videotaping the freaking gunmen as they shot at them!

"What the hell are you doing?" he shouted.

"I'm a journalist. If someone is shooting at me, I'm

going to film it," she explained, trying to hold the camera steady as he pulled her away.

Then Mackenzie frantically motioned to the left, her camera dangling from her wrist. "I saw a building over there."

The "building" was a barn. Unfortunately, it didn't have any doors. But right now, they didn't have a better option.

He headed for the back of the barn, then tugged Mackenzie down to the hay-strewn dirt floor with him.

"Are you okay?" he asked. "Did you get hit?" The thought alone was enough to almost make his head stop working.

"No, I'm fine." She searched his face. "What about you?"

"I'm fine."

Gage took out his cell phone and swore. No service. So much for more bars in more places.

Mackenzie held up her camera, pointing it at the entrance. He knew she was scared because he could hear her heart thundering, and yet she kept filming. Damn, she was amazing—or insane.

"What are we going to do?" Mackenzie asked.

Gage shoved his phone back in his front pocket, hoping for inspiration to tell him how to answer that question when gunfire sounded from the front of the barn.

He pushed Mackenzie to the floor, covering her body with his as bullets zipped over their heads. Ragged chunks of wood went flying every which way thanks to the six men and their automatic weapons.

No, not six—four. Where the hell were the other two?

He lifted his head as he caught their scent. They were in the barn, just inside the door. All at once, the gunfire stopped. It had only been a diversion to make him duck so he wouldn't see the men come in.

Shit.

In a minute, they'd start spraying the place with bullets. He and Mackenzie would never survive that much firepower in this small barn.

Gage pushed himself up to his knees and took aim around the support post he was using for cover. Both gunmen had taken up defensive positions similar to his, which didn't leave Gage with much of a target. But he had to shoot. Every second he wasted gave the bad guys more time to shoot at them.

He leveled his Sig and squeezed the trigger. He was pretty sure he grazed the guy, but he didn't have time to check. The moment he fired, the second shooter immediately emptied a full magazine in his direction.

Gage felt a bullet hit his right shoulder, then another clip his left leg. He ignored the white-hot flash of pain and adjusted his sights on the second gunman. He caught the guy just as he was reloading, putting two rounds in his chest. Then he turned his attention back to the first guy to find him lining Gage up for the kill shot.

Gage squeezed off a round in the man's general direction, praying it found its target. Unfortunately, it was about half a foot above the shooter's head. It made the man flinch and jump out from his hiding place, though. That was all the opening Gage needed. He put the gunman down with a shot dead through the center of his chest.

Gage waited for the four men outside to rush in, guns blazing. Maybe they'd figured things hadn't gone according to plan. They probably thought Gage had killed their buddies and was waiting for the rest of them to come in so he could do the same to them.

They had no way of knowing Gage had been hit twice,

but neither shot was life-threatening for a werewolf. Right now, he was more concerned with the fact that he only had two rounds left in his Sig—and four gunmen still waiting outside.

"Oh, God. Gage, you're bleeding!" Mackenzie cried.

She caught his arm, trying to pull him down with her. He resisted, keeping his gaze trained on the door. If the bad guys came at them now, he wasn't going to have many options. But he'd protect Mackenzie, no matter what.

"Gage," she said. "You've been shot."

If he thought her heart had been beating fast before, that didn't compare to how it was racing now.

He glanced at her. "I'm okay. It's just a graze wound."

"Let me see," she insisted.

"Not now. The rest of those assholes could come in here any second and I'm almost out of ammo."

That got her attention. "You're not carrying another magazine?"

He shook his head. God, what he wouldn't give to get his hands on those two machine guns lying on the ground on the far side of the barn.

It'd be crazy to try it, though. The men outside knew those weapons were there, too. Going for them would require him to step directly into their line of sight. In his human form, he wouldn't be fast enough to pull that off without getting hit a lot. And contrary to pop culture, you didn't need a silver bullet to kill a werewolf. A good old-fashioned lead one would do the job just fine.

But what choice did he have? If he could have shifted, it would have drastically improved his odds, but with Mackenzie here, he couldn't do that.

Gage tensed, ready to sprint across the barn, when he smelled smoke. "What the hell?"

The men had set fire to the barn. If they couldn't come in, they were going to burn him and Mackenzie out.

Shit.

He jerked around to see flames creeping along the walls behind them.

"Gage, the barn's on fire."

Mackenzie's voice was much calmer than it should have been in a situation like this. She was even filming again. No doubt about it—she was crazy.

Or maybe she didn't realize how screwed they really were. The men had started the fire to drive their prey out of the barn. They were standing out there with every weapon pointed at the entryway and the weapons lying on the floor in the opening. When Gage made a move for them, they'd take him out before he even had a chance to pick them up.

And then they'd come for Mackenzie.

But if they stayed where they were, they'd roast. And Mackenzie would still be dead.

His mind raced at a thousand miles an hour as Mackenzie began to cough. There was a third option. A way to take out the men, or at least distract them long enough for Mackenzie to escape.

He was going to have to shift. He might still not survive the hit he was going to take from their automatic weapons, but Mackenzie would be safe. And that was what mattered.

But if he did this, everything would change—no matter how it turned out.

Gage took the camera out of Mackenzie's grasp to let it hang by its cord from her wrist, then he gently pushed his pistol into her hand. "I have to get rid of those guys before this whole place goes up in flames, and there's only one way to do it. And it's going to the scare the hell out of you."

She tried to push the gun back into his hand. "Gage, what are you talking about? How can you get those men without a weapon? It's..."

He didn't know if she had been about to say it was crazy, or stupid, or impossible because she started to cough from the thick smoke rolling off the back wall.

He wrapped her fingers around the pistol grip and curled her index finger in the trigger guard. "This is going to be hard on you, but you have to do it, no matter how scared you are. I need you to count to five, then follow me outside. You only have two rounds. If there's anyone left out there when I'm done, you need to make those two rounds count. Do you understand?"

She coughed again, tears running down her face. He told himself it was the smoke making her cry, but he knew that was bull.

He slid his hands in her hair and kissed her hard. He wanted to tell her what she meant to him, tell her how he felt about her, tell her what he really was, but one kiss was all he had time for.

When he lifted his head, she was gazing up at him with tear-filled eyes, and the sight of them tore at his heart. "Remember—count to five, okay?"

"Why? Gage, what are you going to do?"

"Whatever I have to do to protect you."

The whole back of the barn was engulfed in flames now. He rose to his feet, ignoring the pain of his wounds.

"I'm sorry," he said raggedly, then turned and ran toward the door, shifting as he ran.

It was almost a relief to finally allow his teeth to elongate and his claws to come out. He wouldn't need the MP5s on the floor now. With his speed, strength, claws, and fangs, he was a killing machine.

Mackenzie didn't know that, of course. And as he ran out of the barn, she screamed his name.

———∾———

Mac knew Gage was going to do something reckless and dangerous when he'd shoved his pistol into her hand — she just hadn't known what.

When he'd said he was going to get rid of the men, she thought he was going to grab one of the machine guns the thugs had dropped, but he hadn't. Why would he do something so insane?

She wiped away a tear with her free hand. She had to get it together. Gage was depending on her to go out there in five seconds.

How long had it been?

Longer than five seconds she was sure.

Outside, the sounds of gunfire filled the night, followed by shouting. Mac's blood turned to ice in her veins. There was no way Gage could survive that many bullets.

She jumped to her feet and ran across the barn. The fire and smoke had sucked the oxygen out of the place and it was hard to breathe. Pieces of hay and wood floated through the air like dandelion fluff, burning her skin, but she ignored them.

Fresh air hit her like a slap to the face when she got outside, but it was nothing compared to what she saw that completely took her breath away again.

Two of the gunmen were already dead, their bodies

torn and bloody. A third lay on the ground trying to reach a machine gun a dozen feet away, his leg twisted at an odd angle and badly bleeding. Dear God, the men looked as if they'd been mauled by a wild animal.

She searched around wildly for Gage and saw him locked in a struggle with the fourth man. They each had a hand around the other's throat, trying to squeeze the life out of their opponent. The man twisted the machine gun in his free hand and pointed it at Gage.

Suddenly remembering the pistol in her hand, Mac aimed it at the man and squeezed the trigger, praying she shot him and not Gage. The bullet hit the man in the leg, and he made a strangled sound, relaxing his grip on his weapon.

Gage let out a growl, then lifted the man off the ground and flung him into the air. Mac cringed as he smashed into the burning barn to be consumed by the flames. She didn't realize she'd made a sound until Gage spun around to face her.

Mac gasped. At first she thought the smoke from the fire was still affecting her, or that shock was making her too dizzy to see straight. Because what she saw couldn't be real.

Gage's shoulders were broader; his brow heavier and more furrowed; his hair longer; his stubble thicker; his ears slightly pointed at the tips; his jaw wider; his canine teeth now long, dangerous-looking fangs; and his eyes no longer a soulful brown, but a deep yellow-gold so bright they almost glowed. And on each hand, his nails had turned into wickedly sharp claws.

She was so focused on Gage, she completely forgot about the man with the leg wound until Gage growled and leaped fifteen feet to land behind the guy. The man grabbed the machine gun on the ground and rolled over to shoot, but Gage caught the weapon and ripped it out of his hands. He punched the guy in the face—hard.

That was it—one punch and it was over. But Gage still picked him up and slung him at least ten feet through the air to land in a crumpled heap near the entrance of the burning barn with his companions.

Gage turned to her, his body tense, his eyes on fire, and his lips pulled back in an angry snarl. Mac took a step back, her hands bringing up the pistol before she even realized what she was doing. That was when she noticed she was holding the camera, too. She was a journalist. Catching action on film was second nature to her—she did it without thinking.

When Gage stepped closer, she stepped back. He stopped and raised his hands in a silent gesture. He locked eyes with hers, and despite how afraid she was, the sadness there made her heart squeeze in her chest.

Mac shoved the camera in her rear pocket so she could use two hands to steady the gun. She wanted to think Gage wouldn't hurt her, but she didn't even know if the thing in front of her was Gage anymore.

"What are you?" she asked.

As she watched, the monster in front of her slowly shifted back into the form of the man she knew—or thought she knew. But the four dead bodies made it impossible to forget what she'd seen.

"I'm sorry you had to see that," Gage said quietly. "And I'm sorry I scared you."

The hurt in his eyes tore at her, but she refused to give in to it. "Answer my question. What are you?"

The muscle in Gage's jaw ticked. "I'm a werewolf."

A werewolf?

It was insane.

And if she hadn't seen the sharp claws and wicked fangs with her own eyes, she wouldn't have believed it.

But she had seen them, and every suspicious thing she'd had no explanation for now made perfect sense— the feeling that Gage and the rest of his SWAT team were hiding something, the fact that they didn't use their night vision goggles during their missions, the lack of concern over Martinez's injury.

She looked at Gage's shoulder. The gunshot wound that had been bleeding freely just a few minutes ago in the barn was now miraculously healed.

She thought back to how the SWAT team had reacted at the restaurant when Hardy's men had come in, how hard they trained, how they'd survived a freaking house collapsing on them. And finally, she remembered the wolf-head tattoo that every member of the team wore.

She lowered the gun. "You're all werewolves, aren't you? The whole SWAT team?"

Gage's eyes widened in alarm. "I know what you're thinking, Mackenzie, but you can't tell anyone."

Was he kidding? This was huge, bigger than huge— the biggest story she'd ever stumbled on. Werewolves were real and she'd captured one on camera.

She took a deep breath. Crap. Werewolves were real, and a whole…pack…of them were employed by the city of Dallas. Did the chief of police know? What about the mayor? Were they werewolves, too?

How was any of this possible?

There was so much she wanted to know. Like who'd

turned Gage into a werewolf and whether he'd turned all the other men in the unit.

But she couldn't ask any of those questions yet. "The public has a right to know the truth."

The worried look disappeared, replaced by one of irritation. Gage snatched the gun out of her hand and shoved it back in his ankle holster.

"Damn it, Mackenzie, this isn't a game."

What the hell did he have to be angry about? He was the one who'd lied to her.

That thought led to a place she didn't want to go. Had Gage played her over the last several days, had he slept with her, because he was worried she'd find out he was a werewolf?

She opened her mouth to ask him when he slipped one arm under her legs and the other around her shoulder and swung her up in his arms like he was some damn caveman. She immediately struggled to free herself. "Let me go!"

He did, but only after carrying her thirty feet away from the burning barn. She stumbled backward and fell on her butt.

She glared up at him. "What the hell was that about?"

"That."

Gage pointed at the barn, which was nothing more than a huge bonfire now. As she watched, the front wall fell in on itself, beams and flaming pieces of wood going everywhere, including where she and Gage had been standing.

He had saved her life—again.

She frowned as she realized the structure had collapsed on top of the three bodies lying outside the door of the barn, too. There'd be no mangled bodies for Gage to have

to explain. If she didn't know better, she'd think he had
orchestrated that.

He held out his hand for her. After several long moments, she finally took it and let him help her up. But
the moment she was on her feet, she put some distance
between them. It was a joke—she'd seen how fast he
could move.

In the distance, she could hear sirens approaching.
Someone had called the cops. Gage swore under his breath.

"Mackenzie, you have to promise me you'll never tell
anyone about what you saw. If you breathe a word of this,
my life, and the lives of every man on the SWAT team
will be destroyed."

His face was so earnest, it almost brought fresh tears
to her eyes. "It won't be like that, Gage. You're a cop.
You were defending us. You'll be a hero. That's the way
I'll write it."

The sirens got louder as they drew closer.

Gage's jaw tightened. "Yeah, if your editor doesn't
demand you change it," he said bitterly. "Even if he
doesn't, what happens after that, huh? When the other
reporters who aren't as idealistic as you get ahold of the
footage on that camera of yours and see how I tore that
man apart? You think they'll treat us like heroes? They'll
think we're monsters."

Mac flushed. She couldn't very well say he was wrong
when she'd thought the same thing a few moments ago.
"It's like I told you back at the restaurant. Secrets are
better when they're out in the open."

"You don't get to decide that," he growled.

"People like me have a right to know that people like
you exist."

"Do you even hear yourself?" he demanded. "You were terrified of me, and we've spent the past two days in bed together. How do you think the rest of the world is going to react? The ones who don't want to hunt us down and kill us outright will want to capture us and cut us up for research."

"That's not true." Mac shook her head. She refused to believe they lived in a world where people would allow something like that to happen. "This isn't the Dark Ages. People don't go around in mobs carrying torches and pitchforks anymore. Not everyone is as bad as you seem to think."

He snorted. "You're right. Sometimes they're worse. Walter Hardy comes to mind. Or have you forgotten he just sent men to kill us?"

"No, I haven't forgotten," she said. "All the more reason to let him and people like him know what you are. What the whole SWAT team is. He'd be terrified to go after you."

The lights from the police cars flashed against the trees, getting closer. Gage muttered something under his breath. "I'm not going to be able to talk you out of writing this story, am I?"

Mac didn't answer. It was her job to keep people informed. Why couldn't he understand that? More importantly, why couldn't he trust her to handle this in the best possible way?

The same look of sadness was back in his eyes, this time mixed with hurt. "At least give me twenty-four hours before you run it. I think you owe me that much, don't you?"

If it were anyone else, she never would have agreed, but he was right—after what they'd shared, she owed him that much. In truth, she owed him a hell of a lot more. But she wouldn't be doing her job as a journalist if she didn't write this story. And maybe after it ran, he'd see that she was right and they could get back to that place they'd been before Hardy's hired guns had tried to kill them.

Realizing she hadn't answered his question, she nodded.

Half a dozen police cars came into view, their lights bouncing off the farmer's field as they navigated the uneven terrain.

"I can't protect you and my pack at the same time, Mackenzie," Gage said. "You're still a target. Be careful."

Gage didn't wait for a reply, but turned and strode across the clearing toward the police cars. Mac had been a target before and she'd always taken care of herself just fine, but for some stupid reason, knowing he put his pack ahead of her hurt. For the first time in her life, she wasn't sure if she was doing the right thing.

Chapter 11

IT WAS ALMOST 0200 HOURS BY THE TIME GAGE GOT TO the compound. Between giving a statement to the cops who'd responded to the incident, then the duty captain who'd come out after hearing who Gage was, he'd barely had enough time for a quick call to tell Mike he was okay before Deputy Chief Mason had shown up with a half dozen detectives and Internal Affairs. The newsies hadn't been far behind. Cops getting called out to a rural farm area about reports of automatic weapons fire was one thing. Finding out that a member of the city's SWAT team had been targeted and ambushed by seven foreign killers armed with those automatic weapons? That was something completely different, and it drew a lot of attention.

It had taken a long time to answer Internal Affairs' questions. It was tough making up a story that explained everything that'd happened, especially when he was thinking of Mackenzie and what a damn fool he'd been to trust her. Luckily, the entire department had heard the rumors about Hardy bringing in some hired killers, so they were more than ready to believe the men had come to kill him and Mackenzie. The part they had a hard time believing was how one man—even if he was SWAT—managed to kill seven cold-blooded killers with just his off-duty weapon and his bare hands.

Gage had really outdone himself on that part of the story. He should get a freaking Oscar for his acting skills.

And while they were handing out awards, Mackenzie should get one, too, because she'd really made him believe she gave a damn about him. But all she'd ever wanted was a fucking story, and he'd been so convinced she was *The One*, he hadn't even seen it. Fool that he was, he'd thought he might be able to make one last appeal to her after Internal Affairs had finished with him, but Mason told him she'd asked if one of the uniformed officers could take her home.

While he was still mad as hell at Mackenzie, Gage was also worried about her. He hadn't been making that crap up about her being a target. But as much as he wanted to protect her, his first priority was to his pack. Besides, she'd made her decision. She was probably back at the newsroom going over her video evidence and writing the first draft of a story that'd earn her another award for her wall, and end his life, and those of men who were like brothers to him.

It was his own damn fault. He never should have let her get so close. Hell, he should never have let her into the compound. But he'd been fooled by her smile and her pretty face—and yeah, her sexy body, too—and ignored the fact that she'd been after one thing and one thing only—a story. And when her smile and pretty face hadn't gotten her anywhere, she'd used her body to get what she wanted. She'd slept with him and made him feel things that weren't real. And when he'd gotten careless, she'd been there to record the whole thing.

So, why didn't he hate her? Because he was in love with her. He had to be, right? Why else would he feel as if his soul had been ripped out?

Gage punched his code into the control on the compound's gate and let himself in. The deputy chief had wanted him to relocate to a protective services safe house immediately, but Gage refused. When Mason insisted, Gage had told his boss he'd quit right there on the spot. That hadn't earned him any future favors with his division chief, but it had ended the discussion, which was all Gage cared about. After tonight, he wouldn't be working for the Dallas PD anymore anyway.

Gage closed the gate behind him, then headed for the training building. The guys were waiting for him inside. They looked concerned—and wired.

"Where's Mac?" Cooper asked. "Is she okay?"

Gage set his duffel bag on the floor. "She's fine. She's probably at the *Dallas Daily Star* working on her story."

Cooper frowned. "Probably?"

"What story?" Becker asked.

There was no easy way to say it so he might as well rip off the Band-Aid. "The story telling the world that the Dallas SWAT team is made up of werewolves."

No one said anything. They all stared at him like he'd announced he'd just been abducted and probed by aliens.

"You *told* her?" Mike asked.

"I didn't have to." Gage couldn't keep the bitterness from his voice. He quickly recounted the night's events, keeping it as brief and to the point as he could. "I didn't have a choice. I had to shift to fight them."

Xander swore.

"Did she see you kill those men?" Mike asked.

"Worse," Gage said. "She caught some of it on video."

Xander wasn't the only one who swore this time. Or shifted. They were all looking at Gage with yellow-gold eyes as if they wanted to tear him apart. But Xander was the only one brave enough to come at him with claws extended and fangs flashing.

Gage braced himself, letting out his claws and baring his teeth. Unfortunately, Mike and Nelson grabbed Xander, holding him back. Too bad. He wouldn't have minded putting his fist in someone's face right then, and something told him Xander would have given him a good fight.

"This is all your fault," Xander snarled.

"Don't you think I fucking know that?" Gage roared. He clenched his fists, welcoming the pain as his claws dug into his palms. "I never should have let Mackenzie step foot in this compound, but I did, and saying I'm sorry isn't going to change it."

"He's right," Mike said. "Our faces are going to be on every newspaper and television station in the country by tomorrow night. Let's just worry about that right now."

Xander pinned Mike with a glare, but only shook off his pack mate's hold and stepped back.

"So, what are we going to do?" Lowry asked, his golden eyes filled with concern.

"Disappear," Gage said. "Change our names and go somewhere no one can find us. There are already fake IDs and passports in the safe in my office, along with burner phones for each of us."

They all looked stunned by that. He couldn't blame them. Besides having a job they all loved, they had parents and siblings and friends they'd never be able to see again. Parents, siblings, and friends who'd be hounded by reporters like Mackenzie for a sound bite. She wouldn't only destroy his pack in her quest for truth, she'd destroy the lives of everyone close to them.

Becker shook his head. "Damn. How long have you been planning this? Us going on the run, I mean."

"Right after I recruited Xander and Mike," Gage said. "I always knew there was a chance someone would find out what we are, and I wanted to be prepared."

Xander looked at him scornfully. "And because you let some woman lead you around by the dick, we have to go on the run like the criminals we put in prison."

Gage let out a soft growl. He didn't need the reminder. "We don't have a choice."

"Yeah, we do," Xander said. "We can get the video back from Mac and make sure she doesn't talk."

The entire room went still. Though whether it was because the rest of the Pack was shocked by Xander's words or because they agreed with him, Gage didn't know and he didn't care. He fixed his senior squad leader with a hard look.

"Anyone who wants to try it will have to come through me first." Gage slowly and deliberately locked eyes with every member of the Pack. "And you'd better be ready to kill me."

No one seemed to want to take him up on it, not even Xander.

"Mackenzie said she'd give us twenty-four hours before she ran the story, but I want you all out of here before noon tomorrow," he continued.

"Wait a minute. What about you?" Becker asked. "You're making it sound like you aren't coming with us."

"I'm not. At least not right away," Gage added. "I can't leave until I make sure Hardy is no longer a threat to Mackenzie."

Xander cursed. "I can't believe you can even give a damn about her after what she did to us."

"He gives a damn about her because she's *The One* for him," Cooper said.

"That's bullshit! There's no one perfect mate for any of us." Xander gave Gage a disgusted look. "And if you think there is, you're a damn fool." He shook his head. "I'm going to get some air."

Gage watched him go. He was tempted to follow just to make sure Xander didn't do something stupid, like go after Mackenzie. Because he'd meant what he said. He'd fight his entire pack before he'd let them hurt her.

Instead of running up to her apartment the minute the police officer dropped her off so she could start her story, Mac jumped in her car and drove straight to Zak's apartment. She needed someone to tell her she was doing the right thing—or the wrong thing. Because she was so confused right then she didn't know what to think.

As she knocked on his door a half hour later, she realized she probably should have called first. It was after midnight.

But Zak jerked open the door before she'd even finished knocking. He was wearing jeans and a Texas A&M T-shirt. The way his hair was sticking up all over the place made her think she'd woken him up.

"Mac, thank God! I've been worried as hell about you."

Mac brushed past him. "I think I really screwed up."

Zak shut the door. "I've been calling you for the past two hours. You're all over the news. Something about machine guns and a barn catching fire. What happened?"

"Hardy sent a bunch of hired guns to kill Gage and me," she told him. "But that's not important."

His eyes went wide behind his glasses. "You almost get killed and it's not important?"

She waved her hand. "No. I found out what SWAT's been hiding. And it's huge."

"O-kay." When she didn't elaborate, he frowned. "So, what is it?"

She opened her mouth, then closed it again. "Maybe you should sit down first."

Zak gave her a curious look, but did as she suggested, parking himself in the overstuffed chair he'd had since his college days. Mac sat on the adjacent matching couch.

"Well?" he prompted.

Mac felt as if he was looking right through her. But he could always do that. The difference now was that she had something to feel guilty about.

"Gage is…"

A werewolf.

It sounded crazy. She'd seen Gage turn into one and she could hardly believe it herself.

"Gage is…what?" Zak asked.

"He's…" She tried again. And failed miserably. "Maybe I should just show you."

She took out her camera and turned it on. Her finger hovered over the video playback button, but she didn't click on it.

"Mac, I thought you dropped the whole idea of doing a story on SWAT."

"I did. But then I found out what Gage has been hiding and I…"

"Damn Mac, you just couldn't let this one go, could you?"

She looked up, shocked. He actually sounded mad at her. "It could be the biggest story of my career."

Zak sat back, studying her from behind his glasses. "But if you run with it, you'll lose Gage."

She gave him a miserable look. "I think I already have."

He sighed. "Maybe you should start at the beginning."

Mac told him everything. Well, not everything. She didn't talk about the sex, of course. Which meant there were huge periods of time throughout the weekend she didn't mention at all. And she didn't tell Zak the things Gage had shared with her about his life before SWAT, when he was an Army Ranger. She didn't feel right sharing that.

But she told Zak the most important parts. About hanging around her apartment for hours doing nothing more than talking. About the feelings she had for Gage. And believing he'd felt the same things for her.

"So, what changed?" Zak asked.

She told him about going to her favorite restaurant out in Bonham and about Mike calling to tell them Hardy had sent men to kill them, then about the car ramming them, the chase through the woods, and finally the fight in the barn.

"Then when I went outside and saw Gage... Zak, he was..."

Mac faltered—again. Damn it. Why couldn't she just say it?

"Was it illegal?"

She looked at Zak in confusion. "What?"

"Whatever Gage did," Zak explained. "Was it illegal?"

"No."

"Immoral?"

"No."

"Did it save your life?"

She remembered the burning barn and the gunmen waiting outside to shoot her and Gage the moment they ran out. "Yes."

"Now for a tough one," Zak said. "Is Gage—or anyone else on the SWAT team—going to be hurt if you write this story?"

Exposing the truth was her job. She wasn't responsible for what other people did with that truth once she exposed it. But then she thought about what Gage said—about people hunting him and his pack, conducting research on them, killing them—and she felt ill.

"Yes," she said softly. "I don't know what to do, Zak."

He gave her a small smile. "I'm pretty sure you do, or you wouldn't have come here to talk to me. You're looking for someone to tell you it's okay to do something your gut tells you is wrong. Sorry, but that's not going to be me."

Zak was right. "But there's never been a time in my life when the story didn't come first. I'm not sure if I know how to let this one go."

"Mac, you just said Gage and the rest of the guys on the SWAT team would be hurt if you told anyone about what you saw him do tonight, right?" When she nodded, he continued. "Don't you think Gage knew that?"

She remembered the terrified look on his face when he'd told her she couldn't tell anyone what he was. "Yes."

"And yet he did it anyway, even though he knew what it might cost him."

Oh, God. If it hadn't been for her, Gage would never have been in that barn in the first place. He would have taken out the bad guys in the woods. He'd changed into a werewolf because it was the only choice he had.

Tears welled up in her eyes.

"Gage loves you, Mac," Zak said. "And I'm pretty sure you love him, even if you haven't admitted it to yourself yet."

Mac covered her face in her hands. How could she have been so stupid? And why could Zak see everything so clearly when she'd been so blind? She'd just screwed up the best thing that had ever happened to her for the sake of a stupid-ass story.

"Go talk to him, Mac."

She lowered her hands to look at Zak. He made it sound so simple. "But how do I even begin to apologize to him?"

"It's not that complicated. Just open your mouth and say, I'm sorry." His mouth edged up. "It's pretty easy after that."

She turned off her camera and shoved it in her pocket, then got to her feet and gave Zak a hug. "Thank you."

He grinned. "For what? You already knew what you were going to do."

She laughed. "Maybe, but I just needed my big brother to tell me I was doing the right thing."

He opened the door for her. "Tell Gage I said hey."

"I will."

On the way to her car, she pulled out her phone and called Gage, but it went to voice mail. Damn it.

Gage lived across town, so Mac had almost half an hour to rehearse what she was going to say to him. If he even let her in. She'd bang on his door until he opened it if she had to. And when he did, she'd tell him she didn't care that he was a werewolf. Then she'd make him see what he meant to her.

But when she got to his place and knocked on the door, there wasn't any answer. His car wasn't in its parking space, either. She took out her cell and called him again. Again, it went to voice mail. Maybe he was asleep.

Though she didn't know how he could sleep after what happened tonight. He probably knew it was her and was pretending he wasn't home.

At the risk of looking like a complete stalker, Mac climbed behind the hedges to peek through the window. The living room was empty. So was the kitchen. She cupped her hands against the glass and leaned closer. Then she frowned. In the light coming from the kitchen she saw that the framed photos were no longer on the wall above the bookcase. That was odd.

She shifted to see better into the kitchen. But all she saw was a neat pile of stuff on the counter. She couldn't make out everything from this distance, but she recognized Gage's cell phone sitting on top. Okay, that was even weirder.

Oh, crap. What if he'd asked her to wait twenty-four hours so he and the rest of the team—his pack—could leave town?

She suddenly broke out in a cold sweat. Gage had left, and she was never going to get the chance to tell him she'd made a mistake. Or tell him that she loved him.

Tears blurring her vision, Mac stumbled out from behind the hedges and ran to her car. Gage wouldn't leave without making sure his pack was safe first. Hopefully, they'd still be at the compound planning or coordinating, or whatever it was werewolves did before they went on the run.

She didn't take her foot off the gas the entire way there. It was only by some miracle she didn't get pulled over.

She breathed a huge sigh of relief when she stopped outside the gate and saw that the parking area was full of vehicles. Gage's Charger wasn't there, but again, that didn't mean anything.

Please let him still be here.

Mac hurried over to ring the bell, only to jerk to a halt when she heard a low, menacing growl. Yellow eyes gleamed in the darkness. She cringed when she saw it was Xander. Why couldn't Gage have been the one prowling around out here? Or Becker. Hell, anyone but Xander. The senior corporal had never been warm to her, but after the explosion at the meth lab, she thought maybe he'd thawed a little. He probably hated her more now. One more thing she'd damaged.

Eyes narrowing, he scanned the darkness behind her before giving her a look that could have melted paint off a car.

"I knew Gage was stupid to believe you'd actually give us time to get out of here." He snarled, showing her a pair of wickedly sharp canine teeth. "What, did you decide you need some more footage before you wrote your story? Maybe get some pictures of the freaks running for their lives?"

Her face flamed. "It's not like that."

"Really? Then how is it?"

Xander's eyes flashed and she had to force herself not to take a step back at the anger rolling off him.

She moved closer to the gate and looked him straight in his yellow eyes. "I'm here to apologize to Gage. And to tell him that I won't be telling anyone about your…pack."

Xander couldn't completely hide the surprise that came over his face, but he sure as hell tried. "And you expect me to believe that?"

She swallowed hard. "I know you don't have any reason to trust me or believe anything I say, but I'm hoping you'll at least give me a chance to talk to Gage."

He snorted. "Trust me, Gage isn't interested in seeing you right now. He's a little busy trying to get us all out of the country before the mob of angry villagers shows up with their torches and pitchforks."

She hooked her fingers in the chain link. "I don't blame him for not wanting to see me. I said some really stupid things tonight. I only want to make it right."

Mac thought she saw doubt creep across Xander's face, but it disappeared too quickly to be sure. "You don't get it, do you?" he asked harshly. "You didn't just hurt him. You definitely messed him up good, that's for damn sure. But more than that, you threatened the safety of his pack. That's not something you can fix by batting your eyelashes at him and saying you're sorry."

His pack. When Gage had used the word before, she hadn't truly realized what it meant. The SWAT officers weren't merely a team—they were a family. She'd not only ripped out Gage's heart, she'd threatened his family. Why the hell would he listen to a word she had to say?

Tears flooded her eyes and she blinked them back. She had to talk to him. If for no other reason than to let him know that she'd never tell a soul about his pack. Even if she couldn't get him to listen to anything else, she wanted him to know he wouldn't need to look over his shoulder for the rest of his life. After all the damage she'd inflicted, that was all she could hope for. It would have to be enough.

She gave Xander a beseeching look, not caring that her eyes were wet with tears. "I don't know if I can fix this either, but I have to try. Five minutes, that's all I'm asking for. If Gage wants me to leave after he hears what I have to say, I'll go. I promise."

Xander was silent for so long she was afraid he'd turn around and walk away. But instead he unlocked the gate and jerked it open.

"You've got five minutes," he told her. "You'd better make them count."

Mac had to practically run to keep up with Xander as he led the way to the training building. When they got there, he yanked open the door and waited for her to go ahead of him. She took a deep breath and walked in...and immediately felt like she'd stepped off a bus at the wrong stop.

Fourteen pairs of yellow eyes turned her way. There was shock in some of them, disbelief in others, and outright hatred in the rest.

Gage wasn't with them.

The place looked as if it'd been ransacked. Maps covered one whole table. Passports and cell phones were scattered across another. And in the center of the room there was a pile of black duffel bags. They were getting ready to leave, and they were traveling light.

Where would a pack of werewolves go to disappear? And would Gage split them up or try to keep them together?

It didn't matter. If she didn't convince them to stay, she'd never know.

"What the hell are you doing here?" Cooper demanded.

Mac flinched. "I have to talk to Gage."

Her words were met with deep-throated growls that made her shiver. If she wasn't so in love with Gage, she probably would have turned and fled. Not that she would have gotten very far with Xander behind her, breathing down her neck.

"You should leave now, Mac," Cooper said. "Before this gets ugly."

She swallowed hard. "I can't leave. Not until I talk to Gage."

Trevino advanced on her, teeth bared, claws extended. Brooks, Martinez, and Nelson joined him, their golden eyes on fire.

Mac was thinking she might have to run for the door after all when Xander stepped in front of her, putting himself between her and the men. She barely had time to recover from her shock before Becker and Lowry moved to stand beside Xander, appointing themselves her protectors.

The growls around the room got louder.

Crap.

Mac wanted to think they wouldn't fight each other, but she realized she didn't know a damn thing about how werewolves behaved. Maybe they fought each other all the time.

"That's enough."

Gage's deep voice cut through the snarls and the growling immediately stopped.

Mac stepped out from behind the solid wall of muscle in front of her to see Gage standing in the doorway of his office. She started to hurry over to him, but he froze her with a glare.

"What do you want, Mackenzie?" he demanded. "You agreed to give us twenty-four hours before you told anyone. It's barely been five."

Had it really? It felt like it had been a lifetime to her. She glanced at the other men, then looked at him. "Can I talk to you alone?"

"I don't have time for this, Mackenzie. We're leaving in ten minutes. Anything you came to say to me can be said in front of my pack. So, just say it and get out."

The anger in his voice was almost more than she could bear. Tears clogged her throat and she couldn't find her voice. But she had to say something, and fast. Gage looked as if he was ready to walk back in his office and close the door.

She took a deep breath and let it out halfway—just like Gage had taught during their shooting lesson. "I'm sorry."

Gage shrugged. "No need to apologize. You're just doing your job, right?"

"No! Well...yes, but..." Mac shook her head. This wasn't coming out the way she'd rehearsed it. "You were right when you said it wasn't my secret to tell."

Gage's brows drew together. "What are you saying, Mackenzie?"

"I'm saying that I'm never going to tell anyone about what you are." She looked at the other men. "Any of you."

Becker cocked a brow. "And we're supposed to just take your word on that?"

She reached in her back pocket and pulled out her camera, holding it out to him. "Take it. I have no story without it. No one would believe me."

Becker took the camera. "How do we know you didn't already download it?"

They weren't going to make this easy on her, were they? "Would I be here now if I did?"

"Maybe you're trying to keep us in town long enough for your story to hit the street," Gage said softly.

She turned to see him standing a few feet away. It broke her heart to see the distrust in his eyes. "I wouldn't do that."

He snorted. "Forgive me if I find that a little hard to

believe. A few hours ago you had absolutely no problem telling the whole world about us, regardless of what it cost."

Mac blinked back tears. Xander had been right—she couldn't fix this. She'd burned every bridge behind her and there was no going back. Why hadn't she thought before she'd opened her big mouth back at the barn?

"I know it's no excuse, but I've spent my whole life chasing one big story after the next. When I realized what I stumbled onto, the journalist in me took over." She moved to close the last little distance between them and looked up forlornly into his beautiful eyes. "But when I stopped to think for just a few minutes, my head had a chance to catch up and I knew I'd done something really stupid. I'd thrown away the chance to be with someone special. Someone I wanted to spend the rest of my life with."

Gage didn't say anything. He just stared at her like he didn't know what the hell she was babbling about.

A tear trickled down her cheek and she wiped it away with a hand that shook. "When we were back at your apartment, I said you could tell me anything. When you decided to trust me with your biggest secret, I betrayed that trust. And for that I'm sorrier than you'll ever know. I know that I have no right to ask you to trust me now, but I'm begging you to believe me when I say I won't tell anyone about you or your pack."

Another tear found its way down her face, and then another. This time she didn't wipe them away. There was nothing left to say. Either Gage would believe her and stay, or he wouldn't, and she'd never see him again.

Golden eyes held her captive. "What made you change your mind?" Gage asked.

Mac thought it would have been obvious why she was standing here in front of him pouring out her heart. But maybe it wasn't. Maybe Gage assumed it was because she had a guilty conscience.

She looked around the room. The other men were regarding her just as intently as before. Only now, the open hostility that had been on their faces had been replaced with curiosity.

Could she tell Gage what was in her heart in front of them? But if she didn't, nothing she already said would mean anything.

Mac wiped away the tears on her face. Then she took a deep breath, lifted her chin, and told him the truth.

"I love you."

She held her breath, waiting for him to say something. And waited...and waited...and waited.

But Gage just stood there still as a statue, his face unreadable.

"Um, Sarg. I'm not real familiar with this part, but I think you're supposed to say something," Cooper said softly.

Gage still didn't say anything. Instead, he took her hand and led her across the room toward his office. Before she had time to think, they were in his office and he'd closed the door behind them. He was standing so close to her that it was almost hard to breathe.

"Just like that?" he asked hoarsely. "You're going to just spring that on me in front of everyone?"

Was he angry? Her stomach lurched at the thought. But she'd said it, and there was no taking it back. "I wanted to talk to you privately, but you wanted to talk right there in front of your pack, so I said it in front of them."

He slipped a finger under her chin and tilted her head up. "And were you telling the truth?"

Mac pulled away from his finger. He might be the injured party in this whole thing, but that didn't mean she wasn't hurting, too. And right now, his attitude was annoying. "Of course I was, but I doubt you'd believe me no matter what I said."

He slipped his finger under her chin and very gently lifted her face up again. "Try me. Say it again—just to me."

His eyes were glowing that deep gold-yellow they'd been back at the barn. It was hard to look into those eyes and not be drawn in. She licked her lips. It had almost been easier to say those words with a crowd around her. But it was impossible to be this close to him and not say what she felt.

"I love you," she told him softly, not pulling away this time. "Is that so impossible to believe?"

"Impossible? No," he murmured. "But surprising? Yes. Just a just a few hours ago, you were ready to expose my secret to the world. Now you've decided that you're in love with me?"

Before dropping his finger, he let it trace down the line of her throat just a bit. She tried not to let herself shiver at his touch. She'd never expected to feel it again.

"Can I ask what brought on this epiphany?" he said.

"I'd like to claim that I figured it all out on my own, but to be honest, it was Zak."

Gage frowned. "You told Zak about us?"

She took a step back so she could think straight. "That you and the rest of the SWAT team are werewolves? No. But I did tell him about you and me. It didn't take him long to point out that I was destroying the best relationship I've ever had, with the only man I've ever loved."

Gage smiled just a little, but it felt like the sun finally coming out after a really long rain. "Pretty perceptive… for a guy."

"True," she agreed. "He's good at seeing the things I frequently miss, and he's never afraid to tell me when I'm being stupid."

Gage was the one to close the distance this time, and she sighed when she felt his big hands slide down her arms to pull her even closer. "So you love me, huh?"

She dropped her head. "I know you don't have any reason to believe me, but it's true."

"I believe you."

She looked up at him. "You do?"

He nodded. "I'd know if you were lying. When a person lies, their pulse races, their breath hitches, their muscles tense. They even release certain pheromones. You're not doing any of that."

She frowned. "You can smell if a person is lying?"

"Uh-huh. And hearing you say those words and knowing you aren't lying…that means a lot."

Her pulse kicked into high gear. "Does that mean you won't be leaving?"

His mouth curved. "I suppose I don't have a reason to leave now, do I?"

She shook her head, fresh tears forming in her eyes—the happy kind this time.

Gage searched her face, his yellow gaze bright. "Does it bother you when my eyes are like this?"

She shook her head, not trusting herself to speak, afraid she'd say something wrong again and destroy everything.

"And is it hard for you to be this close to me—to have me touching you—knowing what I am?"

"No." She gave him a sheepish smile. "I'm just glad you're still willing to touch me."

He pushed her hair back, gently cupping her face in his hand. "I never wanted to stop."

Mac caught her lip between her teeth. As much as she loved hearing him say that, it only reminded her that even though they were standing close together, and even after all that had been said—the apologies and declarations of love—there was still a tremendous yawning chasm between them. There was one more leap of faith she'd need to take before they could completely close that gap. If she didn't make the first move, he might always think she feared what he was.

She went up on tiptoe and gave him the gentlest of kisses, hoping it would convey how much she loved him.

The glow in his eyes flared, then he bent his head and kissed her back. That kiss started out tenderly, too. But as her hands found their way to his chest and he pulled her against him, his mouth moved more urgently over hers, his fingers twisting into her hair.

And just like that, it was as if none of the idiocy had ever happened.

When he broke the kiss, Gage's eyes were back to their normal deep, honeyed brown, and he stared at her with the hunger she yearned for. Mac pulled him down for another kiss, but he stopped her with a look.

"I love you, too," he whispered.

Gage's actions at the barn had proclaimed his feelings for her far better than any mere words, but still...the words were nice. Really nice.

Then he was kissing her again. Knowing she'd regained what she'd been so sure she'd lost made her so giddy she felt like screaming. But with Gage's pack—she still couldn't believe how easily that rolled off the tongue—right outside in the other room, a scream probably wasn't a good idea.

So, she did the next best thing and started undoing the buttons on his shirt.

Gage lifted his head to look at her with an arched brow. "You know werewolves have really good hearing, right?"

Huh. No, she didn't know that. She smiled up at him, working at his buttons until they were all undone and she had a view of his chest and abs all the way down to his belt. She slid her hands under the edges of his shirt and caressed those exquisite muscles.

"Then I guess we'll just have to be quiet," she said softly.

Mac leaned forward and nibbled at the lines of his pecs. A low rumbling growl slipped out of him.

She pulled away to give him a reproving look. "What part of quiet didn't you understand?"

He slipped his fingers in her hair, urging her to go back to what she'd been doing. "Quiet, right. Got it."

When she kissed, nibbled, and licked her way down his chest and stomach, Gage did a better job of holding his tongue—but just barely. Still, she had to smile a little as she unbuckled his belt. If he'd had a problem staying silent for the first part, this part was really going to be tough on him.

Once she had his belt undone, she struggled to work his jeans and underwear together down over his hips. He helped some, but let her work for it, which she appreciated. Anticipation always made things better.

When Mac had everything down around his thighs, she nudged him back so he was perched on the edge of his desk. She wanted him to be able to lean back and relax because she was going to make sure he never forgot what he meant to her.

His cock was already hard and jutting out eagerly before her. She ran her hands up his thighs until she reached the base of his cock. Then she carefully curled one hand around his shaft and tilted her head up to look at him.

"Quiet, remember?"

He gazed down at her with heated eyes. "I'll try."

That was good enough for Mac. She dipped her head and wrapped her lips around him. Gage didn't exactly remain silent, but the groan he let out wasn't much more than a deep sigh. She doubted even a werewolf would be able to hear it unless he was standing right outside the door.

She worked her mouth up and down his shaft, moving her hand in smooth counterpoint to the rhythm of her tongue. Gage tasted so damn good it was difficult not to cut loose with a few moans of her own. She could do this all night, letting him come in her mouth, then getting him hard so she could do it all over again. The thought alone made heat pool between her thighs.

Gage slipped his fingers into her hair, guiding her movement, urging her to go faster…deeper. But just when liftoff seemed imminent, he used that hand in her hair to bring her to a slow halt, then tug her mouth off his cock.

She started to complain, but he'd already tugged her to her feet and urged her back against his desk before she had the chance. He had her shoes off before she even found her voice.

"Um, I was still working down there."

He gave her a sly look as he yanked open the buttons on her jeans and pulled them off. She had to grab hold of the edge of his desk to keep from being dragged off with them.

"Maybe," he agreed. "But it's my turn now."

Gage tossed her pants and panties over to the couch that lined one wall, leaving her leaning back on his desk wearing nothing but her top. He reached around her and shoved stuff aside, then urged her back. When he dropped to his knees between her spread legs, his eyes were once again gold. Was he flipping them back and forth to freak her out?

Maybe, but that wasn't the effect it was having. In fact, it was just plain turning her on.

"Remember," he said in that low, rumbling growl she was already coming to love. "No screaming."

He lowered his head and nibbled his way down her inner thigh, and for one crazy moment, Mac wondered if Gage's teeth were sharper when his eyes were gold like they were now. If he nipped her hard enough, would she turn into a werewolf, too?

But those thoughts disappeared the second his warm mouth came into contact with her pussy. If his teeth were any sharper or longer than normal, she didn't notice it when his tongue slipped into her folds.

She tried hard to keep her head up so she could watch him go down on her, but as tantalizing as the view was, she couldn't do it for very long. As Gage's tongue glided up and down her folds over and over, then finally focusing on her clit, she got so dizzy she had no choice but to drop her head back and give herself over to the pleasure.

Right then, she was far beyond worrying about whether Gage's pack heard her, but she bit down on her knuckle anyway, hoping it would muffle her moans.

Mac gripped the edge of the desk with her other hand and lifted her head. The sight of Gage lapping at her pussy—his glowing eyes locked with hers—was the most erotic thing she'd ever seen. She forced herself to keep watching him as he made love to her with his mouth, drawing her orgasm out longer and longer until she was sure she would scream.

Only when her whole body was shaking and spasming like she was holding a bolt of lightning did Gage finally let up and move his mouth off her clit. Even then, he continued to slowly lave his tongue across her folds, making little sparks dance in her vision.

She dropped her head back to the desk and gasped for air as Gage went back to nibbling on her inner thighs. At some point he stopped that, too, but she didn't know what he was up to until she heard his jeans hit the floor.

She looked up to find him grinning at her.

"I love watching you come, did you know that?"

Mac returned his smile. "No, I didn't."

She licked her lips, waiting for him to climb up on the desk with her, but he simply stood there gazing at her.

"Thank you for coming back to me," he said, his voice rough with emotion. "I don't like to think what my life would have been like without you."

The words made her heart squeeze in her chest. What did a woman say to something like that? *You're welcome* just didn't seem to cut it.

She beckoned him closer. "Care to show me your appreciation in a gratuitously physical manner?"

He hesitated. "Yeah, about that. I don't have a condom. One of the other guys might, but…"

She grimaced. "Let's not. Fortunately, one of us was planning ahead. I started taking birth control pills Wednesday morning."

"Wednesday?" He frowned. "The morning after I took you to dinner at Chambre Francaise? How did you know we'd sleep together?"

"I didn't," she said softly. "But I'd hoped."

Mac motioned him closer again, spreading her legs wider in open invitation. Gage stripped off the rest of his clothes and moved between her legs. He ran a hand up the outside of one thigh, making her quiver all over.

"And you've been taking the pill long enough for it to work, right?" he asked.

She nodded. "Most experts recommend seven days, but I think six days is okay. Unless you're not planning to stay with me if I get pregnant? Now that we're mentioning it, can you get me pregnant?"

Gage trailed his hand down her thigh and across her stomach. He left it there, caressing her lightly. "Yes, I could get you pregnant. And before you ask—no, the kid wouldn't come out growling and howling at the moon. That's not the way it works. And no, if I got you pregnant, I wouldn't leave you."

He leaned over and she wrapped her legs around him, pulling him closer and preparing herself for the rush that came whenever he slid inside her. He didn't enter her, though. Instead he gazed down at her so intently she started to worry he wouldn't make love to her without protection. But then he licked his lips and she knew he was trying to figure out how to say something…big.

"Mackenzie, there's something you need to know. Something important."

O-kay. "Is now the best time for this?"

"Now is the perfect time for this," he said. "Werewolves have an urban legend that's been around as long as there have been werewolves. Whether they'll admit it or not, they all believe there's one special person out there for them. As in *The One*—capital *T*, capital *O*. Unfortunately, while the legend is so common as to be cliché, I've never met a werewolf who found *The One*."

Gage leaned closer, so his lips were only millimeters from hers. "But I've found mine. You can't understand the significance of that until I tell you that none of the werewolves in my pack have ever been in a serious relationship—not one. Sure, they sleep with women, maybe even live with them for a while, but it never lasts. Hell, I've never been involved with a woman that I even wanted to be around for more than maybe two weeks at the longest, until I met you."

His mouth traced along her jawline and settled next to her ear, his voice dropping to a whisper. "I knew from the moment you stepped into the operations vehicle that first day that there was something different about you. I didn't know at first that you were *The One*—I never believed in that kind of stuff—but some of the guys knew. Cooper. Xander."

"Xander?" she repeated. "He didn't even like me."

"Regardless of what he tells people, Xander believes the legend more than any werewolf I've ever met. But he figured you'd use the irresistible attraction I felt for you against me to get your story."

She winced. "Which is basically what I did. No

wonder he looked like he wanted to bite my head off when I showed up tonight."

"It doesn't matter now," Gage whispered. "We're together, and I'm never going anywhere. I never could have."

She wrapped her arms around him and pulled him more tightly against her, burying her face in his neck. "But you were leaving when I got here."

He lifted his head so he could gaze down at her. "I was, but only long enough to make sure my pack got out of town and someplace safe. I was coming back to make sure Hardy was no longer a threat to you. Then I intended to watch over you from a distance for the rest of my life."

The look in his eyes told her he wasn't kidding. She didn't let herself dwell on the part about making sure Hardy was no longer a threat. She was just comforted by the thought that Gage would have willingly lived on the street outside her apartment just to be near her. It was insane, but romantic at the same time.

She threaded her fingers in his hair, pulling him down for a kiss. He growled, kissing her back with an urgency that left her gasping for breath by the time he lifted his head.

Straightening, he grabbed her ankles and spread her legs wide. Mac did her best to be quiet, but she couldn't hold back the moan that escaped her lips when he pushed inside her. Right then she didn't want to be quiet. She wanted to shout her pleasure to the world—and if his pack heard, oh well.

Gage took her slowly, sliding his thickness deep with steady, even strokes that made her whole body tremble. He moved in and out of her over and over, and the whole time, he gazed down at her with those vivid gold eyes.

She was so in love with him that it hurt, and right there

in the middle of their lovemaking, she thanked God for helping her repair the damage she'd done and for making this moment possible.

Her orgasm built higher and higher, but it wouldn't crest, even though Mac was sure she was about to explode at any minute.

"Harder," she begged softly.

"You sure you won't scream?"

She nodded.

It was possible that a little cry slipped out when she orgasmed, but she was too busy coming to care. And when Gage stiffened and came inside her? It was like heaven. The closeness she felt with him at that moment was the only thing that could ever rival the pleasure she'd felt from the orgasm he'd given her.

Then Gage was leaning over her, kissing her hotly on the mouth while his cock still pulsed inside her. It was impossible not to whimper a little with the aftershocks of her orgasm vibrating through her.

Mac felt wetness on her face and realized that she was crying. Gage gently kissed away her tears.

"That was amazing," she said softly.

"Yeah, it was." He gave her another kiss, then gently pulled her into a sitting position. "We should probably get back out there."

But he made no move to get dressed. Instead he stood there between her legs, gazing down at her.

Mac traced her fingers over the tattoo of the wolf on his chest. The design certainly held a lot more meaning than it had the first time she'd seen it.

"So, what's up with this tattoo?" she asked softly.

Gage chuckled. "It's the ultimate inside joke. For us,

SWAT stands for Special Wolf Alpha Team, since we're all werewolves and alpha-male types. Get it?"

She poked him hard in the ribs. "Yeah, I get it. I'm sex-addled, not slow."

Gage laughed again.

Mac went back to playing with his tattoo. She'd never get tired of seeing the way the wolf image moved over his well-muscled skin. Who was she kidding? She'd love playing with his chest if there was a hippo tattooed on it.

She thought back to what Gage had said about her being *The One*. Maybe he and the werewolf legend were onto something. How else could she explain why she'd tossed aside a once-in-a-lifetime story for a man she'd met less than a week ago? Or that the thought of not having him in her life made her hyperventilate? They were truly made for each other. And if that meant there was some mythical force at work here, she was more than ready to believe it. If werewolves could be real, why not a cosmic love connection?

Mac lifted her head to look at him. "So, what I saw tonight—is that as werewolfy as you get?"

His mouth twitched. "Not exactly. I get a little bit more werewolfy."

"How much more?"

"Think four paws and a tail."

Her eyes went wide. "Like a real wolf. Seriously?"

He nodded.

"Can I see?"

He chuckled. "Not right now. Let's take baby steps with this, okay?"

She made a face. "Okay. But you have to promise to show me."

A few hours ago, she was freaked out about him being a werewolf, and now she couldn't wait to see him turn again. Love could do that to a woman.

Mac went back to playing with his tattoo again. "Did you bite all the guys in your pack to turn them into werewolves?"

He snorted. "Hell, no."

"Then how did you do it?"

"I didn't. You can't turn someone into a werewolf by biting them like in the movies. We're born like this." When she jerked up to look at him, he laughed. "I don't mean we're born with claws and fangs. That might be a little hard to hide."

"What then?"

"From what we've been able to figure out, there's something in our DNA that triggers our change into werewolves when the right set of circumstances come along."

"What kind of circumstances?"

"A person carrying the werewolf gene, or whatever you call it, has to be exposed to a high-stress, life-threatening situation. If the person makes it through the situation, they come out the other side a werewolf."

She chewed on her lips as she considered that. "That's what happened to you in Iraq, wasn't it? When all the other members of your squad were killed?"

He nodded. "That's why I had to get out of the Army. I didn't have a clue what was happening to me, and I needed time to figure it out."

As if seeing all his friends killed wasn't enough, he then had to figure out what it meant to be a werewolf, too.

"Is that how it happened to your pack, too? Combat?"

"Some of them," he said. "Cooper got blown through a building in Iraq. McCall's convoy got hit in Afghanistan.

That's where Duncan, our senior medic, was turned, too. He got trapped in a small, forward-operating base that was completely overrun. Most of the others changed while they were on the job, after getting shot."

"And you just found them and recruited them?"

"Pretty much." Gage ran his hand up and down her arm. "I didn't understand the significance of the Pack thing until I had about a half dozen of them together. That's when I realized we all work better—and are happier—in an environment like this."

Mac smiled. Gage just couldn't help it. He was the kind of man who worried about others. "But how did you find all of them? I assume there isn't a website you can look on."

"I wish." He let out a short laugh. "Over the years, I've gotten good at knowing what to look for. I read a lot of news articles about cops and stuff, looking for the right clues."

Clever, she thought. "How do you think your pack's going to handle it when you tell them that we're back together again?"

He chuckled. "They already know. It was sort of hard to miss."

"I was quiet!"

"Not to a werewolf. Even if they couldn't hear your sexy little moans—which they did, by the way—they wouldn't have been able to miss that scrumptious smell you put off when you're aroused."

Mac groaned, her face hot. "I'll never be able to look any of them in the eye again."

Gage cupped her cheek. "There aren't any secrets in the Pack, babe. You're just going have to learn to accept it. These guys are going to know every time we have sex because they'll smell my scent on you, and yours on me."

"Will that—you and me together, I mean—cause problems?"

She didn't know much about wolf packs in the wild, but she thought she remembered reading something about how female wolves in heat caused all the males to go crazy.

But Gage shook his head. "They won't have a problem with it. You give them hope."

She frowned. "What do you mean?"

"They look at you and know the legend is true, that there really is someone special out there for every one of them." He grinned. "And if they tease you now and then, it's just because you're part of our pack now."

Part of the Pack. She liked the sound of that.

He gave her a kiss. "Come on. Let's go see what they're up to out there."

Remembering what Gage had said about werewolves and their keen sense of hearing, Mac would rather have put off facing the Pack as long as possible, but she got dressed and let Gage lead her out of his office and into the main room anyway.

She'd hoped the guys wouldn't be there, but the entire Pack was sitting around casually in their chairs, holding up cards with Olympic-style scores on them. She had more than enough imagination to figure out what they were grading them on. Her face turned bright red. Embarrassed didn't even begin to cover it.

But after a good laugh, every one of the guys gave her a hug and welcomed her into the Pack. She tried not to make a big deal out of it, but she was touched. She could see Gage was touched, too.

Chapter 12

"THE JUDGE SIGNED THE WARRANTS AGAINST HARDY," Gage told Mackenzie when he walked back into his office.

She didn't exactly look thrilled to hear his news, but then again, he hadn't expected her to be. They'd spent a good part of the early morning hours talking about what going after Hardy would entail, and Mackenzie had been pretty clear about her feelings that she thought someone else in the department should be kicking in the man's front door instead of him and his team. They'd barely survived Hardy's first attack, and now Gage wanted to put himself right in the crazy bastard's sights.

"I have to do this, sweetheart," he'd told her.

She'd tried hard not to cry, but he'd seen the tears. "Why?"

"Because there's a good chance Hardy will resist when the DPD shows up on his doorstep." Gage gently wiped a tear from her cheek with his thumb. "If that happens, a lot of cops will die. Unless my pack and I are there."

Mackenzie still hadn't liked it, but at least she'd understood.

With the twenty-four-hour news outlets already plastering Walter Hardy's face all over the TV and Internet, sensationalizing the attempted murders and detailing the supposed connections between him and the dead gunmen at the barn, it hadn't been hard finding a judge to sign the search warrants the police needed.

"When will you serve them?" she asked as she sat up from the couch where she'd been napping. Her hair was a wild tumble around her shoulders and she looked more tired than she had when he'd left to go downtown for the meeting at police headquarters at dawn this morning. Gage doubted she'd gotten any sleep.

"We're going to hit all of his major business locations and his residential addresses simultaneously at noon." He glanced at his watch. "In a little less than three hours."

Mackenzie sat up straighter, alarm clear in her eyes. "That fast? Don't you need more time for planning?"

"Normally, we'd want at least a full day to plan out an operation this ambitious, but in this case, our biggest concern is that Hardy will get wind of what we're doing and flee the country before we move on him. He likely has people on his payroll planted throughout the police department and the prosecutor's office, so our only hope is to limit the number of people who know the details and hit him faster than he expects."

Gage could already hear his men getting ready outside, talking in low voices about team assignments and how they would deal with the possibility of serious resistance at multiple locations around the Dallas area at the same time.

Mackenzie stood up and crossed the room to hug him. "When do you leave?" she asked, the words muffled against his shoulder.

"Thirty minutes." Gage hated seeing her worry like this. "I'm leading the team into Hardy's main residence. The prosecutor thinks that's where we're likely to find the most evidence."

"What happens if he's already gotten rid of any

evidence that could tie him directly to the people who tried to kill us—if there ever was any?"

Gage didn't want to think about that. They had this one shot to find something worthwhile on Hardy. If they did, they had a good chance of getting him off the street. If they blew it, Hardy would hit back even harder than he had the last time Gage had come for him. And the son of a bitch had already shown a penchant for aiming at Mackenzie.

But he didn't voice any of those thoughts. Mackenzie needed to hear that this was all going to work out okay.

"That's not going to happen. We'll get him, one way or the other."

Fortunately, Mackenzie was so preoccupied that the anger in his voice escaped her notice. That was good, because this was another topic they'd argued about in the early morning hours, when he'd made the mistake of saying he'd track Hardy down and tear him into several small, Butterball turkey–sized pieces before he ever let the man get near her again. Mackenzie had come seriously unglued, complete with finger waving and foot stamping.

"You aren't a murderer, and I'm not going to stand by and let you turn into one," she'd told him angrily.

Yeah, he realized as he stood in his office and hugged her tightly. *She's still an idealist*. Learning about werewolves hadn't changed that.

Mac chewed on her lip as Gage loaded more equipment into the operations vehicle, then climbed in with Delaney and Lowry. There were way too many different locations to hit and not enough SWAT officers to go around. Which meant that one or two would go in with regular cops for backup at each target. Gage, Delaney, and Lowry were hitting Hardy's home out in Southlake. Gage had assured her it wasn't any more dangerous than the other locations, but if that were true, he wouldn't have insisted on taking that one himself, and there wouldn't have been two other SWAT guys going to the same location.

The anxious feeling that had been growing all day suddenly turned to fear. She jumped up on the running board on the passenger side of the vehicle. Grabbing Gage by the collar, she pulled him close and kissed him, not caring if she embarrassed him in from of Delaney and Lowry.

"Be careful out there, okay?" she whispered.

His mouth curved. "I will. And you stay inside as much as possible. If you come out, I want someone with you."

Mac nodded. Cooper, Becker, and Brooks were staying back to supposedly man the compound, but in reality, they'd been pulled out of action so they could be there to protect her. She expected them to be unhappy about being left behind, but they weren't nearly as upset as she thought they'd be. In some bizarre way that only a man could understand, the three werewolves took it as some kind of distinction that their alpha leader had selected them to stay back and watch over his woman. She was already comfortable with Becker and Cooper, and Brooks was so damn big that she couldn't help but feel safe around him.

Still, as she watched Gage drive off, she couldn't deny she was terrified, not for herself, but for Gage and all the other guys in the Pack. They might be stronger and more capable than ordinary men, but that didn't mean they couldn't get hurt, or worse.

Mac and the guys spent the next few hours listening

to the drama unfold over the police radio, with frequent updates from the teams. During the initial entry, there had been some resistance, but not anything extreme—yet.

Of course, when the press got wind of what was going down, every TV news channel lit up like a Christmas tree, so they were able to watch the whole thing going down live. Around seven that night, Gage called to talk to Cooper. Mac worried her bottom lip as she waited for a report.

"Hardy wasn't at his house or any of the places the teams have searched so far," Cooper said when he hung up.

Crap.

"But on the upside," Cooper continued, "Gage says they've already found evidence tying Hardy to the gunmen he hired. Apparently the man was so obsessed with getting someone who could kill the two of you that he didn't even slow down to hide his tracks. Arrest warrants are on a judge's desk right now."

Hearing about the evidence helped, but she'd feel a whole hell of a lot better if they could locate Hardy.

Mac tried calling Zak to see if he'd heard anything, but it went to his voice mail. She left a message asking him to call, then hung up. Her cell rang before she could even get it back in her pocket. Zak's name popped up on the display. That was fast.

"Hey," she said.

"Mackenzie Stone?" a woman's voice asked.

Mac frowned, not recognizing the voice. "Yes."

"This is Amy Bronson. I'm a nurse in the Intensive Care Unit at Mercy General. We found your name listed in Mr. Gibson's phone under his emergency contact."

Oh God. "Is Zak okay?"

"We've been able to stabilize him, but he was beaten pretty badly."

"Beaten? Where? By whom?"

"We're not sure. A few tourists found him in an alley and brought him to the emergency room about thirty minutes ago," the nurse said. "Does Mr. Gibson have any family we can call, or would you rather do that?"

"I'm the only family he has," Mac said.

"Then you might want to come quickly."

Mac clutched the phone to her chest. "It's Zak," she told the three werewolves. "Someone beat him up. I have to go to the hospital."

She jumped to her feet, but Cooper caught her arm. "Hang on. Let me call back and make sure Zak's really there. Which hospital?"

Crap. Cooper thought it might be a trap. She hadn't even considered that. "Mercy General. The nurse said he was in ICU."

Mac listened impatiently as Cooper identified himself and gave his badge number to whoever answered the phone. The look on his face told her all she needed to know.

"He's there, and he's in bad shape," Cooper told her when he hung up. "Come on. We'll drive you."

Fifteen minutes later, Brooks pulled the SUV up to the emergency entrance. Mac would have jumped out right away, but Cooper stopped her.

"Wait until Becker gives the all clear."

Becker got out and scanned the surrounding area, then nodded.

Mac was out of the car and running toward the building

when she heard gunshots—a lot of gunshots. She whirled around to see Cooper and Becker falling to the ground, blood staining their uniform shirts. More gunfire echoed as whoever was shooting riddled the SUV with bullets.

Mac froze for a moment, then sprinted toward the downed SWAT officers. But she didn't make it more than a few steps before someone grabbed her and dragged her across the parking lot to a four-door sedan that squealed to a stop.

When the guy tossed her in the back, she immediately lunged for the opposite door, but a second man jumped in, trapping her. The man who'd first grabbed her shoved her back against the seat as the driver punched the gas.

"Yeah, boss, we have her," the man in the front passenger seat said, turning to give her a smirk.

Roscoe Patterson. Mac would recognize that smug face of his anywhere—even with bruises covering half of it. There was a soft cast on his right wrist, too. She wondered who had beaten him up.

"She ran straight to the hospital, just like you said," Patterson continued. "We put down three of those fucking SWAT assholes, too. Told you there was no reason to bring outsiders in to deal with this. We'll be at the hangar in thirty minutes."

Mac swallowed hard. She wasn't sure how badly Cooper and Becker had been hit, but Hardy's thugs must have put a couple hundred rounds into the SUV. There was no way Brooks had made it through unscathed. Gage had told her werewolves weren't immortal. Could Hardy's men have killed them? Tears stung her eyes. She didn't even want to think about that.

"What are you going to do to me?" Mac asked.

Patterson ignored her as he said something into a hand-held radio. Since he kept looking in the side mirror, he must have been talking to someone in a car behind them. She was right. A moment later, another sedan passed them and took the lead.

Patterson gave her a nasty smile. "Honestly, I don't know what Mr. Hardy has in store for you. But considering that your boyfriend is responsible for the destruction of his entire business empire, killed his son, then had the balls to walk in and threaten him in his own home, I assume it's going to be something very painful. I really wouldn't want to be you when the boss gets his hands on you."

Mac didn't have a clue what the man meant about Gage threatening Hardy in his own home. But if Hardy had gone to the effort of grabbing her alive, it meant he had something specific in mind for her. If he'd wanted her dead, his men would have gunned her down like Cooper, Becker, and Brooks.

They must have been the ones who'd beat up Zak and used him as bait to draw her out of the compound. She had no idea how Hardy could have known about her relationship with Zak and that it was one thing that would pull her out of hiding, but somehow he had.

Mac saw a blur of movement out of the corner of her eye. Up ahead in the darkness, something big slammed into the side of the car in front of them, sending it spinning out of control. The driver of the car Mac was in swerved, barely avoiding it, then slowed to a stop.

"Shit," muttered the guy beside her. "That was a freaking man who hit them."

"No way," Patterson said, turning to look over his

shoulder at the other car that was now thirty feet behind them.

"I know what I saw," the other man insisted. "It was a man. He hit them like he was tackling the damn car."

Mac had seen it, too, but she wasn't going to clarify that the man they'd seen wasn't really a man at all. She didn't know how it was possible, but Brooks had survived the ambush and chased down two speeding cars to rescue her. She hadn't realized a werewolf could do that. Then again, she didn't really know what a werewolf was capable of.

Gunshots echoed in the air. Mac turned to see orange flashes of light in the dark.

Patterson swore. "Get us out of here."

"What about the others?" the man driving asked.

"Screw them if they can't take care of themselves."

Over her shoulder, Mac saw a dark shape hurtling toward them. Even though she knew it was Brooks, she still screamed when he slammed into the passenger door hard enough to shatter the glass and dent the door panel. She screamed again when he yanked off the door and dragged out the man beside her.

She had enough sense to get out while she could. Or would have if the man on her right hadn't grabbed her at the same time the driver floored the gas and sped away. As they did, she caught sight of movement behind them.

"What the hell was that?" the driver asked.

Patterson was looking around everywhere at once. "How the fuck should I know? Just get us the hell out of here."

Mac jerked around, trying to get another glimpse of the werewolf chasing them, but it was too dark. It wasn't big enough to be Brooks, so it had to be either Cooper or Becker.

She braced herself, expecting whoever it was to slam into the car again, but nothing happened and the blurred shape fell back. She kept looking around, but twenty minutes later, they drove through a small gate somewhere on the backside of the airport and stopped in front of a series of hangars. The man beside her dragged her out of the backseat.

"Keep an eye out for Mr. Hardy," Patterson ordered the man, grabbing Mac's arm and pulling her toward a metal building. "We'll be leaving as soon as he takes care of her."

Mac fought Patterson, trying to jerk out of his grasp, but it was no good. Even with the soft cast on his arm, Patterson easily overpowered her and dragged her toward the door that another man was holding open for them.

"Stay out on the gate, and make sure no one followed us."

Before Patterson shoved her through the door, she got a chance to see the man alternating looks between the ripped-up car and the darkness beyond the gate. He didn't seem like he wanted to be out there, either.

Patterson dragged her across the hangar and around the big, sleek jet in the middle of it until they reached a door on the far side. Without a word, he opened the door and shoved her inside, slamming it behind her.

The room was almost completely dark except for an orange glow leaking through the row of small windows near the top of the outer wall. She looked around, but couldn't see much more than some shelves and a lot of boxes.

Mac ran her hand along the door for the knob, but it was locked. She jerked on it a few times, but it didn't give. She felt her way around the room, looking for another way out, but there weren't any other doors, and the only windows were nearly fifteen feet off the floor. There was no way she could get up there.

She didn't like thinking about what Walter Hardy had in mind for her. He was a vicious man with nothing left to lose. As Patterson had said, Hardy blamed Gage for everything that had happened to him, from the death of his son to the cops being on his trail. The powerful man had tried to take his anger out on the commander of the SWAT team, and failed. Mac could only assume that he'd decided to go after an easier target—her. Somehow Hardy knew she and Gage were together. He figured that if he couldn't hurt Gage directly, he'd do the next best thing and hurt someone who was important to him.

That thought terrified her so much it made her tremble, but one thing helped her keep it together. Gage and his pack would come for her—no matter how many of Hardy's men stood in their way.

—◆—

Gage had been pissed as hell to find out Hardy wasn't home. He'd really wanted to serve the man the warrants personally. But the search of the Southlake residence had still gone well. Not only had they connected Hardy to the men who'd come after him and Mackenzie, but they'd also gotten enough to put the guy away for years on racketeering charges, tax evasion, money laundering, illegal drugs—just to name a few. Gage couldn't believe Hardy had been so sloppy as to keep records of all his dealings. It was like he didn't think the cops would dare come after him.

He was still worried no one had seen Hardy yet, though. Gage was just about to go check to see if the deputy chief had heard anything when his cell phone rang.

"Dixon."

"Hardy's men grabbed Mac," Brooks said simply.

Gage's heart stopped. "What? When?"

"About ten minutes ago. The bastards beat up Zak to lure Mac to the hospital. We chased them for a couple miles, but they got away."

Shit.

"I'm on my way. Where are you?"

After Brooks gave him the location, Gage shoved his phone in his pocket, then shouted for Delaney and Lowry to get in the vehicle. He saw Mason glance his way. Gage pretended not to see him. They didn't need SWAT on the scene now anyway.

Brooks had obviously alerted the whole team, because there were several SWAT SUVs parked along the side of the road where the senior corporal had said to meet him.

The road had been blocked off around what looked like a traffic accident. A dark sedan was lying in the ditch with the driver's side door smashed in and the windows missing. Bullet holes riddled the car, and there were four dead bodies lying in the grass, automatic weapons alongside them. Hundreds of shell casings were scattered around the area.

Gage's whole pack was clustered around the first SUV in the line. Well, not all of them. Becker and Xander were missing. Cooper was sitting on the hood of the car with his shirt off, a stoic look on his face while Trevino dug a bullet out of his shoulder. The team medic dropped it to the asphalt to join the others he'd already taken out. Shit, there were a lot of bloody bullets lying there.

Brooks turned. There was a dark purple and black bruise running down the big man's neck and into his collar that probably stretched across his shoulder and chest. It looked like he'd been hit by a freaking car.

"Any idea where they took Mackenzie?" Gage asked.

"We don't know for sure. All we know is that she was taken by Roscoe Patterson."

Brooks briefly outlined the call Mac had gotten from the hospital, the ambush they'd walked right into, and the subsequent chase.

"You rammed a car off the road?" Gage asked.

Werewolves were strong, and Brooks was stronger than most. But tackling a car? That was extreme.

"Yeah, I thought it was the car Mac was in." His jaw tightened. "It wasn't until I started yanking people out that I realized I'd hit the wrong one."

"That's when I ripped the door off the other car, but one of Hardy's thugs got in the way," Cooper said. "They sped off before I could pull Mac out. I tried to keep up with them, but I couldn't. Sorry, boss."

Gage appreciated the effort they'd gone to get her back. He knew there was nothing more they could have done. "And no one here has any idea where the car was heading?"

"No one who's alive," Cooper said. "We're hoping Becker gets lucky."

Gage frowned. "Where is Becker?"

"Trying to get in to talk to Zak," Brooks answered. "According to the nurse at the hospital, a couple of tourists brought Zak in. We assume those tourists were actually some of Hardy's men, and that Zak might have overheard something—either while they were beating the hell out of him, or while they were taking him to the hospital to be bait."

Gage wasn't sure what they could expect out of Zak. The guy didn't exactly seem like the kind of man who could pay attention to details while in the middle of an ass whooping. "And Xander?"

"He's there to make sure the doctors don't try to drag Becker in for surgery," Cooper supplied. "He got hit a few times, too. Not as many times as I was, but I think that's because he was using me as a shield."

There wasn't much they could do until Xander and Becker got some information, but that didn't mean they couldn't search the car and the men who had been in it. Maybe they'd get lucky.

Gage was digging through some suitcases in the trunk of the sedan when three police cruisers and an unmarked car pulled up beside them.

He spotted Deputy Chief Mason's salt-and-pepper hair in the front seat. Mike came over to stand next to Gage as Mason got out of the car. Shit, this was all he needed.

Mason's jaw was tight as he took in the bodies on the ground, the automatic weapons, and the bullet holes in the car. His eyes narrowed when he saw Cooper sitting on the hood of the SUV with blood covering half his chest and a SWAT medic leaning over him with a pair of forceps.

"What the hell is going on here?" he demanded, his gaze snapping to Gage and Mike. "First, I find out there was a shootout in front of Mercy General involving three of my SWAT officers. Then I learn you've ordered your entire team here. Have you lost your mind, Sergeant?"

Mason walked over and looked down at the first body he came to—a body that didn't have any obvious bullet wounds but had clearly been killed in an extremely brutal fashion. He made a face, then turned to Gage again.

"As if that isn't enough, I got a call on the way here that one of Hardy's enforcers is dead in a ditch about a mile up the road. The patrolman said it looked like someone threw the man out of a moving vehicle. What's left of him, anyway. They still haven't found his arm." The deputy chief strode over to Gage. "Maybe you can explain it to me."

Gage wasn't going to pull any punches with his superior. He didn't have the time, and neither did Mackenzie.

"Hardy's men abducted Mackenzie Stone about forty minutes ago and have taken her who the hell knows where. My guess is that they're delivering her to Hardy as we sit here on our thumbs."

Mason looked at him sharply. "The reporter? What would Hardy want with her?"

"Payback," Gage said simply. "I took away someone who was important to him, so he wants to take away someone who's important to me."

Mason's brows rose. "You and Stone?" He swore under his breath. "Fuck, you should have told me. You don't have a clue where she was taken?"

Gage shook his head. "Not yet, but I hope to soon."

Mason regarded him thoughtfully. "What do you plan to do once you figure out where Hardy took her?"

Gage didn't hesitate. "I'm going to get her back."

"By yourself?" his boss asked drily. "Without telling anyone else in the department?"

Gage didn't answer. He didn't give a shit about proper police procedure in a case like this. There was nothing that'd keep him from going after Mackenzie.

Mason sighed. "I'll get a BOLO out on Ms. Stone. Maybe we'll get lucky and someone saw where they took her. Then I'll get a team out here to take care of this mess."

The deputy chief walked away, leaving Gage to wonder if the man was really going to look the other way on something like this. Then his boss stopped and turned back to glare at him. "And get Cooper to the hospital before he bleeds to death."

Gage nodded as the deputy chief reached in the car for the radio. A few minutes later, Xander called.

"Tell me you talked to Zak," Gage said as he put the phone on speaker.

"We did," Xander replied. "Hardy's men really beat the shit out of him. Probably figured he'd die from it, but he's tougher than he looks. The doctors didn't think he'd even come to for a couple of days, but he was already awake and shouting to talk to someone from the SWAT team when we walked in."

"Does he know where Hardy's men took Mackenzie?"

"Maybe. After kicking in his door and doing a number on him, they tossed him in the trunk of their car for the drive to the hospital. Through the backseat, he heard them talking about a private hangar where Hardy keeps a jet. Zak thinks that's where they'd take Mac—so Hardy can kill her before he leaves the country."

That last part made Gage flinch, but he forced the image aside. He had to stay focused on the fact that he was going to get Mackenzie back safely. Zak's information wasn't as concrete and definitive as he would have preferred, but it was the best intel he was going to get at this point.

"Okay. I'm heading to the airport," he said. "Is Becker in good enough shape to do that computer thing he does and figure out where Hardy keeps his plane? There has to be some record somewhere that'll give us a clue where that hangar is."

"Don't worry, Sarg." Becker's voice came on the line. "I'm already on it. If it's a private hangar, it'll be on the north side of the airport. Riggs and I will meet you outside the airport on the expressway. I'll have something specific before you get there."

Gage hadn't been asking them to join him, but he appreciated it anyway.

"Gage." Xander's voice came back on. "You know Hardy is bound to have a lot of his men around the place. Who else is going in with us?"

Gage didn't answer. He turned to look around the blocked section of highway and was surprised to see that his pack had stopped digging for clues and come to stand in front of him, their faces set and determined. His gaze lingered on Brooks and Cooper, still torn and bloody from their last encounter with Hardy's men. Their faces were no less determined than the others.

He couldn't ask any of them to do this with him. Hardy was going to have an army of thugs around him, and whether Mason looked the other way or not, this operation wasn't likely to go down well with Internal Affairs and the politicians down at police headquarters. They were going to figure out that Gage had broken every rule in the book because his girlfriend was involved. He didn't care what they did to him, but if any of his men went in there with him, they'd be risking their futures in the department as well. He couldn't ask them to do that.

But as he looked at each of their faces, he realized he didn't have to ask them.

"We're all going," he told Xander.

Chapter 13

MAYBE SHE'D HEARD WRONG. PUSHING THE HEAVY shelving unit under the window had made a lot of noise. But no. She'd heard just fine. A car had pulled into the hangar. That squeal of tires had to be Hardy. She was out of time.

Heart racing, Mac glanced over at the door to make sure the pieces of the ruler she'd broken and wedged underneath it were in place. They wouldn't keep Hardy and his men out, but they would slow them down long enough for her to escape. She hoped.

Of course, she would have been out of here fifteen minutes ago if the shelf hadn't been so damn heavy to move. She was probably taking her life in her hands climbing up on the precariously balanced boxes she'd put on the top shelf so she could reach the window, but she didn't have a choice. She couldn't wait around for Gage and his pack to show up and save her. Oh, she knew they'd come—she was just worried she'd be dead by the time they got here. She hated to think about it, but there was a real possibility that Brooks, Cooper, and Becker had succumbed to their injuries after trying to rescue her. Gage might not even know what happened to her.

Mac swallowed hard at that painful thought and reached for another box just as footsteps sounded outside the door. She froze, holding her breath. *Go away*, she prayed silently. *Just give me one more minute.*

The doorknob jiggled. Muttering a curse, she hefted another case of paper to the top shelf, then scrambled up after it. The boxes of paper made the unit top-heavy as hell, and it wobbled wildly under her weight.

Just stay together long enough to let me reach the window.

It would be just her luck to have the shelf collapse. Hardy wouldn't have to kill her. She'd break her neck all on her own.

The door shuddered as someone big slammed against it, but her wedges held. She quickly finished stacking the two cases of paper, then climbed on top of them. The shelf swayed dangerously, but she kept herself balanced in the center of her makeshift ladder and kept going.

"I don't know what you think you're gaining by this, Ms. Stone," Hardy shouted over the whir of a nearby jet engine. "I was only going to shoot you in the head, but if you make me work for it, I'm going to make it so much more painful for you."

Not exactly a great motivational speaker, was he? Unless he was trying to get her to hurry even more.

Mac grabbed the windowsill as a gunshot rang out. The bullet went clean through the door and smacked into the wall near the shelf she was standing on. If she wasn't so focused on keeping herself from tumbling off her precarious perch, she would have screamed for sure.

She grabbed the handle and levered it upward, then pushed open the window. It only tilted out about a foot, but that was more than she needed. She yanked herself up to the window frame and shimmied through the narrow gap as more bullets tore through the door. If Gage and the Pack were anywhere nearby, they had to have heard the gunshots, right?

Mac didn't exactly climb through the window as much as she fell through it. She tried to hold on to the edge of the frame so she could hang down then drop to the ground, but she ended up tumbling out the window in a nearly horizontal position. The asphalt came up to smack her faster than she expected, and for a moment, everything sparked, then went dark as pain engulfed the entire right side of her body.

But the sound of shooting coupled with Hardy's furious shouts jarred her out of the blackness. She winced and crawled to her feet. Crap, it felt like she'd broken everything important in her body.

"Get outside and find that bitch!" Hardy ordered.

Damn it. They were already in the room. It wouldn't take them long to figure out where she went.

In the darkness, Mac looked from the open runways and planes on her right to the long continuous row of hangars on her left. She'd never make it very far if she tried to run in a straight line across the open airfield. Hardy's men would see her and shoot her down before she went a hundred feet. So she turned left and stumbled along the hangars as fast as her beat-up body would allow. She needed to find someplace to hide until Gage and his pack could find her.

Hurry up, Gage. If you were planning to make a dramatic entrance, please do it now.

"South Salinas Air," Becker called out from the backseat of Xander's SUV. "North Twenty-Fourth Avenue."

"Are you sure?" Gage had to fight to keep from snarling as he glanced over his shoulder. Finding

Hardy's hangar had turned out to be harder than the IT guru had thought.

They were all parked on the side of the expressway waiting on Becker to give them a location. For about the thousandth time, Gage questioned the intelligence of putting all his eggs in one basket and bringing the whole team out here based on a muffled conversation a beaten man had heard while locked in a trunk. He glanced at his watch again and this time, he didn't even try to hold in the growl that escaped his lips. It was after midnight already. Hardy's men had taken Mackenzie over an hour ago. This was taking too damn long.

"I'm sure," Becker said. "I gave up trying to find a connection between Hardy and one of the general aviation operations out here. Instead, I tapped into the security feed for the cameras that surround the airport. I found the car that brought Mac here and followed it camera to camera until it stopped at a small charter service called South Salinas."

Gage wanted to believe Becker, but this was Mackenzie's life here. "How do you know it's the car she was in?"

Becker spun his laptop around so Gage could see it. "Not many dark sedans driving around at this time of night with the rear passenger-side door ripped off."

Gage grabbed the radio and thumbed the button. "Northeast quadrant of the airport," he ordered. "East Sixteenth to North Twenty-Fourth. Stop three blocks short and follow the plan."

Xander floored it and shot onto the expressway, heading to the general aviation side of Dallas/Fort Worth.

Gage glanced at his watch again, then looked down at

the map of the airport spread out on his lap. He locked on to the spot where the hangar for South Salinas Air was located. He'd been staring at the map so long over the past hour that he'd practically memorized it. He wished he knew exactly where in that building Mackenzie was being held.

It didn't matter. He'd be able to pinpoint her location the second he got within a couple hundred feet of her; then he'd get Mackenzie back. Assuming she was still alive, a part of his mind whispered darkly.

He swore, refusing to even consider the possibility.

"We'll find her in time," Xander said quietly as he took the off-ramp that led onto airport property.

Gage didn't say anything.

"Mac's smart. And she's spunky as hell." Xander shook his head. "I tried to scare her the other night when she came to the compound to see you, but she didn't back down. My eyes were yellow, my claws were out, and I showed her my fangs. Even growled. But she didn't flinch."

Gage smiled. That sounded like Mackenzie. If anyone could keep herself alive in a situation like this, it would be her.

He forced himself not to look at his watch again. They'd be outside the hangar in minutes; then it would be up to him and his pack to get Mackenzie out safely. That was what they did for a living—they got hostages out alive.

And that was what they were going to do. They were going to get Mackenzie out alive, and if Hardy or his men had harmed a single hair on her head, Gage was going to shred the fucking lot of them.

Mac half walked, half ran for as long as she could, praying the whole time she'd find someone willing to help her. But all the open hangars she passed were dark and empty. Her knee and ankle throbbed so badly she thought she was going to drop to the ground at any moment. Not that she could keep running out in the open like this for much longer. One of Hardy's men was bound to see her sooner or later. Time to stop trying to find help and fall back on her original plan—hiding.

She staggered past the next three empty hangars before settling on a big aluminum building filled with half a dozen small planes, rolling toolboxes, and wall lockers. There had to be a place to hide in here.

Mac hobbled as far back in the hangar as she could, then slumped to the floor behind a big toolbox. Just bending her knee that much made her want to yelp in pain, but she bit her lip and tried to make herself as small as possible.

She wasn't a moment too soon. Within twenty seconds of slipping to the floor, she heard footsteps thudding against the pavement. *Keep going. Please don't look in here.*

She'd been beyond lucky so far, but this time, her prayers weren't answered. She didn't know how many people were out there, but they'd stopped in front of the hangar she was in.

"I've got this one. Check the next," Patterson shouted. "She couldn't have gotten very far."

Mac tried to crawl underneath the toolbox, but the space wasn't big enough. Damn it. If Patterson walked around behind this line of toolboxes, he was going to see her, even in the darkened interior.

She looked around for another hiding place, but as badly as her leg hurt, she wasn't sure how well she'd be able to get to it even if she found one.

"If she gets away, I'm going to kill you in her place, you know that, right?"

The sound of Hardy's voice made her jump. Hardy and Patterson were both searching the hangar. Her luck was getting worse by the second.

She heard a clicking sound that she recognized from her shooting lessons with Gage. One of the men had thumbed the hammer back on a pistol.

"Unless I shoot you first," Patterson answered his boss.

Oh please, shoot each other.

Hardy laughed. "Find her and I'll let you bring her with us to Mexico. You can do anything you want with her until we get there. Then I'll shoot her and mail the parts back to Dixon in a box."

Crap.

"Deal," Patterson said. "But we need to get out of here soon. All that shooting is going to bring the cops out here."

"Carlos and the others will keep them busy." Hardy snorted. "What, did you think I was going to bring them down to Mexico with us?"

Patterson blew out a breath. "Damn. You can be a bastard sometimes, you know that?"

"When we find Stone, I'll show you what kind of bastard I really am."

Footsteps came into view on the other side of the toolbox Mac was hiding behind. She cringed and quickly looked at the shelves to her right. Could she make it there without being seen?

She was about to risk it when a long, low wolf howl filled the air.

Gage.

"What the hell is that?" Hardy asked.

The howl came again, closer this time. It was followed by another, then another, and another, each from different directions, each bouncing and echoing off the metal buildings until it was impossible to figure out where the eerie sounds were coming from.

"We need to get the hell out of here," Patterson said. Footsteps headed away from her. "Let's forget about Stone and get on the plane."

Mac grinned. *That's right. You'd better run.* It wasn't just Gage out there; it was his whole pack. For the first time since Hardy's men had grabbed her, she started thinking that maybe this was going to end okay.

"What the hell are you talking about?" Hardy shouted. "It's just a bunch of coyotes howling at the moon."

"I don't think so." Patterson's voice was farther away now. "Something attacked us when we grabbed the reporter. It took out Don's sedan and everyone in it. Then it ripped Jasper right out of the backseat of my car, taking the door with it. I tried to stop it, but it was too fast."

The howls sounded like they were getting closer. Mac took a quick peek around the side of the toolbox. Patterson was standing all the way out by the big roll-up door at the hangar's entrance, looking back toward the building she'd escaped from. He shifted from foot to foot, like he was about to take off running at any second.

Hardy laughed. "What, do you think the big, bad boogeyman is out there coming to get us?"

Shouts came from somewhere outside, followed immediately by the sound of gunfire.

"I don't know," Patterson murmured. "But I'm not hanging around to find out. Something tells me you're not making that plane to Mexico."

Mac held her breath, waiting for Hardy to say something snide in reply, but instead loud gunshots filled the building. She covered her ears with her hands and hunkered down. What the hell was that?

"Come back here, you fucking coward, so I can shoot you like the piece of shit you are!"

Hands still over her ears, she peeked out from behind the toolbox again and saw Hardy standing in the open doorway, a huge automatic pistol in his hand that dwarfed the ones she'd fired at the SWAT compound. She couldn't believe he'd shot at Patterson. Now she just had to wait for Hardy to leave and she'd be home free.

She knelt down behind the toolbox again, listening for the sounds of Hardy's retreating footsteps. When she didn't hear anything, she leaned close to the floor and looked under the rolling toolbox. Hardy was nowhere in sight. She frowned. Why hadn't she heard him leave?

He was gone. That was all that mattered.

Mac slowly started to get up, only to scream when a hand grabbed her hair from behind and yanked her to her feet.

"Looks like I'll be making that plane after all," Hardy whispered in her ear as he shoved that big cannon of a gun to her head.

Gage slipped quietly through the narrow alley between the two hangars, soundlessly making his way along the metal wall on one side while Xander and Brooks moved along the other. He inhaled deeply, sifting through the barrage of scents on the night breeze that moved across the airfield. He couldn't smell Mackenzie yet, but he hadn't expected to—not this far from where she was being held.

He and his small team would slip quietly around to the airfield side of the hangars, approaching from downwind, while the rest of the Pack headed straight for the front entrance of South Salinas Air and the crowd of armed men they'd seen there. He told Mike and his team to be as loud as possible when they initiated contact to draw Hardy's men away. Then he and his entry team would slip into the hangar, find Mackenzie, and get her out before anyone even knew they were there.

This would have been a pretty simple hostage rescue op if it wasn't for one factor—a lot of the hangars in this part of the airfield were constructed of lightweight metal. Without knowing exactly where Mackenzie—or any other innocent bystanders—were, there was no way his team could risk firing their weapons in the direction of the hangar. The bullets were likely to go straight through every wall in the place and keep on going.

Mike and his team were going to have to deal with Hardy's men without weapons. Well, without traditional weapons anyway. For the first time ever, Gage had given his pack the freedom to fight the way they preferred.

"Claws, fangs, or muscles. I don't care how you do it," he'd said. "Those men took Mackenzie. By the time we're done, I want them to be sorry they were ever born."

Gage only prayed the pure and simple shock value of a pack of werewolves hitting them would be the kind of distraction he needed.

When they reached the airfield side of the hangars a few buildings down from South Salinas, Gage tapped his radio mic three times in rapid succession—the go signal.

Immediately, a long, drawn-out howl shattered the normal background noises of the airfield. Moments later, another howl sounded a little farther away, and then another one closer. At the same time, Gage knew Mike would be killing all power to the hangar, throwing everything in the area into total darkness.

"I think that should do the job of attracting some attention," Xander whispered.

A few seconds later, Gage heard gunfire coming from the front of the South Salinas hangar, followed closely by shouts as Mike's team hit the men there.

"Yup, that's a distraction all right," Brooks agreed.

Gage started toward the hangar when the sounds of running footsteps caught his attention. Shit, Hardy must have had some of his men stationed along this side of the hangar, too.

Time for Plan B.

He pointed at Xander and Brooks, then in the direction of the footsteps. He pointed at himself and motioned he'd continue on to the hangar.

Xander frowned, clearly less than thrilled with the idea of Gage going in alone, but his squad leader didn't argue. The goal here was to get Mackenzie out, and Gage wouldn't be able to do that with bad guys chasing him from behind.

Gage hesitated for half a second as Xander and Brooks stepped out from behind the concealment of the little alley they were in and streaked toward the approaching men. Their attack was so sudden and vicious that Hardy's men barely had time to raise their weapons and fire.

Gage didn't wait to see more. Turning, he sprinted toward the target, hoping the noise on this side of the hangar didn't ruin their plan.

The savage growls behind him told him Xander had shifted at least partially—human vocal cords couldn't make those sounds. He had no doubt that at some point Brooks would be dropping his tactical gear and shifting to his full wolf form. While several of the team's members could handle a full wolf shift—Xander, Cooper, Brady, Remy, and Carter included—Brooks was the only one besides Gage who could handle anything close to an instantaneous transformation. Gage imagined when that happened, the shouts were going to get a lot louder. He needed to get to Mackenzie out before that.

Gage was nearing the big open doors of the South Salinas hangar and the private jet running its engines when an unexpectedly powerful scent hit him, forcing him to slow. It was Mackenzie's. But the scent wasn't coming from inside the hangar. It was coming from outside. And it was close.

Then he saw Mackenzie step out from an entry alcove twenty feet away. Gage almost dropped to his knees in relief. She'd gotten away and was already safe. That was when he realized she wasn't alone. Hardy was right behind her, holding that big Desert Eagle of his to her head.

"You and your cop friends are going to let me get on my plane and fly out of here," Hardy ordered from where he hid behind Mackenzie. "If you don't, I'll shoot your girlfriend right in front of you."

Mac tried to run to Gage, but Hardy tightened his hold in her hair, yanking her back. She stifled a scream and attempted to twist in his grip, but it was useless. He literally had her by the scruff.

She tensed, ready to jab her elbow back and smash the jerk in the face, but immediately went still as Hardy pressed his pistol harder against her temple.

"Drop it, Dixon, or I'll shoot her right now." Hardy pulled her backward so that most of his body was hidden by the edge of the door. "I swear I'll put a bullet right through her head."

It took everything in Mac not to give in to the overwhelming urge to struggle against Hardy. Now wasn't the time to do anything stupid. Gage was here and obviously had a plan on how to deal with the situation. This was what he did for a living. She just had to be ready to react once she figured out what his plan was.

She searched Gage's face, silently begging him to give her a hint, but he was focused on Hardy. Then, faster than she could have imagined, he moved in a blur, slipping inside the open door of the hangar with them, and disappeared into the darkness. The rapid move shocked Hardy just as much as it shocked her. The man turned, yanking her around with him like a shield.

"I'm telling you—I'll shoot her!"

A low chuckle came out of the darkness. "Then what will you do without a woman to hide behind?"

Hardy moved slightly away from the corner he was hiding behind, careful to keep her in front of him as he tried to get an angle on Gage. Now the thug couldn't seem to figure out who he wanted to cover with his pistol—her or the patch of darkness where Gage was hiding.

"Come out and show yourself, Dixon," Hardy ordered. "And you'd better not be holding a weapon, or we'll both get to find out what I'll do without her to hide behind."

No answer.

Mac strained to see in the darkness. She couldn't even guess where Gage was. Could he shoot Hardy while the man was hiding behind her?

Hardy backed out of the hangar and onto the tarmac, the pistol still firmly planted against her head. "Come out where I can see you, Dixon, or I'll kill her!"

Mac gasped as a shape moved out of the shadows. For a moment, her eyes couldn't comprehend what she was seeing. The tall, broad-shouldered figure she'd expected was instead replaced with a large gray wolf.

Gage.

He'd told her he could turn into a wolf, but she hadn't expected him to be so...so...*huge*. Or so beautiful. All Mac could do was stare at him, transfixed by his amazing presence.

"What the hell...?" Hardy muttered.

Gage bared his teeth in a snarl as he charged, moving so fast he was nothing more than a big, gray blur.

Mac barely had time to scream before Gage slammed into her and Hardy. The blow probably would have broken her in half if Gage had actually struck her squarely, but his big front paws skimmed over her right shoulder, hitting the taller Hardy with the force of a moving truck.

Still, the glancing blow sent her flying. She hit the ground hard enough to knock the air from her lungs.

Hardy's gun went off, but the sound was drowned out by Gage's snarl. Heart in her throat, Mac rolled onto her hip to see Gage clamp down on Hardy's arm with his enormous teeth. After a few savage shakes, Hardy cried out in pain and dropped the gun.

Mac lunged for the weapon. She didn't know if Gage needed her help, but she was determined to give it to him anyway. She scrambled to pick up the gun, cursing as she fumbled to get her hands around the large grip. She turned around just in time to see Gage going for Hardy's throat.

She quickly looked away. Even after everything that Hardy had done to them, she knew this wasn't something she wanted to see.

When she looked back a few moments later, Gage was standing over Hardy's lifeless body. As if sensing her eyes on him, Gage turned his big head toward her. He gazed at her with those mesmerizing gold eyes she'd come to love. They were filled with so many emotions that she almost cried.

He took a slow step toward her, then another and another until he was right in front of her. He seemed even bigger up close. She set the gun on the ground, then went up on her knees so she could look him in the eyes. Then, because she couldn't help herself, she wrapped her arms around his neck, burying her face in his soft, thick fur.

Movement off to the right caught her attention. She

lifted her head a little, expecting to see the rest of the Pack, but instead it was Roscoe Patterson. Something glinted in the glow of a distant airfield light—a gun.

And he was aiming it at Gage.

Without thought, Mac grabbed the pistol from the ground, somehow getting both hands around it on the first try, then instinctively aimed it like Gage had taught her. She squeezed the trigger as smoothly as her thundering heart would allow.

The boom from the thing was deafening, but that was nothing compared to the shockwave that reverberated through her. She'd planned to fire a second shot, but found herself sitting on her ass, the gun somewhere on the ground. She threw a quick glance in Patterson's direction as she frantically searched for the weapon and was stunned to see him lying on the ground. He wasn't moving, and in the darkness, she could see the big stain slowly spreading across his chest.

Oh, God. She'd killed him. She'd done it to save Gage's life, and would do it again if she had to, but still…

Gage ran over to check anyway. He sniffed the body once, then loped back over to her. His eyes searched her face, as if asking, *Are you okay?* She sank her fingers in the fur around his ears, tugging him closer. Then, she wrapped her arms around his neck again and buried her face in his scruff like before.

She might have cried a little then—she was doing a lot of that these days—but she couldn't be sure. Gage didn't seem to mind. He simply rubbed his muzzle against her face and let her hold him. God, she could really get used to doing this.

After a while, Mac realized she couldn't hear gunshots

anymore. That must mean it was all over. She prayed the rest of the Pack was okay.

She pulled back to find Gage appraising her with questioning eyes. She smiled at him.

"I'm fine," she assured him, but he didn't look convinced. "They didn't hurt me."

That seemed to appease him. He nuzzled her neck with his huge snout and chuffed quietly.

"Yes, I love you, too," she said with a soft laugh.

If someone had told her that one day she'd be carrying on a one-sided conversation with a werewolf, she would have called them crazy. But as she gazed into Gage's expressive eyes, she decided that maybe the conversation wasn't one-sided after all.

She ran her hand over his fur. "Thank you for coming to get me."

He chuffed again in answer, then jerked his head toward the hangar. It took her a moment to realize he wanted her to follow him. When she nodded, he began walking that way. Now that Gage was here, the pain in her knee didn't seem as bad as before and she fell into step beside him, admiring how graceful he was for a creature so big. It was like walking with a pony.

They hadn't reached the hangar yet when she heard the sirens approach. Inside the building, Gage stopped beside a pile of something on the floor. It took Mac a second to figure out what she was looking at, then it struck her.

"I never thought about that. You're naked under all that fur."

It probably should have been obvious, but she hadn't actually thought about it until now.

He chuffed again. Not once, but three times. When his

big, red tongue came rolling out, she realized she was hearing the werewolf equivalent of a laugh.

"What? You think that's funny?" she asked, as she crossed her arms and looked at him. "Wonder how much you'll be laughing if the cops show up and find you standing here naked after you turn back into a man—I'm assuming you are planning to change back before the cops get here, right?"

Now it was her turn to laugh as she got to see what a werewolf looked like when he blushed.

Chapter 14

"YOU STILL WORKING ON YOUR STORY?" ZAK ASKED, gesturing to her laptop as he slowly sat down at the picnic table where she'd been parked for the last fifteen minutes enjoying the unseasonably mild day and the very pleasant view of Gage and his pack playing volleyball with their shirts off.

She was never going to get tired of that.

Mac dragged herself away from all that eye candy to turn her attention to her friend. Zak had been out of the hospital for a full ten days, and he still looked beat-up. The swelling around his eyes and mouth had gone down, but it would take time for the bruises on his face and body to heal completely, and he was going to have to baby those broken ribs of his for weeks. She just thanked God he was up and about. Judging by the pile of food on his plate, his appetite was finally coming back, too. That was a relief. He was tall and lanky at the best of times. She was pretty sure he'd lost at least ten or fifteen pounds since Hardy's goons had beaten the crap out of him.

"Yeah," she said in answer to his question. "But I'm having a hard time coming up with a story that won't get Gage and his men into hot water—or me for that matter."

Zak glanced up from cutting his burger into small pieces. "I can see why you might have a problem with that. It's kind of hard explaining how the SWAT team came to your rescue on their own, killing Hardy and most of his men before the rest of the DPD even knew where they were."

"And don't forget the part about me shooting Patterson," she added. "I'm pretty sure that little tidbit doesn't even show up in the official police report."

He laughed, then winced.

"Sorry," she said.

He waved a hand at her until he could talk again. "Just a suggestion. I know how much it'd bother you to drop the whole thing and let people figure out for themselves what happened to Hardy, but I think this is a case where the world is better off not knowing the whole truth and nothing but the truth."

Mac didn't say anything. Actually, that same thought had been bouncing around in her head for the past few days. There'd be questions, but most people would assume the ruthless business mogul had gotten what he deserved. Would it be so awful if the world didn't know the details?

"You know, you might be right about that," she told Zak.

He did a double take before going back to cutting up his burger. "Well, damn. Getting engaged to Gage must be good for you. I never thought I'd hear you agree to drop a story, even if it's for your own good."

She grinned, glancing down at the beautiful diamond ring on her left hand. Funny how a piece of jewelry could change your perspective on a lot of things. "He's taught me there are some things more important than the great and almighty journalistic search for truth."

Zak nodded as he ate. Then he closed his eyes and groaned in appreciation. Mac couldn't blame him.

Apparently, SWAT held these cookouts at their compound at least once a month, and it turned out that they really knew what they were doing. Xander—the officer in charge of the grill at today's cookout—had put out a spread worthy of that cute chef on the Food Network. She'd eaten more than her fair share of barbecue as proof.

She put her hands on the table behind her and leaned back, happy to sit there with Zak while she watched Gage run around playing in the sand. He was going to look like a sugar cookie by the time he was done. Not that she minded. She definitely enjoyed spending time with him in the shower getting squeaky clean.

Taking a shower was the first thing they'd done when they'd gotten back to her apartment after the rescue at the hangar that night. Then Gage took her to bed and made love to her until they were both exhausted. When they woke up, they did it all over again. The only time they got out of bed was to get something to eat. Well, that wasn't quite true. Gage had insisted on leaving once so he could run some mysterious errand.

And when he'd come back, he'd taken her back to bed again, then slipped the diamond ring on her hand and asked her to be his *One*.

They'd made love, then spent the rest of the day talking about the future. Mac even convinced Gage into shifting into his wolf form again.

He'd looked stunned. "Right here?"

She'd nodded, refusing to let up until he did. Then she'd curled up against his big, furry body and fallen asleep while he'd rested his chin on his huge paws. It had been perfect.

Laughter coming from the volleyball court interrupted

her daydreaming. Mac jerked out of her thoughts to see the game breaking up.

"Sure you don't want to play in the next game?" Gage asked as he swept in and hugged her.

"Nah. My knee's still a little sore. I'd rather watch anyway," she said.

"Okay. But if you change your mind, there's always room for you." He leaned in to kiss her, groaning softly. "Mmm, you taste good enough to eat."

"Said the Big Bad Wolf." She laughed as he nuzzled her neck. "Down, big boy."

"I'm right here," Zak reminded them. "My face might be messed up, but I can hear just fine. And if you keep talking like that, I'm going to be ill."

Mac laughed. She knew she should behave herself because Zak was still recovering, but she couldn't resist teasing him. "Maybe we can slip off to the operations vehicle again," she said to Gage. "You know I love all those cameras in there."

"Okay." Zak picked up his plate and got to his feet. "I'm going to find another place to eat that's better for my digestion. See you two lovebirds later."

Gage chuckled as Zak slowly walked over to join Xander by the grill.

"Keep an eye on Zak, Xander," she said softly. "I don't want him wearing himself out."

Even though the grill was at least a hundred feet away, Xander gave her a nod. There was something to be said for extra-sensitive hearing. Becker, Cooper, and the two team medics—Trevino and Duncan—moved over to join them. Without a word, Cooper plunked down a folding chair, which Zak sank down into without complaint.

Gage climbed up behind her and pulled her back against his chest. "What are you smiling at?"

Mac pulled his arms around her middle and snuggled closer to all that muscle. He was covered in sand, but she didn't care. "I was just thinking how nice it is being part of the Pack. I hope they don't get tired of me hanging around all the time."

"Not going to happen," he assured her. "Like I told you, you're one of the Pack now. You're also a beautiful reminder that *The One* isn't just an urban legend. There's a reason for all the guys to believe they might find the woman who was meant for them—like I did."

She tipped back her head and kissed him, only to pull away as a thought came to her.

"What is it?" Gage asked.

"I was just wondering if there might be a way for me to help each of the guys find their *One*."

He pressed a kiss to her forehead. "Unfortunately, I don't think it works that way. They just have to keep looking until they stumble across the right woman. Besides, I don't think my team would appreciate you getting involved in their love lives."

Mac sighed. He was probably right. Then again, maybe not. She smiled up at Gage. "You sure about that?"

He looked across the yard to survey his pack, who'd all stopped what they were doing to give her their full attention. One by one, each werewolf grinned.

"For some reason, I don't think your pack agrees," she said.

Gage groaned. "Why do I think this has the potential to get really messy?"

Mac only laughed and kissed him again.

Acknowledgments

My husband and I came up with the idea for the SWAT series by accident. I originally wanted to write an erotic set of stories in which all the heroes were cops, but I kept getting derailed by all those police procedurals we watch on television. Every story line I came up with begged for more story and less of the erotic stuff. So, after a very frustrating few days, hubby suggested scrapping the whole cop thing and writing about a zombie who falls in love with his dermatologist. I said, "Honey, I want to write a book that sells. Like something with wolf shifters. Better yet, wolf shifters who are cops." Hubby thought a minute and said, "You know, you may be on to something." So, we went to P.F. Chang's (our favorite restaurant!) and batted ideas back and forth over spicy chicken until we came up with SWAT (Special Wolf Alpha Team), a series about sixteen hunky wolf shifters/cops and the women who make them howl!

In addition to another big thank-you to my hubby for all his help with the action scenes and military and tactical jargon, I want to also thank my agent, Bob Mecoy, for believing in me and encouraging me and being there when I need to talk; my editor, Cat Clyne, for loving this series and hot guys in tactical gear as much as I do; and all the other amazing people at Sourcebooks, including my publicist, Amelia, and the crazy-talented art department. I'm still drooling over this cover!

I also want to give a big thank-you to the men, women, and working dogs who protect and serve in police departments everywhere, as well as their families.

And because I could never leave my readers out, a huge thank-you to everyone who has read my books and Snoopy Danced right along with me with every new release. That includes the fantastic girls on my street team. You rock!

Hope you enjoyed *Hungry Like the Wolf* and look forward to reading the other books in the series as much as I look forward to sharing them with you. Look for book two in the series, *Wolf Trouble*, this summer.

Happy reading!

About the Author

Paige Tyler is a *USA Today* bestselling author of sexy romantic suspense and paranormal romance. She and her very own military hero (also known as her husband!) live on the beautiful Florida coast with their adorable fur baby (also known as their dog!). Paige graduated with a degree in education, but decided to pursue her passion and write books about hunky alpha males and the kick-butt heroines who fall in love with them.

Visit Paige at her website, www.paigetylertheauthor.com. She's also on Facebook, Twitter, Pinterest, Instagram, and Tumblr.

READ ON FOR A SNEAK PEEK AT BOOK THREE IN
PAIGE TYLER'S X-OPS SERIES

HER WILD HERO

AVAILABLE MAY 2015
FROM SOURCEBOOKS CASABLANCA

AFTER TEN YEARS OF WRITING PERFORMANCE REVIEWS,
training schedules, and after-action reports, she was finally going on a mission. Kendra Carlsen was so excited
she was practically bouncing in her chair. But getting
all geeked up wasn't going to get the work on her desk
done—and she had a ton to do before she left.

She was just finishing up the semiannual performance
evaluation on Trevor Maxwell's team—outstanding as
usual—when intel specialist Evan Lloyd stuck his head
in her office.

"Some of us are heading out for lunch. Want to come?"

Kendra was sorely tempted, but she was heading to the
airport in—she looked at her watch—three hours. Yikes!

She shook her head as she kept typing. "Thanks for
the invite, but I can't. I have way too much to do before
I leave."

Evan frowned. "You going on vacation?"

Kendra had a hard time keeping the silly grin off her
face. "Mission in Costa Rica."

His eyes went wide. "Seriously?"

"Uh-huh. John wants me to evaluate a big international, interagency training exercise down there."

"You're going down there alone?"

She printed out the report on Trevor's team and signed it, then attached the secret cover page on it and slid the document into an envelope. "Of course not. I'm going with Tate's team. They're taking part in the exercise."

"Oh." Evan shook his head. "Damn, that sounds cool."

Kendra grinned. "Yeah, it does, doesn't it?"

"Well, I'd better let you go then," Evan said. "Watch yourself out there, okay?"

"I will."

Kendra checked her email once more before logging off and thumbing the power button. It felt weird to shut down her computer. The only time she ever did it was when she went on vacation. And running around the hot, sweaty Costa Rican jungle for a week was going to be anything but a vacation. But she'd been begging her boss John Loughlin for months to go into the field, and now that he'd finally agreed, she was damn well going to make the most of the opportunity. Sure, she would have preferred if her first real mission had been going with Ivy and Landon to check out a hybrid research lab. Or maybe tagging along with Clayne and Danica to serve as backup the next time they took down a bad guy.

But John wasn't ready to go that far...yet. He probably thought that if he sent her into the hot, humid, bug-ridden Costa Rican jungle, she'd hate it so much she'd never bother him about going into the field again. He was wrong. She was going to kick butt out there.